HASTENED

THE BLOODSTORM
BOOK 3

VAUGHAN W. SMITH

FAIR FOLIO

Her growth is hastened.

For Ana

1

HULKING IN THE SHADOWS

Maya edged around the corner, peering into the gloom. She could see the black-armored security guard finishing his loop and disappearing behind a far building. Turning quickly, she signaled for Anders to follow her and darted along the wall, keeping a low profile, and staying quiet.

As the security guard emerged again, Maya was behind him in a flash. With expert precision, she activated a Binding curse. Targeting a critical area near a Chakra point, the light touch on the back of the security guard's neck was incredibly effective. He crumpled into a heap, his helmet clattered against the ground.

Maya paused to see if anyone noticed. The yard around the warehouse was completely still. She glanced back at Anders.

"You know, if you wanted to be stealthier you could have ditched the signature red jacket," Anders said. Maya sized him up. Anders was wearing a long coat, no doubt stuffed full of gadgets.

Can't even make a retort, his coat blends into the darkness.

Maya sighed.

"I like the jacket, it's not a problem. I just don't want to get ambushed, that's all," Anders said with a shrug.

"I'll watch your back, don't worry."

Maya continued around the outside of the building, searching for a way in. The powerful floodlights cast strong shadows, which she used as much as possible to avoid being out in the open. As she crept along, she continually looked for any signs of security guards or cameras that might alert anyone to her presence. There were none.

"This looks too quiet. Are you sure this is the right place?" Maya said.

"Trust me, this is it. Let's just keep going." Anders slipped his hand into his coat and pulled out a tiny device, scrutinizing it carefully. Maya noticed what looked like a door up ahead. She picked up her pace, darting over to examine it.

"Hey Anders, look at this." Maya pointed to the door. Anders quickly joined her, peering at the large steel door with an electronic lock in the middle.

"Hmm," Anders said, lost in thought. He retrieved a different gadget from his coat, a compact circular device, and clipped it onto the lock. It started flashing green and red immediately. Maya looked around, worried.

"Relax, this won't take long." Anders pointed back to the circular device and soon it made a tiny beep and glowed entirely green. Maya heard the lock click open. Anders quickly pocketed the electronic device and stood back. Maya shoved the doors open, and they peered into the gloomy warehouse.

There were no lights, and it took a moment for Maya's eyes to adjust to the dark. She stepped inside carefully, looking left and right to get her bearings. The warehouse seemed empty, and her footsteps echoed more than she would have liked.

I have a bad feeling about this. But I have to keep going. It's our only shot.

Maya walked around the edge of the warehouse, slowly

moving toward several large shapes looming in the distance. As she closed in, she realized what she'd seen were two buildings standing in the middle of the space. Both had large glass panels and she could see tiny lights flickering inside, most likely from some sort of machinery.

"What's your take on this?" Maya asked Anders.

"I think that's what we're here for," Anders said. He gestured with his hand for Maya to keep going, and she took the lead.

They slowly advanced, looking for traps and guards. But there was nothing. Once they reached the closer of the two, Maya examined the door in front of her. It was made entirely of light-colored wood with a silver handle shaped like a lever.

"Here goes," Maya whispered as she turned the handle and pushed on the door, it didn't budge. Maya looked back at Anders, and he shrugged.

"I think you're gonna be opening this one." Anders chuckled and stepped back, giving Maya some space. She turned back to the door and took a deep breath. Focusing her energy, she gathered her Chakra in her right hand and let it out in an explosive attack. The door flew open, rattling on its hinges. The sound reverberated around the entire space, giving Maya a moment of pause.

That was a bit louder than I had hoped.

Maya stepped into the room, taking care to look over all the machinery. A lot of it seemed to be just panels with no decipherable information. She ran her hand along the metal as she walked the length of the room, looking for something she could use. At a corner junction, she found a small inset panel with a red button.

"Should I press it?" Maya said.

"You have to. It's too inviting," Anders said. Maya reached closer and pressed the button, quickly turning to see what happened. She heard the loud shift of machinery coming from the center of the warehouse. She darted back to the doorway to observe.

A large opening was now visible in the center of the floor and Maya could see stairs leading down to another area.

"This is it. This is what we've been looking for." Maya strode ahead toward the stairs, not hesitating at all. Anders stayed close behind and kept looking around for signs that they were being watched.

Tiny lights illuminated the sides of the stairway as Maya made her way down. The stairs opened out into a tunnel with minimal lighting along the walls. It looked like she was now somewhere way more technologically advanced than how it appeared on the surface.

"What kind of facility do you think this is?" Maya said.

"Most likely research and development. The kind of place we want to explore," Anders said. They continued down the corridor until they reached a security door. It looked like it was for a secure area or even an airlock.

"Who should open this one?" Maya said.

"You did so well last time why not try this one too," Anders said with a smile. Maya looked closer at the locking mechanism and the handle. It didn't look like it was actually locked. She turned the handle and leaned into the door. With a bit of effort, it opened, and she stopped immediately.

Before them was a wide-open space with all the telltale signs of a Degeneration Field. Red lights shone from the ceiling, giving the room an eerie look about it. However, what really grabbed Maya's attention was the figure standing in the center of the room. He was gigantic and tall, clad entirely in metallic black armor. He turned to acknowledge their presence, and Maya could feel waves of fury coming off him.

"A friend of yours?" Anders said.

"Unfortunately, yes. That's the Iron Hulk. I defeated him

back in the LifeDeath tournament. But it was a close one," Maya said.

"Didn't you need to drop him into the water?"

"Yes. But I'm tougher now. Stay back, don't get caught in the field." Maya walked forward, standing halfway between Anders and the Iron Hulk. She paused and waited for him to react. The Iron Hulk raised his right arm and pointed at Maya, before making a cutting motion on his neck.

I think I get the message. He doesn't look back on our last meeting fondly.

"We don't have to fight. Things will still go the same way this time," Maya said. The Iron Hulk surged forward at considerable speed, not even trying to respond with words. With Maya's enhanced senses she anticipated the move and dodged to the side. As the Iron Hulk turned to adjust his assault, Maya activated her Chakra vision. She suddenly gasped.

"What have you done to your body?" Maya dodged backward to keep distance between them. The Iron Hulk didn't respond and dashed forward into a follow-up attack.

His Chakra points are a mess. All that enhancement work they've done on his body has messed with his Chakra flow.

Maya decided to test how far she had come. Instead of dodging, she held out her hand to catch the Iron Hulk's punch.

The impact hit really hard. But Maya was ready. She activated her Root Chakra and held firm, not shifting backward at all. Once her body was steady, she pushed a Binding curse through her hand into the Iron Hulk's fist. He immediately withdrew his hand and stared at it. Maya used his hesitation to her advantage. She rushed forward and crouched, attacking his legs. In a flash, she applied two pinpoint Binding curses on his knees. Before the Iron Hulk could react, he toppled to the ground. Maya reached down and grabbed his other arm, using a final Binding curse to disable it as well.

Now that the Iron Hulk was still, she crouched next to him.

Using both her hands she gently removed his helmet. The Iron Hulk stared at her with a mix of fury, disbelief, and defiance.

"I'm sorry. I wanted to stop this from escalating too quickly. Now we can talk," Maya said. The Iron Hulk didn't try to speak, just continued staring at her. His skin was pitch black and had the look of metal about it, as she had observed in their last meeting. She reached forward slowly with her hand, brushing it across his forehead.

It doesn't even feel like skin. How much has he suffered?

"The curses I used are not long acting. I don't mean you any harm at all, I'm just looking for answers. I'm sorry for what they've done to you. I'm going to make them pay." Maya looked directly into his eyes, showing him the depth of her resolve. She slowly stood and turned to look at Anders.

"Don't enter the room until I make it safe. I'm not sure what level it's been tuned to." Maya started to search for some controls to deactivate the Degeneration Field. She spotted a small control panel in the far right corner. Maya walked closer, leaning in to examine the panel. It was quite simple, a couple of dials and a display to show the current strength. It was set to thirty.

I can't believe it. Back in the Academy, I nearly passed out at level 18.

Maya turned the dial all the way to zero and watched as the readout slowly counted down until the Degeneration Field was entirely deactivated. Suddenly everything felt easier. Even though she hadn't really noticed the effect when she entered.

So, I'm quite powerful now, huh?

Maya walked back into the center of the room and waved Anders over. He took a few tentative steps and then confidently strode through the room, keeping an eye on the Iron Hulk.

"How long will he be down?" Anders said.

"Only a few minutes. We should just get what we need and leave." Maya led Anders deeper into the room where they found an unlocked door. Maya wasted no time in searching the adjoining room. It was completely white and full of computer towers with a single screen and accompanying keyboard on a desk in the middle of the room.

"I hope this has something because the trail ends here," Maya said.

"Maybe I should take care of this, and you can keep an eye on our friend in the other room." Anders rushed off to the computer terminal without looking back. Maya quickly turned and stepped through the doorway to watch over the Iron Hulk.

He was no longer on the floor but was instead standing at the far end of the room, waiting for her. Maya tensed her body as a reflex and then took a breath to prepare herself for a fight. However, the Iron Hulk remained still. After a few moments, he raised his right fist and placed it against his chest, in a form of salute.

Maya nodded at him, and before she could speak, he abruptly turned and left the room at surprising speed.

"I've dealt with our Hulk problem, how are you going in there?" Maya said.

"I think it's working. We'll find out in a few seconds," Anders said. Maya walked back into the room just in time to hear an alarm blaring from speakers hidden in the walls.

"Does that mean it's working? Or did you break something?" Maya said.

"I think it's a good alarm? Maybe you should just hold them off while I finish up here." Anders continued typing furiously.

Here we go, I wonder what type of response we're going to get.

Maya walked into the main room and paused, staring at the control panel.

If this doesn't affect the computer room, this could be quite useful.

Maya darted over to the Degeneration Field controls and turned it back up to level thirty. She turned at the sound of footsteps and watched as a security team rushed down the stairs toward her. The first one ran straight into the room and instantly collapsed onto the floor. The rest of the team quickly stopped, but the closest man was not so lucky and was shoved into the room by the ones behind him. He too joined his friend on the floor.

"I don't think you want to be in here with me. And since I'm fine in this room and you're not, I think that speaks to the difference in power between us." Maya walked ahead and the security team started to back away. As they left, Maya immediately deactivated the Degeneration Field.

"I bought you some time," she said.

"Thanks, but I'm done. We found something." Anders walked into the room, waving a data disk triumphantly. Before Maya could ask what it was, an explosion from outside rocked the room.

2

WAVES OF DESTRUCTION

Maya looked at Anders and he shrugged.

"That definitely wasn't me, I think they're upping the ante." Anders pulled out a tablet and started reviewing a map of their location.

"Are you picking up anything?" Maya said.

"I'm only picking up a few heat signatures closing in. We should make a move, but I'm not sure what it looks like out there."

"Let's go." Maya charged ahead, steeling herself for what lay beyond the stairs. She bounded up the stairway, two steps at a time until she reached the open warehouse space. The doorway they had used to enter was now a pile of rubble. Anders was with her in moments.

"Looks like they took out the exit. Where's the security team?"

"Over there." Maya pointed at the far corner, where the security team had set up in a defensive formation. A large groan sounded above them, and Maya dragged Anders back into one of the small buildings nearby. As she peered out, she saw a giant tear being ripped in the ceiling, and a spotlight illuminating the ground below. Three figures descended through the hole, landing neatly in the middle of the spotlight.

One figure stepped forward, clearly the leader.

"There's no way out, just come quietly," the woman said. She was dressed all in black with a red hood obscuring her face. As if to demonstrate, the woman became a blur and reappeared right in front of Maya.

"I wouldn't stay that close if I were you," Maya said. She grabbed the woman's arm before she could dash away. Panic flashed across the woman's features. Not wasting any time, Maya spun the woman in a single motion and planted a Binding curse on her back. She collapsed onto the floor.

The other two figures stepped from the light. Maya used her Chakra vision to observe them.

"The big one is a LifeDeath user, the other one is an Elemental. What's your pick?" Maya said.

"I'll take the Elemental. Do you know what type?" Anders started stepping to the side.

"I haven't seen enough of them to judge properly yet, but maybe water?" Maya walked toward the larger man. He was dressed in green and black robes covering an all-white leather outfit. His hood was thrown back, showing off his red hair. His dark eyes watched Maya intently.

"If you let us be, we will be out of your hair in moments," Maya said. The robed man started to laugh. He advanced toward her, and his partner started to circle around. Maya sensed Anders moving and quickly turned to see what he was doing. His attention was entirely focused on the Elemental, and he was moving to intercept and preparing some gadgets.

He can take care of himself. Focus on the big guy. I'm taking you down, Green Robes.

Maya noticed something strange about the man's life force. She dashed in and tried a quick strike. He didn't try to block her, letting her hit his chest. Maya applied a Binding curse, but it didn't stick. Green Robes lunged at her, but she quickly stepped back out of reach.

Maya kept her distance and looked carefully at the man's aura and energy. Within moments, she had figured it out.

He's using his LifeDeath power to create a barrier, so my curses won't work. I'll have to work on that.

Just as Maya was about to test her theory, a huge blast of water shot at her from the Elemental. Maya narrowly dodged it but started to lose her footing. Green Robes used this opportunity to attack again. Instead of dodging, Maya caught his hand and held on tight. She then began to yank out his life force.

At first, he laughed it off and prepared to strike her with his other hand. But Maya surprised him, getting a life drain going very quickly. As she tugged on his life force, she could see the barriers he had been sustaining with it start to fade away.

It's working just keep it up.

"Anders, are you okay over there?" Maya couldn't divert her focus to look over at what he was doing.

"All fine here just a little puddle to deal with." Anders said no more, and Maya left him to it.

I'm sure he's got a gadget for this.

Maya kept her attention on the life drain and searched for which areas of Green Robes's body became vulnerable. The man had extracted his hand and launched into a full-on assault, with a Dante Sphere in one hand and a Binding curse in the other. Maya had to use all of her attention, speed, and skill to keep herself away while continuing the life drain.

One slip-up and it's all over.

A cry of pain from across the warehouse distracted them both.

That didn't sound like Anders.

Turning back to Green Robes, Maya saw that his left arm was no longer being shielded. She pretended to stumble, inviting him to attack with that arm. At the last second, she pivoted, slapping a Binding curse on the arm. It dropped limply to his side, the curse he was preparing disappearing entirely.

One down. One to go.

Unfortunately, Green Robes seemed to have expected this. Rather than pause with shock at the loss of his arm, he leaned into it, closing the gap. Maya had no room to maneuver, and the Dante Sphere connected with her arm. As it hit, she yanked harder on Green Robes's life force. Using that, she sought for the feeling of connecting her two powers. It took a moment, but she found it.

C'mon this better work.

With her powers flowing together in sync, she stopped the spread of the Dante Sphere and reversed it. A few moments later she was free of it entirely, a brief flash of light signifying her victory.

Maya wasted no time celebrating. She flowed straight into a heavily reinforced palm strike, targeting Green Robes's chest. He flew backward and landed awkwardly, struggling to get up with only one usable arm. Maya glanced at Anders, he was circling behind the Elemental, attaching Bloodcuffs. The Elemental hung his head in shame, his mop of blond hair obscuring his face.

"Nicely done over there," Maya said.

"Pretty sure I finished mine first too," Anders said with a smirk. Maya shrugged and turned her attention back to Green Robes. He remained seated on the ground, staring at her.

Not a danger currently.

Maya looked around the room. The original entrance was still blocked, but the other walls were untouched. She started to get an idea.

"Anders, follow me." Maya ran over to the nearest wall in the warehouse. She used her hand to feel the surface, trying to gauge the thickness of the wall.

"You trying to punch through?" Anders said, with a puzzled expression.

"Probably not that, something better." Maya took a step back and then focused her energy internally.

There's a curse that might work here. If I mix my powers, I might be able to create a new effect. Worth a try.

Maya prepared a Decay curse, one that was normally used to wither an opponent. As before, she mixed her powers together. The aim this time was to use her Chakra to disperse and change the effect of the curse. Working with the two powers in sync was like trying to hold onto two slippery and oily objects at the same time. But she persisted and unleashed the new variant of the curse onto the wall in front of them.

A humongous circular shape was impressed upon the wall. The affected section started to crack, then began rocking back and forth. Almost like it was rippling. Suddenly the wall started to deteriorate, flaking away, then crumbling, and turning to dust. In only a few moments, a perfect circular hole existed in the wall.

"Wow, that worked." Anders sped over to the new exit and peered at the edges.

Maya didn't even stop to examine it, continuing through the hole into the cold air outside. It only took a few glances for Maya to get her bearings, and she started off toward their escape vehicle.

Anders kept pace with her easily, occasionally turning back to see if anyone was in pursuit.

"Are they following?" Maya said.

"They don't appear to be. I think the disintegrating wall gave them pause." Anders had a smile in his voice, and it was infectious.

I can't believe I just did that. What else am I capable of?

Soon they approached the gates of the facility, and Maya forced them open with no effort, holding them to create a gap to pass through. After Anders slipped through, Maya followed and let the gate slam closed behind them. The well-maintained road ahead of them was poorly lit, but they could see the lights from many vehicles approaching in the distance.

"I recommend we make a hasty exit, before the cavalry arrives." Anders rushed over to a dark shape. After a beep, the camouflage technology faded away and Anders quickly opened the driver's side door of a very sleek black sports car. Maya dove in after him, slamming the door behind her.

"Maasvlakte is not a very big place. We need to get to the airport fast," Maya said.

"Should be fine, once we're off the peninsula. We can lose them on the way."

"I'm going to message the pilot." Maya pulled out her phone, almost dropping it as Anders slammed the car around a corner way too fast. The collection of vehicle lights was starting to converge into a large mass behind them.

"There's a problem up ahead," Anders said. Maya looked up and noticed the only road was blocked by a massive gate.

"I don't remember seeing that on the way in."

"Can you do something about it? If we hit it, our car will become a pretzel."

"Let me see." Maya racked her brain. The new Decay combination attack would be ideal, but they didn't really have the time to stop the car and let her prepare it.

Maybe there's another way. How good is your Chakra?

Maya retreated deep within, removing all distractions. She started a meditation, building her Chakra through all her points methodically. She could almost hear Anders trying to say something but tuned it out. She couldn't be distracted. As she gathered her Chakra within, she began to focus and compress it.

"Open my window," Maya said, her eyes still closed. As soon as she was ready, her eye snapped open, and she could see the gate looming right in front of them. Shoving her hand out the window, Maya built and fired a sizable ball of pure Chakra as big as her head. It zoomed ahead of the car, slamming into the gigantic steel gates. The impact was incredibly loud, almost deafening her enhanced senses. But it had the desired effect.

The gates not only swung open but each half was ripped off its hinges and tossed effortlessly to the side. It all happened just fast enough for their car to sail through.

"Maybe next time we could get that going just a smidge faster," Anders said.

"A smidge faster? I just ripped that gate apart in seconds, and you want it faster?"

"Well, we almost became a part of the gate."

"You maybe, I'm tougher than that." Maya grinned at Anders, and he returned an uneasy smile.

"Well, why don't you just sit back and relax, and I'll lose our tail." Anders pressed down on the accelerator and Maya was forced back in her chair. She glanced back, seeing that the pursuing lights were getting further away.

Too close for comfort. But at least we got a result. I wonder what they're trying so hard to recover.

ONCE IN HER private jet and in the air, Maya could finally relax.

"Now that we're about to leave the Netherlands, can you fill me in on what you found?" she said. Anders inserted the drive into his laptop and started reviewing the contents.

"Give me a moment, I need to confirm what I think I am seeing." Anders typed furiously on the keyboard, running some sort of search queries. Maya looked on, not sure what he was doing.

"This is it. Good news."

"Out with it!"

"I've found data linking test subjects with this location. Not surprising, given we saw your old friend there." Anders paused the constant activity and looked over at Maya.

"He was definitely training or something like that. You don't sit in Degeneration Fields for fun."

"So, it's a location of interest. And going from the records, it was often supplied from a restricted facility. Which looks like this." Anders brought up some photos showing a large complex. First, he scrolled through exterior photos, showing a rather featureless concrete building. However, the next few were photos of the inside. There were vaults and a gigantic, cavernous space filled with rows of shelves and boxes. Maya gasped.

"I know this place!"

3

———

ACCESS DENIED

nders stared at Maya expectantly.

"And?"

"Sorry, I need to gather my thoughts. I don't know where it is, but this is the place I saw in my Chakra vision. The place where the Master Sage hid something," Maya said.

"Fantastic. This is where we need to be next then. I have the coordinates, let me go brief the pilot and try to get a new destination filed." Anders carefully stood and wandered toward the cockpit. Maya grabbed his laptop and paged through the photos more.

This is definitely it. I wonder what the Master Sage was hiding here. And why I need to find it.

Anders returned within moments with a triumphant look.

"Success?"

"You should expect no less. Next stop Madrid."

"Madrid? As in Spain?" Maya blurted out.

"The one and only. Fine food and football await us. Oh, and that facility." Anders eased into his chair and took back possession of his laptop.

"It's a Haste facility. There's a major hub of Speedsters in Spain, particularly Madrid."

"And they're related to the LifeDeath training facility we just busted into?"

"So it would seem. We already have the data showing they're trying to enhance people to have both Haste and Life-Death. And there's records indicating some of the monitored people have the seventh bloodline."

"Actively?" Maya said with excitement.

"No, latent. But it's a useful clue. Maybe there's something about the presence of this bloodline that makes them more useful test subjects for the Master Sage?" Anders kept paging through the information he had available.

"Even if the power can't be activated?"

"It's my best guess. We will have to find out more." Anders resumed searching for more information, and Maya let him continue without extra questions. She stared out the window, letting her mind work over the new information.

It's great that something is finally happening. But why do I feel so uneasy all of a sudden?

ANDERS PARKED THE RENTAL CAR, a sporty red convertible, and assessed the facility. It was ultra-modern, consisting of two main buildings. The first was smaller, filled with floor-to-ceiling glass, and looked like an office. The second building dwarfed it, a giant metallic cube.

This is definitely it. Let's see how their security is.

Anders left and locked the car, sauntering over to the foot-path. There was a steady flow of people going in and out of what he had dubbed the office building. He looked around as he walked, trying to take stock of who they were.

Are they Speedsters? Probably.

The people seemed to be walking at regular speeds. But Anders noticed the occasional strange behavior, such as someone adjusting their shoes a little faster than you would expect. There was a large revolving door at the entrance, with a smaller side door a few yards away.

Anders headed straight for the revolving doors, stepping through them successfully and emerging into a surprisingly small foyer. There were a few cushioned chairs around the edge, and straight ahead was a security scanning machine. It was monitored by a woman with red hair who was staring off into space. She had a red and black uniform on, with obvious shoulder pads. Anders approached her.

"Hola," Anders said.

"We speak English here too, sir," the security guard responded. Anders smiled.

"Fantastic. Glad I didn't have to murder any more Spanish than was truly necessary. I have a friend who just activated the Haste bloodline. I wanted to give the facility a tour to see what you could offer her."

"And you are?"

"I'm a good friend," Anders said. The security guard sighed.

"Do you possess the Haste bloodline?" she said in a way that sounded like she repeated it often.

"No."

"Then I'm sorry, I can't allow you to enter."

"Is there some sort of security screening I need to pass?" Anders pointed to the machinery.

"Yes. It checks you for the Haste bloodline. If you don't pass, you don't get in." The security guard crossed her arms.

"I can't even..."

"No." The security guard pointed at the door behind Anders.

"Fine, fine. I'll be on my way. Thank you for your time." Anders waved and quickly turned. He stepped around the queue of people that had formed behind him and made his way back outside.

Time for plan B.

Anders took a few steps outside the building, before pulling out a pair of sunglasses. He put them on and continued walking, going for a lap around the building. Anders looked over the walls, picking out any distinguishing features, and focused on building access and vents. Once he was outside the larger building, a man appeared before him. He wore a similar black security uniform to the guard inside.

"Excuse me, this is a restricted area." The guard glared at Anders.

"Oh, my apologies. I was trying to find my car, but I think I got turned around."

"I'll escort you, sir." The guard moved in a blur, stopping behind Anders and beckoning him to follow. Anders walked in step with the guard, looking at as much as he could on the way back. His eyes wandered over the space around the facility, and even the distant fences. Soon enough they were on the main path again.

"Your vehicle will be in that direction," the guard said, pointing at the stream of people leaving the building.

"Thank you for your assistance, I don't know how I would have found my way otherwise." Anders gave the guard a big smile and waved. He then casually walked down the path, along with the other people. He glanced back once, noticing the guard staying in his position and watching.

I think I touched a nerve.

Anders returned to the car, unlocked it, and got inside. Pocketing the sunglasses, he quickly typed out a message to Maya.

Initial scoping done. Security is tight and access is restricted to Haste bloodline. Let's discuss more when I'm back.

With that done, he started the car and sped off.

This is not going to be straightforward.

Maya read and re-read all the information that Anders had collated about the facility. It wasn't enough. She closed the laptop and headed over to the window. Their hotel room was high enough that she could get a good view of the city. The sight of buildings instead reminded her of the facility Anders was investigating.

Why isn't he back yet?

Maya couldn't shake the feeling that urgency was required. But she had no reason to be urgent. Not yet at least. She heard the front door opening and practically ran over to the door.

"Well?" Maya said.

"It's complicated." Anders walked over to the couch and dropped down into it. Maya sat next to him, waiting.

"Can you get in?" she asked.

"Probably not. There's a security protocol preventing people who aren't Speedsters from getting in. The exterior is well secured and is patrolled by Speedster guards." Anders sighed.

"Still, that's not a complete no. What other options do we have?"

"There may be a way to infiltrate from above. But we are working blind. We have no information on the inside. Breaking in is a one-time thing. Once we are in, if we don't get what we need we won't get another shot at it." Anders leaned back and stared at the ceiling.

"Sounds like you're giving up," Maya said quietly.

"Not at all, I just don't like our chances right now. It's good news, in that we have something real on our hands. But it's going to take time and preparation to get inside. There's no easy way." Anders stood and strode over to his laptop. He opened it up and started to work again.

"There is another way," Maya said. Anders paused what he was doing and looked up. After a few moments, a look of recognition went across his features.

"No. Don't make any rash moves."

"It solves all our problems. I activate the Haste bloodline, waltz through the front door, and infiltrate the place. I'll get all the intel we need from inside." Maya stood and started pacing around the room. "Only I can do this. They can teach me about the bloodline too."

"It's too risky. Once you activate it, you become powerless again. You're back at the start."

"I'll have you to protect me," Maya said with a smile, trying to hide her fear.

He's right. I'll be a sitting duck. I won't be able to fight back.

"How about I phone a friend? Mikael offered to help me if I went for the Haste bloodline," Maya said, her voice tinged with hope.

"Oh, right. That's actually a good idea. Can you still get in contact?"

"I think so." Maya pulled out her phone and tried Mikael's number. A few rings, and it kept going. He didn't answer and there was no voicemail.

"I'll send a message." Maya switched to the messaging app and typed.

·　·　·

Hi Mikael, I hope you're doing well. I need your help if you're available. It involves the Haste bloodline. Let me know if you are as it would be great to see you.

"Well, I guess I can put a hold on that for now. How are you doing with the facility research?" Maya wandered over and sat next to Anders peeking over his shoulder. He had what looked like blueprints up on the screen.

"I got lucky with some plans. I don't think they're final, but they should be helpful."

"How'd you get them?" Maya blurted out. Anders gave her a sly smile.

"I have my ways."

"You asked Kora, didn't you?" Maya said, laughing. Anders's smile broadened.

"I might have. I am pretty resourceful too, you know."

"Resourceful, yes. But you're not this fast." Maya gave Anders a deadpan look and he burst out laughing.

"Fine. I've still got my gadgets." Anders zoomed into the blueprint, studying the building in detail.

"It looks like quite a large space, with levels underground. And space for vaults."

"Sounds like a place we want to explore."

"Absolutely. Hang on. Kora is calling me." Anders picked up his phone and answered. He stood and started to walk around, just listening.

"I see. And you're sure?" Anders said. Maya watched him, observing his body language on the phone.

He seems like he's getting bad news. He looks closed off, defensive.

Anders paced a few more times before saying goodbye and hanging up the phone.

"So, we've got good news and bad news."

"Good news?" Maya said.

"Kora is coming up to help." Anders projected his voice and put on a big grin. Maya saw right through it.

"And the bad news is that Kora thinks she has to come help. It's that hard to get in," Maya said. Anders's fake grin persisted.

"Got it in one." Anders wandered over to the kitchenette and pulled out some coffee.

"We'll take care of it. When will she arrive?" Maya said.

"A few days I think," Anders called out while pouring coffee beans into the grinder. Maya heard her phone beep and darted over to check the message.

"It's Mikael," she said before reading the message.

HELLO MAYA, fantastic to hear from you. I'm also glad that you have decided to join me as a fellow Speedster, even if only for a limited time. I wish I could be there to support you in person, but I will send through the guide we use for bloodline activation, and I should be able to answer my phone. Good luck and good speed to you.

MAYA SIGHED and quickly typed out a thank you message.

"Who is it?" Anders said, once the coffee grinder was finished.

"Mikael. He can't come, but he can offer help from afar." Maya started reading through the guide Mikael sent.

This looks pretty useful. I should seek this kind of information out for future bloodline activations.

Maya sat on the couch, thinking over what she had just read. Anders brought over coffee, and they sat together.

"So, what's it look like?" he said.

"There are multiple ways to do it, but it boils down to two styles. Relaxed style or intense style." Maya took a sip of coffee and closed her eyes, enjoying the flavor.

"Let me guess, you picked the intense style?" Anders said, taking a big sip of coffee. Maya chuckled.

"It's actually really sensible. You get a better boost to the power to start with."

"Something to consider, when it's time for that."

"I've already decided. And as soon as the coffee is done, I'm activating it." Maya took a big gulp of her coffee.

4

VIRAL STAR

Maya strode over to the lift, resolute. Anders was close behind.

"I think you're jumping in a little early here. Kora will be here in a few days. We have time, so there's no ticking clock just yet. For what's probably the first time, we have a chance to take things at our own pace," Anders said. Maya pushed the lift call button and then turned to look at him.

"If I'm a Speedster, I walk in. We can't be breaking in as a starting point. I'm going to do it, anyway, let's face it. May as well get the benefits of activating the bloodline." Maya stepped through the open doors and Anders hastily joined her. Maya pressed the basement button and the lift sped away.

"How bad is this activation?"

"Intense style requires a desperate need for speed. We just create the conditions. I have a few examples."

"And the best example is?"

"Chasing me with a vehicle," Maya said carefully.

"What?" Anders blurted out. Maya walked through the open lift doors.

"It creates a sense of urgency and danger, while being somewhat controlled." Maya walked confidently through the underground car park.

"This sounds a little extreme." Anders jogged ahead and stopped in front of the car with his arms crossed.

"What's the big deal? Do you think your car can actually seriously hurt me? I'm actually more worried that this won't even work. I'm not normal anymore." Maya gave Anders a worried look and he nodded.

"I get it. Sorry, I overreacted."

"It's alright. C'mon, let's get this done." Maya quickly entered the car and Anders started the engine.

Before my nerve runs out and I chicken out of this.

They drove out to an abandoned lot nearby. It was in a poorly lit section of an industrial zone. Anders pulled the car to a stop, stepping out to expertly remove the chain barring access. He drove in carefully, looking around for any security.

"It's definitely empty. The perfect place," Maya said.

"What's going to work best in here?" Anders said as he drove around. There were large warehouses on the edges, with an empty square in the middle. Maya noticed a few wrecked cars, long since picked clean for any useful parts.

"I've got a good idea. Stop over there." Maya pointed out a spot in the middle. Anders slowed the car and stopped.

"How is this going to play out?" he said.

"When I signal, drive at me."

"When do I stop?"

"Don't total this car?" Maya shrugged and left the vehicle.

He's in more danger than you. Probably.

Maya picked a car and made her way over to it. She soon stood before an old pickup truck. Peering closer, Maya could see there were massive holes in the front.

I hope my tetanus shot is still good. Is that even still relevant?

Maya put her leg inside one of the holes, taking care to

make sure her shoe was jammed in and snug. She tested getting her leg out a few times, and it felt stuck.

This oughta create a sense of urgency.

Maya took a long slow breath, making sure that she exhaled it just as slowly. Once she was ready, she waved at Anders. It was hard to make out his reaction.

Did he get the signal?

The black sports car sped off, the wheels squealing as it accelerated.

This is happening awfully fast. When do I try and get out?

Anders sped closer and closer. Maya felt panic start to set in.

He can't stop in time. I need to get out immediately, so he has time to stop.

Maya struggled to get her leg out. She felt the need to move faster. She just needed to move so fast that her leg could escape the trap she had engineered for herself. A shift happened and the world seemed to tumble. Maya staggered and found herself in a heap on the ground.

Dazed, she looked around and saw the car had stopped right in front of where she had been trapped. Only inches away. Anders opened the door and ran over to Maya, crouching next to her.

"Are you okay? What happened?"

"Don't let me question your driving again," Maya said slowly, trying to gather her thoughts. She reached out, and Anders helped her up.

"Something happened. I'm not stuck anymore, and I felt a change happen. Hang on." Maya tried to activate her Chakra vision, but it felt out of reach. Tantalizingly close, but not there. She focused on breathing and Chakras. They were there, but not empowered the same way.

You did it. You've triggered the Haste bloodline.

"It worked. My other powers are locked away. Dulled. Here

we go again." Maya tried to smile, but it was more of a grimace.

"Well, you succeeded in your first try with the intense method. That has to be a positive?" Anders said with a little shrug. He walked her around to the passenger side and opened the door for her. Maya eased herself inside and took her time fastening her seat belt.

Anders switched on the car and looked over at her.

"Are you sure you're okay? You seem off?" he said.

"Just got the wind knocked out of me. I suppose this is what untrained use of the Haste power feels like. I'm sure it will pass quickly." Maya tried to sound optimistic. Anders nodded and turned the car around.

"Did you see anything?" she asked. Anders completed the turn and started driving out of the abandoned lot.

"No, I was too focused on playing the part without causing an accident. I'm not sure how you managed to get out."

"I don't know either. But it worked."

"It did. We can try the next part in the morning."

"Good idea. I think I'll be better after a rest." Maya leaned back in the chair, sinking in.

This better work out. You need to master this power quickly.

ANDERS PARKED THE CAR, the morning sun belting through the windows.

"Ready?" Anders said.

"As I'll ever be." Maya took one last gulp of her coffee and put the flask back in the cup holder.

"I'll wait here. They'll get suspicious if they find me snooping around again."

"Got it. Have fun." Maya waved and stepped out of the car. She walked confidently down the path, not looking back.

The concealer worked. You can't see the other Mastery Marks. Just act like a novice. Should be easy.

Taking a slow, deep breath, Maya pushed through the revolving door into the main entry. As Anders had described, it was surprisingly small. The security guard looked bored, and there was a small queue of people waiting to get through the screening.

Maya waited her turn, focusing her attention on what the screening looked like instead of her feelings. The machine brought back memories of the testing Elias had put her through, way back at the beginning. She shoved those feelings deep inside as quickly as possible. Before long, it was her turn.

"ID card," the security guard said, holding out her hand. Maya read the nametag and saw her name was Doris.

"Hi Doris, I'm new to the Haste bloodline. I don't have an ID card yet?" Maya said. Doris sighed. She pulled out a small handheld scanner and waved it over Maya's arm. It showed a green indicator light.

"Travis? I've got another one!" Doris called out. A thin, waspy man with thinning hair and glasses shuffled over.

"Follow me, please. I'm Travis and I do the inductions here." Travis beckoned for Maya to follow and shuffled off down a corridor. Maya followed close behind, gazing around at the building. She could only see featureless white corridors with no signage. Travis paused at the first door and opened it, holding it for Maya.

"Thank you, Travis," Maya said, entering the room. It was an office. Sparsely furnished. There was only a desk, two chairs, a potted plant, and a painting on one wall. Maya sat in what looked like the right chair and waited for Travis to take his place behind the desk.

"Name?" he said, while rifling through a drawer.

"Maya Mills."

"Hmm alright. No records here. Fill this out please." Travis handed over a computer tablet with an application form. Maya skimmed over it.

Just as Anders suspected. Good thing he prepped me.

Maya filled out the application, knowing exactly what to enter based on the details they had agreed they could share. It was only a minimal risk giving her name, the rest was fabricated.

"Done." Maya slid the tablet over the desk to Travis. He spun it around and reviewed the information before entering some extra details himself.

"How long ago did you activate the bloodline?" Travis said.

"Yesterday."

"On purpose or accidental?"

"Accidental," Maya answered easily. Travis made a few more comments.

"That's enough for now. Let's take you across to the testing room." Travis stood and made his way over to the door. He opened it and stepped into the corridor. Maya followed quickly.

They continued to the end of the corridor, arriving at a large set of white double doors. Travis pushed them open easily, not waiting for Maya. She caught the door swinging back at her with her right hand and entered the room. It was entirely white and filled with white equipment.

It's like some sort of stylish gym. There's a bike, treadmills...

"Maya, this way." Travis broke her chain of thought, directing her over to a treadmill. She quickened her pace.

"Have you experienced any powers yet?" Travis asked, standing by the treadmill.

"No. I'm curious to see what I have."

"We will find out shortly. First, we will test for general speed. Please step onto the treadmill." Travis gestured at the one in front of them. Maya stepped onto it.

"Place your arms on the provided arm rests and try and keep up." Travis stepped behind a control panel and waited.

Maya stepped up and made herself comfortable. The treadmill started going at a steady walking pace. Maya walked along naturally.

"I'll be adjusting the speed as required," Travis explained. Immediately after the treadmill speed ramped up. Maya was soon into a proper run. But it was still relatively comfortable.

I can't wait to see some real speed. This is going to be amazing.

The speed jumped again, Maya entered into a full sprint.

This is my limit. Why can't I get faster?

Maya glanced up to look at Travis. His expression was hard to read. He looked like he was about to adjust the speed again. The treadmill suddenly shifted gears, and Maya tumbled off. She landed in a heap on a nearby mat.

"I thought we were onto it, but that was a fail. Perhaps someone in your family was a runner, you had me convinced. Onto the next test." Travis walked over to another machine. It looked like a trampoline. Maya waited in front of it.

"Step onto the machine and jump. We will get what we need." Travis readied himself by another control panel. Maya stepped onto the circular platform and tried jumping. She reached a normal height and bounced higher still due to the bouncy surface.

Takes me back to childhood. Maybe I'll be able to leap over buildings in a single bound?

She continued to jump, the machine propelling her a little higher each time. Suddenly the platform grew rigid. Maya adjusted her jump, but it was tiny. She didn't bother jumping again, seeing the expression on Travis's face.

"Last test." Travis stalked over to the final machine.

Some sort of wind generator?

It was an enclosed space, with clear Perspex for walls. Inside were some mats and some machinery.

"As you may have guessed, this is a flight simulation test. I expect that you will pass this one, as you have not shown aptitude in the other tests. Enter the room and follow any additional instructions," Travis said.

"Sure." Maya pulled open the door and stepped inside. She looked around, seeing fans and jets spread throughout the space. The floor was soft and cushioned. Turning around to look for Travis, she was surprised by a gust of air knocking her over.

Don't have your usual resilience.

Maya tried to get up, but another jet of air propelled her from below. Other jets and fans activated, causing her to float in midair.

What an odd feeling. They're making me fly.

Maya tried leaning into the feeling, to ascend further in the space. She closed her eyes, concentrating on being weightless, flying high, and soaring. She felt herself slowly ascend. Maya opened her eyes.

This is it! You've done it.

She was higher than before, looking down at where she had been. Maya looked over at Travis, triumphantly. Only he was frowning. The room became quiet, and Maya fell to the floor.

Great. Just great.

Maya picked herself up and opened the door. She stepped out with a wobble and found her footing after a few seconds. Travis was already at the door.

"Come back to my office," he called out before leaving.

This guy is not impressed. What did I do wrong?

Maya picked her way through the equipment, wandered down the corridor, and returned to Travis's office. As she entered the room, he handed her a piece of paper.

"Here's the preliminary results. Please go back to the waiting area and someone will come get you." Travis looked down at his tablet again.

"Thanks." Maya left with the paper, not even looking at it.

What a fail. Pull yourself together. You can fix it with the next person.

Maya sat back down in the empty waiting area. She could see others going through the screening process and entering a different area of the facility.

I must be stuck in processing and admin. Not the fun area.

She noticed a television on the wall and started watching. It was in Spanish, but there were English subtitles. Two hosts were discussing a viral video that had just been published and was grabbing headlines.

Slow news day, I guess.

They played the clip. It was a man wearing a black helmet, speaking into the camera. He was speaking English, but the voice was distorted and sounded like a computer. Spanish subtitles were being shown this time.

"This woman has been trying to operate in the shadows. She's fooled two of our clans. But her secret is being revealed today. If you see this woman, watch out. She could be targeting you next," the man said before pausing.

Great, some kind of con artist. I guess it would be helpful to see if I recognize her.

Alongside the man a photo appeared. It was Maya, but she looked asleep.

What the...

Maya stood up suddenly, her attention entirely focused on the television. The man began speaking again.

"Her name is Maya Mills, and she has all the bloodlines. Be alert and on the lookout. You have been warned." The man finished speaking and the video faded to black. Maya gasped and dropped the paper she was holding.

5

——————

A STICKY SITUATION

aya's eyes were glued to the set. The hosts were discussing whether the video was real or not, and why the photo of the woman looked asleep. A shiver ran down Maya's spine.

Was that photo taken while I was in a coma? You need to get out of here.

Maya grabbed the paper she had dropped and hurried back to the entry.

"All that testing took it out of me. I'll drop in tomorrow, Doris," Maya said as she casually walked back through the screening area. Doris was distracted, reviewing something on her phone.

She could be watching anything, just keep walking.

Maya walked past the people in the entry and rushed through the revolving door. As soon as she was outside, she broke into a run.

The second they put two and two together I'm toast. They'll be on me in a flash.

Maya ran faster and faster, pushing her limit. She noticed strange looks from people walking in both directions but ignored them. The path wasn't long, and she could see Anders leaning on the car in the distance. He was on his phone as well.

Anders looked up and noticed Maya running. He waved her over, and immediately unlocked the car. Maya flew into the passenger seat, Anders driving off before she had even buckled up.

"Are they after you?" Anders said as they sped away.

"Not yet, but I couldn't wait around. Did you see the video?"

"I did. Who could have done that?" Anders threw the steering wheel hard, skidding around a corner.

"Don't go to the hotel. Find a random place somewhere," Maya said, panicked.

If they come after you, you're powerless. You idiot.

Anders kept weaving through traffic, soon emerging into another industrial area. He slowed down, taking random streets but otherwise driving normally. Eventually, he stopped the car outside a tiny park. It was sandwiched between two business complexes which were fortresses of concrete and glass. Anders turned off the engine.

"Let's go sit in the park and talk this over."

"Okay. I need to make sense of this all." Maya took the paper with her and left the car. They wandered over to a park bench, under a large leafy tree. Anders sat first, and Maya sat next to him.

"For what it's worth, here's my report. They don't know what power I have." Maya handed Anders the paper and he studied it.

"This is interesting. Did you read it properly?"

"No. What does it say?"

"Suspected Teleportation Power." Anders chuckled and pointed out the section to Maya.

"Teleportation? No wonder I failed all the tests."

"It's notoriously hard to master. Which won't help you right now," a female voice said. Maya recognized it, swiftly turning.

She looked up and saw a blonde woman in a red jumpsuit approaching. It was Valerie.

"How?" Maya stammered, standing up. Valerie gave her a triumphant smile.

"A little tracker on your car. All that driving was quite entertaining, however pointless though." Valerie chuckled and approached them. Her right hand started to glow black and green.

She's preparing a Binding curse. She has LifeDeath now?

"Don't let her touch you," Maya shouted. Anders nodded.

"I see it." Anders pulled out a stun wand from his coat.

"You won't hit me with that. I'm aware of your tricks, and I came prepared." Valerie kept advancing, heading toward Maya instead of Anders.

What can you do? You can't use your power. You barely have anything from your other bloodlines.

"Stay behind me, I've got this." Anders stepped forward, his other hand hovering near his pocket. Valerie was circling around, watching him carefully.

Don't forget all your training. You're still strong and fast. She doesn't have her speed otherwise she would have beaten you already.

Maya forced herself to take a long slow breath, calming her body. Her Chakras were still there, she just couldn't access the same power. Her body was still strong and resilient.

Just don't get hit by that curse.

Maya stepped out from behind Anders.

"I don't need powers to beat you again, Valerie." Maya raised her hands into a defensive pose. Valerie laughed and closed in. Maya cautiously stepped to the side, not giving Valerie an opening. Valerie suddenly lunged forward, faster than Maya expected. Without thinking, Maya sidestepped, and counterattacked with a palm strike. Valerie was knocked back, her concentration broken. The curse dissipated. But she whirled back in a second.

Valerie didn't need curses to get Maya on the back foot. She used her strength and speed to force Maya back. Each blocked hit reverberated through Maya's body. Pain surged through her hands and arms with every attack.

"This is more fun. I shouldn't have bothered with the curse." Valerie lashed out with a kick, causing Maya to trip over.

Maya scrambled to get up off the ground. She could see Valerie looming over her, ready to strike again. Out of the corner of her eye, she glimpsed movement from Anders. Just before Valerie struck again, something green smashed into her.

Maya stumbled back, steadied her footing, and saw what was happening. Valerie was stuck in an expanding green goo. The more she moved, the more she was stuck. Anders stepped back and chuckled.

"Your speed and strength are not going to help you here," he said. Maya circled around to stand next to Anders and watch what was happening.

"This won't hold me long. You're both dead," Valerie said, while struggling with the goo. It had covered her legs and both her arms and was forcing them down next to her sides.

"Is there something else we should do here, or is that it?" Maya asked.

"Oh, I have one more trick." Anders spun his stun rod and winked at Maya. "You see, not only is this green goo incredibly sticky and troublesome. It's also a great conductor of electricity." With a flourish, Anders jammed the stun rod into the goo and activated it. A pulse of electricity went through the goo and Valerie, causing her to seize up and collapse onto the ground.

"You won't get away with this," she yelled through gritted teeth.

"I think we already did," Anders said. He grabbed Maya's hand, and they ran away as fast as they could, leaving Valerie in the park, struggling with the goo, and straining to get her muscles to work.

"Ignore the car for now, it's too risky," Anders said as they ran.

"Agreed. We need to get to alternate transport." Maya kept pace with Anders easily.

I wish I could teleport around, that would be helpful.

They left the park and Anders led them around the block and across the street. Maya periodically looked back, but there was no sign of Valerie.

"How long do we have?" Maya said as they turned into another street, still jogging.

"Five minutes probably. Ten, if we get really lucky. The goo is very strong and sticky, but it breaks down pretty fast. More if she struggles hard. Which she will." Anders directed Maya down some stairs. She followed quickly, dodging people streaming up and down the stairs. They emerged into an underground concourse.

"Where are we?" Maya asked. Anders slowed to a walk and Maya fell into step alongside him.

"Train station entry. But we won't get the train. We will emerge somewhere else and get a taxi." Anders navigated confidently through the area, weaving between the crowds. Maya noticed lots of eateries and shops but didn't get a good look at them. They soon reached a set of stairs, and Anders bounded up, taking two at a time.

Maya stepped into the daylight and looked around. There was a bus depot nearby, the giant black buses looking like electric coffins. Anders hailed an automated taxi, it was decorated like a New York taxi, in yellow and black. Anders opened the back door, ushering Maya in. She climbed over to the far seat and Anders got in after her.

He directed the taxi to take them to the hotel and relaxed back into the chair.

"We made it. She can't have tracked us this way," Anders said. He gave Maya a reassuring smile.

"Great. That was a close escape. Lucky you had that goo with you. Is that a new thing?"

"Yeah, I was keeping it for emergencies. It won't work a second time. The counter measures are too simple." Anders sighed and pulled out his phone.

"Raising a job to retrieve the hire car," he explained while operating the phone.

"Right." Maya stared out of the taxi, watching the traffic.

Valerie on our tail. I really thought we were clear of all this. And now my identity is out there. What a mess.

"Cheer up," Anders said, putting his phone down.

"I'll be okay, just need a moment." Maya faked a smile and pulled out her phone. She typed out a message to Mikael.

NEW DEVELOPMENTS. Please call ASAP. Need information on teleportation.

MAYA PUT HER PHONE AWAY. She recognized the area. They were nearing the hotel.

"We're going to have to be smart now about our movements. I can be tracked easily," Maya said. Anders nodded.

"I'll organize a few things. Kora can help too when she gets here." Anders paid for the taxi with his phone, and they stepped out, entering the hotel quickly.

"Let's just get up the room and plan our next moves." Anders strode ahead, pressing the button for the lift. He started tapping his foot impatiently.

He looks rattled, as much as he's trying to not be. He thought this was all under control, but we've been blindsided.

They rode the lift up in silence. Anders unlocked the door to their suite and held the door open as he entered.

"Care for a drink?" he said.

"Yeah. Pour some wine." Maya sunk into the couch and stared off into space. Anders bustled around in the kitchenette and returned with two glasses of red wine.

"Here's to being ambushed and escaping." Anders handed Maya a glass. She toasted his glass and took a big sip.

"Here's to my great ideas. Activating the Haste bloodline and having no way to train it!" Maya took a larger gulp. Anders sat next to her and leaned back.

"This is all solvable. You just need a teacher. Let me do some research." Anders put down his wine glass and pulled over his laptop. Maya pulled out her phone and kept rewatching the viral video exposing her.

MAYA PUT down the empty wine glass and also her phone.

"I'm done with this. What have you found out?" she said.

"Not great news I'm afraid. There's a reason why they don't test for teleportation at the Haste facility," Anders said. He paused and looked over at Maya.

"Because it's incredibly rare and nobody teaches it," she suggested. Anders nodded.

"That's the one. I've asked people in my network, and they've mentioned a teleportation user in Madrid. But information is sketchy."

"Sketchy is better than nothing. Show me what you have." Maya shuffled over to look at the screen over Anders's shoulder. He shifted the laptop over to give her a better look. It was a Bounty Hunter message board. Maya read out the post.

"Georgia Santos is a suspected Teleporter operating in Madrid. Linked with some minor burglaries. There's a job posting at the Bounty Center if you're interested." Maya stopped reading and looked at Anders. "Do you think going after her is a good idea?"

"No. Maybe? The official job might have some insider information that we need to track her down."

"And what happens if we don't take her in?" Maya said, giving Anders a skeptical look.

"I cancel the job. It's been open for months, so they will reallocate it." Anders took the laptop back and started looking up information on the Bounty Center.

"Will that have any repercussions? Can you even take jobs over here?" Maya stood up and wandered back over to the kitchenette with her wine glass.

"Yes, I can take jobs. And no drawbacks for failing a few here and there," Anders said, without looking up from his laptop.

"You want a top up?" she asked Anders. He shook his head. Maya filled her glass and eased back onto the couch. She checked her phone and there was no reply from Mikael.

"Get the job. Let's go find Georgia."

"Your wish is my command." Anders packed up his laptop, grabbed his coat, and was out the door in moments.

6

A SMALL LEAP

Maya stood outside the jewelry store. It was tiny, with no valuables in the front windows. Thick bars were behind the glass and the front door was locked.

"Are you sure this is the one?" she said.

"Positive. Doesn't look like much but some expensive stuff passes through here. Georgia made an unsuccessful attempt previously. That information has been left out of any news articles, so it's actionable. I think she will try again."

"Why?" Maya started walking past the window and exploring the dingy lane next to the shop.

"It's a hunch. Her power would make short work of the security."

"We think. Does anyone know how teleportation works?" Maya peered into a side window. There was a dark shape blocking it entirely.

"No, it's a closely guarded secret. Or it just isn't understood. There's a strange stigma against the power." Anders followed the lane around the back of the shop and Maya walked with him, looking around at the nearby buildings.

There are no good vantage points to check for security. Depending on the range of the teleportation, you'd need to get dangerously close to get inside.

"I can understand why. It's not a power that the Master Sage would approve of. Free and unrestricted access to wherever you want to go isn't exactly his style."

"No, it's not at all. Come back here." Anders directed Maya to a nook in the back wall. It looked like it was a building defect, but it was big enough for them to stand inside and not be visible to anyone walking down the laneway without coming closer.

"I get the plan. But why is she coming here tonight?"

"It suits her mode of operating. It's the end of the month. New stock has arrived, and there's also stock awaiting collection. Last time she tried was a similar time," Anders explained patiently, but Maya could sense the tinge of annoyance.

He thinks I don't trust him.

"I just want this to work."

"Me too. Now we wait." Anders motioned for Maya to be quiet, and they stood at the ready.

Darkness fell quickly, and soon after Maya heard the sound of footsteps slowly approaching their position. Anders held up his phone and showed it to Maya. It was displaying a video feed of the laneway before them. A shadowy figure was approaching the rear entry of the jewelry store and paused in front of it. After looking both ways, the figure shimmered then disappeared. Maya gasped.

"Sorry, that was incredible."

"We gotta move fast. Follow me." Anders darted from their hiding spot, running to the rear door. He tossed a metallic object at the door, and it attached itself near the lock. Anders pressed a small remote in his hand and the object exploded, destroying the lock. The door swung open.

Anders wasted no time dashing into the building, with his stun wand drawn. Maya carefully followed. Inside was a haze of smoke from the blast. Past it was a vault room. Shelves of metal boxes lined the walls. A figure stood just past the room, frozen still. Anders was right there, with his stun wand extended.

"Made it in time. Help me, will you?" Anders said. Maya ran forward and grabbed the shadowy figure by one arm. She looked under the hood and saw a woman with blonde hair and green eyes with a pained expression on her face.

"This is not what it seems like," Maya said as they helped the woman outside.

"It looks like you're taking me in," the woman hissed.

"Not today, Georgia. We have a proposition for you," Anders said as they got her outside.

"This isn't how I'd go about winning me over," Georgia muttered.

"He loves his gadgets too much, but he can be charming too. Sometimes," Maya said with a chuckle. They supported Georgia back through the laneway and into a black van.

"I swear this isn't as dodgy as it looks," Anders said. Georgia grunted, unimpressed.

"Not the greatest first impression we're making here," Maya said as she settled in with Georgia and Anders closed the van doors.

"You don't say? He's a hunter, isn't he?" Georgia said.

"Yes. But we're not taking you in. We need your help. We used the contract to find you." Maya shifted in her seat as the van careened around a corner. Georgia was awkwardly lying across the seat.

"Need something stolen? That's all I can do for you," Georgia said.

"No. I need training. I need to learn how to teleport like

you." Maya watched Georgia's reaction. She broke into a pained laugh.

"Oh, that's rich. You have the teleportation power?" Georgia asked. Maya's look confirmed it. "Hah, so you're also cursed."

"We're here," Anders announced from the front of the van. It lurched to a sudden stop, and Maya helped Georgia into a more upright position. Her arms and legs were twitching now.

"Maybe next time don't stun me? Really painful." Georgia wriggled and soon had proper control of her arms. As she was trying her legs, Anders pulled the van doors open.

"Let's move." Anders helped out Maya, and then Georgia. He slammed the doors shut and led them into what looked like a warehouse. Inside though, it was a gym.

They entered a room with exercise equipment. Through the windows, Maya could see a basketball court beyond.

"Not sure what we need to make this work, so I figured a variety of training equipment might help. We have mats, too," Anders said as he walked through the space.

"I never said I'd help," Georgia said.

"We'll pay."

"Well, that's a given, since you've hit me with a stun wand and kidnapped me."

"I'm sorry, we did come in a bit too hard on that. You're here now, what else could we do?" Maya said.

"Hmm." Georgia rubbed her arm and looked at them thoughtfully. "You've ruined my robbery, I don't have any prospects, and you want my help. Maybe a fresh start for me would be nice."

"We can pay you enough to not have to work for a while. If you skip town and don't hit that same jewelry store again, the police have no leads. Our investigation will go nowhere," Maya said. Georgia looked at Maya and crossed her arms.

"It's a good enough. But I can't train you. Not properly."

"Why not?"

"I'm terrible at teleportation. My mentor said so himself. And refused to work with me anymore."

"Looked like you did pretty well back there," Anders said. Georgia scoffed at that.

"That was my max range, and I need a very detailed image to work with. Plus, I can't teleport again for twenty minutes."

"That's why you went back there—you'd already done the work scoping it out," Maya said. Georgia sighed.

"So much effort expended there. But you work with what you can." Georgia looked over at Maya and Anders. "I need the money. I'll help you how I can. But you'll need to find a proper master."

"Who taught you?" Anders said.

"Guy called Eduardo. He was the real deal. I think he was after a partner, but I wasn't up to it. Too many limitations. Not like him, he could do it all." Georgia fully stretched out, almost losing her balance. But she stabilized herself quickly.

"I can talk you through the basics. But I'm not a teacher."

"I'll take what I can get. Let's start." Maya followed Georgia over to an area with mats.

"In case you actually teleport, we better start over here. Less chance of injury," Georgia said.

"I'm not worried about getting hurt," Maya said.

"It's not that. You might shrug it off. But if there's one thing I learned, the pain can become a blocker. Teleportation needs strong focus. If you think you'll get injured, it'll be an issue you need to work through." Georgia walked around and arranged a few mats. She picked up a red cushion and placed it in the middle of the mats.

"Come stand over here," she said. Maya walked over.

"The basic idea is this. You visualize a place and shift yourself there. But you need to umm, understand the location."

"Understand?" Maya asked.

"Yeah. There's some sort of protection built in, so you can't appear inside another object. But it doesn't bump you over or anything. It'll just fail."

"Does that consume your power? Do you need to wait again?" Maya said.

"You betcha. I invested a lot in that store. I was about to get away with it too!" Georgia sighed and returned her focus back to the exercise.

"Stare at the location where the red cushion is. Try and take in all the details," Georgia said. Maya nodded and stared at the cushion. She peered at the mat surrounding it. She noted that the cushion was at the join of two different blue mats. She noted how far off the ground it was. After a minute she looked back at Georgia.

"So, what now?" Maya said.

"Close your eyes and take yourself to that spot. Right in front of the cushion. That easy," Georgia said. Maya closed her eyes and imagined the cushion and the area right around it. She tried to focus on all the details, using her practice of visualizing from when she had trained the Chakra bloodline.

"Move yourself there," Georgia said. Maya tried to get herself there. She willed herself over. She felt something change, but instead, she just fell over.

"See? The mat helps," Georgia said with a chuckle. Anders walked over and gave Maya a hand up. She got back on her feet and wobbled a little.

"It's disorientating. Especially at first," Georgia said.

"What happened?" Maya looked over at the mats and apart from being a bit displaced by her fall, everything else was the same.

"You teleported. A tiny bit." Georgia held out two fingers an inch apart.

"It was like your whole body blinked," Anders said.

"If it worked, then why didn't it work?" Maya bent down to return the mats to their exact position.

"Something wasn't right. You weren't sure of the location probably. Go over and study the cushion and mats up close," Georgia said. Maya walked around the mats, not stepping on them. She crouched and examined the cushion up close, staring next to it, around it, behind it, above it, and even lifted the cushion to look under it, before returning it to its place.

"Will this help? Do I have to wait twenty minutes?" Maya said, walking back to her starting position.

"Yeah, more information never hurt. The delay is worth testing. It's trainable, but I reckon if yours was better, it would start lower than mine." Georgia stood there with her arms crossed, waiting. Maya closed her eyes and tried again.

She continued the visualization and focus. Remembering all the details of the location. She made the destination more explicit in her mind. Commanding her presence to move precisely. Abruptly she felt another change.

Maya collapsed onto the mat again, but this time halfway between her starting point at the red cushion. She thrust her right fist into the air.

"Look at that!" Maya shouted with a grin.

"That was something." Anders kept his expression passive. Maya narrowed her eyes.

"Out with it," she prompted.

"Nothing."

"C'mon."

"Well, the reality bending quality to it is amazing. But it looks a bit funny," Anders said carefully.

"You're basically falling over a distance that you could easily jump and not be helpless," Georgia said with a cheeky grin. Maya's cheeks reddened. She scrambled back up off the floor.

"Well, I don't have to look at myself. Let's go again." Maya walked back to the starting point.

"That was an improvement though," Anders said.

"Go do some cardio, Anders. You're going to need to keep up once I start teleporting everywhere," Maya said.

"Okay, boss," Anders said, heading off toward an exercise bike.

"You noticed a difference though, didn't you? It felt better?" Georgia said, coming in closer.

"Yeah, I did. Small, but noticeable." Maya did some slow breathing and prepared herself again.

"I'm no teacher, but small and noticeable does add up over time," Georgia said.

She's right. Just keep at it.

"At least I don't have to wait twenty minutes," Maya said. She dove into herself and tried again.

HOURS LATER THEY PARTED WAYS. Georgia promised to help again tomorrow before she left town.

"Do you think she'll follow through?" Maya said to Anders as they walked back through the lobby of their hotel.

"Absolutely. We only paid her half. She wants the rest." Anders called the elevator and they both entered.

"I'd like to think she wants to help as well. Seeing as how it was so hard for her to learn." Maya exited first as soon as the doors opened, heading for their suite. She stopped suddenly.

"The solution to all your problems has arrived," Kora said, waiting in the hallway.

7

GOING FOR GREEN

Maya walked up to Kora.

"It's great to see you," she said.

"Well, I knew you needed help," Kora said. "Come this way." She led them down the hall to her suite and opened the door. Anders and Maya followed her through.

As expected, the room was already completely filled with technology. Cables, tables, monitors, towers, and other lab equipment filled the space.

"How do you always set up this quickly?" Anders said.

"I have my ways. And people who help," Kora said with a wink.

Of course, she probably uses her persuasion power to help people along a bit.

Kora led them through the tangled mess to her main workstation.

"It's all good news," she said, "but some things are easier than others. Let's start with the facility. It's definitely the one that we want. The data you retrieved is good. I've paged through it and seen the test subjects we've been reviewing. Most of them went through this location. I think they were picked up from this facility for the test program. This is going to be one we want to look at closely. Do you have a way inside?" Kora said.

"Not yet. Although Maya was working on an angle yester-day," Anders explained.

"Yes, yes, until the viral video came out. Were you actually in the facility?" Kora asked.

"Yes, I had to run out. Then I was tailed and...then we had to fight Valerie. We got away, but it was messy." Maya put on a smile, but she felt really embarrassed.

"Don't worry. You went for broke and sometimes it doesn't work. That's why I'm here. I'm gonna help you come up with a plan to figure out how to get in. Now that you're wanted, we're gonna have to take a very slow and quiet approach."

"Will Maya's new powers help?" Anders said with a hopeful look.

"What is your power?" Kora asked.

"Teleportation, as it turns out," Maya said.

"Oh, that's a good one. I haven't really heard much about it though. Does it work like I think it does?" Kora immediately started searching for information about teleportation.

"Well, we think so, but it doesn't really work properly yet," Maya said. Anders chuckled. "There's a lot of falling over to start with, but I'm sure it'll get better."

Kora was still looking at her screen.

"Teleportation I can work with. The schematics on this place look like it's very hard to get in." Kora brought up some images on her laptop.

"We're going to need a coordinated plan to get in here and it's going to take a bit of time, but with me here we'll succeed. Anything else?"

"Well..." Maya began.

"It sounds like you need a teacher for teleportation. I'll look into that for you as well. Do you have any names to run?"

"Just the one for now," Maya said. "The person helping me now mentioned her mentor was called Eduardo. He might still be in the city." Kora started typing away, reviewing information on the computer.

"I'll probably need more than that but leave it with me. I'm sure there's not that many teleportation users around, let alone in this city."

"We need to look at all the angles. We are really keen to get into this building," Anders said.

"Oh yes, this is not any ordinary building. I can see from the tech that they've got in here that it's very secure. But I'll get you in," Kora said. "If there's nothing else?"

"There is one thing. I really want to find out who launched that video about me. I keep thinking it has to be the Master Sage. But I want to know for sure. And if it is him, then any evidence of that will be useful in the future."

"Yeah, I'll run some diagnostics over it and see what I can pull out. It's an interesting one, and the timing was very awkward," Kora said, with a grin. Maya shrugged.

"Yeah, but now we just gotta make the best of things."

"Alright, well, I will leave you guys to it while I continue my work over here. Have a good night. Let's catch up tomorrow," Kora said. She waved them away and buried herself in the computer screen.

"Come on," Anders said. "You're probably exhausted after all that falling over."

"I am, actually. Let's go before I try and teleport back," Maya countered. Anders laughed and he held the door open for her.

∾

THE NEXT MORNING, Maya awoke to a message on her phone. It was from Mikael.

· · ·

Hᵢ Mᴀʏᴀ. A lot's going on right now. With the recent video released, I have to be careful communicating with you. I can however say this much. There is a teleport expert in your city who is very good. He's hard to find, but worth the effort. His name is Eduardo Estevez. Good luck.

"Finally, a break!" Maya said. Anders wandered over with a curious look on his face.

"What did you get?"

"Mikael came through. He got me the name of a teleport expert who can teach me. It sounds like the same one that was Georgia's mentor." Maya closed her eyes for a moment and just rejoiced.

"Let me text Kora and start doing some searching," Anders said. He quickly grabbed his laptop and started typing away. As he worked, Maya paced around the room.

"Okay, you and Kora can track him down while I do some more training with Georgia. Then, when we meet up with him, I won't be completely hopeless," Maya said.

"Sounds like a plan to me." Anders kept his attention focused on the laptop. "I'm not getting a lot, but the name checks out. We need to do a bit more digging on this one. But we've got a lead."

"We sure do. Can I leave this with you? I'm gonna go meet up with Georgia." Maya grabbed the car keys and ran over to the door.

"Have fun," Anders called out but didn't look up. He was buried in the computer screen.

Mᴀʏᴀ ᴘᴀʀᴋᴇᴅ the orange sports car across the road from the gym they had used. Because the neighborhood was quite industrial, the car stood out a little bit, but there wasn't much she could do about that.

Maybe we should ditch the sports cars for a while. Even without the track device, it's quite conspicuous.I don't want to bring too much attention.

Maya locked the car and jogged through the courtyard and into the building. With a sigh of relief, she saw Georgia waiting there, playing on her phone. Maya noticed the woman's curly blonde hair for the first time. She hadn't really taken it in the night before.

"You came. I wasn't sure if you would if I'm being honest," Maya said. She put on a smile and waited for George's reaction.

"Yeah, I wanted the money. Besides, you need all the help you can get. You're kind of terrible," Georgia said with a grin. Maya chuckled.

"You're right. I do need all the help I can get. Shall we get started?"

"Let's go." Georgia walked over to the mats where they had practiced the previous time. Maya joined her and noticed that the red cushion was gone. There was now a green cushion in its place.

"So, will a different colored cushion help me better? Will it be easier?" Maya said, not disguising the confusion in her voice.

"No," Georgia said with a laugh. "It's just a change of focus. It should help you learn a bit faster. Otherwise, you'll just get fixated on that red cushion way too much." Georgia sounded like she was speaking from experience.

Okay, here we go.

Maya took her position in front of the mats and did the same as before, staring at the green cushion and examining the area around it trying to understand its location and all the things nearby. She stopped and decided to do a proper investigation.

Maya wandered around the entire mat area, pausing, and peering from different angles as she completed her circuit. When she got back to her starting position, she went for a second lap, trying to pick different vantage points and different angles to look through. Finally, after another slow circuit of the area, Maya was satisfied that she'd done all she could do to learn the location and the place.

This better work, or at least not be such a fail.

Maya closed her eyes and focused again. She took a deep breath in and slowly let the breath out, focusing her attention and her mind on the green cushion and the space around it. She really pushed herself to move through space, to be there, in that particular spot. As before, she felt a kind of power building up in her. It was more obvious this time. But she felt like it was slightly more controlled. A little bit easier to grasp.

Channeling the power, she willed herself forward and felt another shift. Maya opened her eyes and saw herself halfway to the cushion in a crouched and ready position. She carefully looked around and noticed that she was stable.

"This looks like an improvement," she said cautiously, standing up slowly. Georgia gave her a nod of approval.

"Yeah, that's much better. You're still not quite to the target, but you're making strides. Try again."

"I will. I'll just keep doing it as much as I need to." Maya steeled her resolve and walked back to the starting position, closed her eyes, and prepared all over again.

MAYA OPENED HER EYES, and her vision was full of green.

What happened?

Adjusting her vision, Maya slowly moved her head back and realized her face was pressed into a cushion. A green cushion.

"I did it?" she said slowly.

"You sure did. I'll give you a ten for location, but maybe a three for your body placement?" Georgia was scrunching up her face as she gave the verdict. Maya stood up fully and wiped a bead of sweat from her forehead.

"I'll take it. Getting there has to be the first priority." Maya smiled and Georgia gave her a thumbs up.

"Well, that's my job done. You did a teleport successfully. I am going to skip town and go enjoy my new winnings. If that's okay with you?" Georgia said, looking at Maya.

"Sure. A deal is a deal." Maya pulled out her phone and completed the funds transfer. A little 'ping' sounded from Georgia's phone and her face broke out into a giant grin.

"This is it. Time to get out of this stinking city." Georgia turned and started off toward the exit. Maya jogged along to catch up.

"Hey, so just a quick one before you leave," Maya said. Georgia stopped and turned around.

"Yeah, what is it?"

"Your old mentor. Was his name Eduardo Estevez?"

"Could be. We never used surnames. Sorry, I can't give you more. I think he'd probably teach you though. You're a fast learner. Faster than me, at least." Georgia gave a shrug and started walking again.

"Thanks. Good luck with whatever you're off to next," Maya said. Georgia held up her hand in a wave without turning around, disappearing through the doors. Maya didn't follow, letting the woman go.

You have other things to focus on now.

Maya pulled her phone out again, checking her notifications. Multiple missed calls from Anders and one message. She read it.

GOT A POSSIBLE LOCATION ON EDUARDO, but we need to move tonight. Let me know as soon as you get this message.

· · ·

Maya typed out a reply.

Heading back now, let's go track the guy down. Thank Kora for me, she did a great job finding him.

Maya put her phone away with a smile.

Time to find a real teacher.

8

REMOTE LOCATION

Maya opened the door and stepped into Kora's suite. She turned and saw Anders and Kora huddled together over a computer monitor.

"So, who actually found Eduardo?" Maya asked.

Anders and Kora looked up, and then at each other. "Fine. It was actually Kora," Anders said, with a sigh.

"Of course it was me," Kora said. "But he was helpful."

Kora went back to working on the computer and Anders walked over to Maya.

"How'd you go today?" he asked.

"Pretty well. I've successfully teleported to a green cushion," Maya said. She couldn't hide the smile on her face. It just bloomed all by itself.

"That's great," Anders said. "What made the difference?"

"I'm not sure. But I think it was just practicing. Georgia was pretty helpful."

Maya walked around and sat on the couch, getting comfortable. Anders joined her.

"So, where is Eduardo, and when do we have to leave?" Maya asked.

"Did you want to handle this one, Kora?" Anders looked over at her. She raised her hand, as if to acknowledge yes, and started speaking without looking at them.

"He's on the outskirts of town, in an abandoned area. I'm actually surprised that I found him. But I got a few tricks, and I pulled in some favors." Kora paused and showed a satisfied grin.

"I think he's trying to plan some kind of job, which is the only reason I found his trail at all. I reckon this guy could hide undetected for a long time if he really wanted to," Kora said. She went back to working on her computer.

"So, we think we have to move tonight," Anders began. "Because..."

"If he is planning something, he might not stay there very long," Kora said.

Anders stood and started pacing around the room.

"Alright, so let's go get him," Maya said, standing from the couch. She looked between Anders and Kora. "Why aren't we going already?"

"Kora's just finishing up some analysis of the area to make sure there's no traps," Anders said. "I guess we can go prepare ourselves and head over. I'm sure she'll give us a call if there's any problems."

"You know I will," Kora said.

"Then it's settled." Maya walked to the door and Anders followed close behind.

"I don't think we should take the bright orange sports car this time," Maya said.

"Yeah, maybe not. I guess it's the van," Anders said with a dry chuckle.

As they drove, the city lights grew fainter and fainter. Soon only the high beams on the van were showing them where the road began and ended.

"This is really remote," Maya said. "This guy likes being alone."

"Well, if you think about it since he can teleport, does it really matter how far away he is?" Anders said. He quickly swerved to avoid some debris on the road.

"Was that a tree trunk?" Maya asked.

"I didn't see," Anders said. "But I dodged it."

They kept driving, but Anders reduced his speed a little.

"I wonder how far I can teleport," Maya said, thinking out loud.

"That's the real trick, isn't it?" Anders said. "Just think, if you can really improve this ability, you'll have the ultimate freedom. You can go anywhere."

Maya liked the sound of that. She stared out the window and let her brain wander.

How good would it be to just be able to move wherever I want, whenever I want? Without having to worry about the space in between. I wonder if I can take people with me. Could Anders and I teleport places?

Maya's thoughts continued to drift, while Anders navigated the now treacherous roads. They were very windy. Going up and down hills with very bad visibility.

Eventually, he slowed and turned off the headlights. They were now in pitch black. Darkness surrounded them as the van came to a stop.

"I take it we're here?" Maya said.

"That's right. We have to approach on foot. We don't want to spook the guy, or he'll just leave."

"I know I would," Maya said, getting out of the van, her eyes adjusted to the darkness. They were in a very dusty area, with minimal shrubs and trees. Maya pulled out her phone and cast a small light on the ground around her.

"This really is the middle of nowhere. He doesn't want people stumbling across him, does he?" Maya said.

"One more reason for us to be careful." Anders pulled out a small gadget from his coat, which ended up being a torch. He lit the ground ahead of them. A small narrow beam lighting just enough so they didn't trip on a stone or an unforeseen obstacle.

They trudged quietly through the underbrush, with Anders periodically checking his phone to see if they were heading in the right direction.

"Are we on track?" Maya asked.

"Yes, we're on track. And Kora just messaged me," Anders said. "She thinks the area is clear."

He went back to studying his phone. Slowly they crept along, Maya almost tripping on the occasional stone or bush. With every step they inched closer, but it felt like it was taking a long time.

"I can barely see two steps ahead," Maya said.

"I know. We've just got to work with this," Anders said, checking his phone again. "It'll be too easy to spot us from a distance otherwise."

"Is this his house?" Maya said.

"We think so. It looks like a house, based on the aerial imagery that Kora pulled up. We know he's here. Well, we saw evidence of him here recently. So, we think that he's still here, but it's a gamble." Anders put his phone away and focused instead on the light and the path ahead of them.

"From here on we can't miss it. We need to be careful. Keep an eye out for any traps and try not to make too much noise."

"I'll do my best," Maya said. She kept trying to peer into the distance, but she couldn't make out any additional details. The building was taking on more of a house-like shape now, with a pitched roof. She looked around for some evidence of a vehicle, but there was none.

Just as they were reaching the perimeter of the building, they were suddenly blinded by a bright light. Maya froze and so did Anders. Standing perfectly still as their eyes adjusted, they noticed flood lamps had been activated on the roof of the house. The entire area around the house was blanketed in bright, white light.

"So, I think we've been spotted, Anders," Maya said. She took a step forward. "Since he knows we're here, we might as well go and knock on the door." With the additional lighting, Maya decided to jog ahead, not seeing anything on the ground that looked like a trap or a danger. Anders jogged behind her, trying to keep up. As Maya reached the door, she slowed down to a walk. It looked like an older house from the 1970s. It was made out of concrete with a tiled roof and a large wooden door.

Maya walked up to the door and rapped on it three times. There was no answer. She listened carefully to hear the sound of someone approaching. Anders stood next to her, peering into a nearby window.

"I can't see anything. You should try the door," he said. Maya turned the round handle and applied a bit of pressure. The door opened. Inside, the house was pitch black. With no lights on, the bright lights from the outside cast eerie shadows.

"Here we go!" Maya said and took a step inside, cautiously looking around. She was in a long hallway with several rooms branching off. She walked confidently down the corridor, her footsteps echoing on the wooden floorboards. She could hear Anders behind her, the uneven rhythm of his steps suggesting that he was checking for danger.

"Don't you have some thermal goggles or something like that in your bag of tricks?" Maya said.

"I actually do," Anders said. He pulled out a headband with goggles and put it over his eyes. Maya turned and looked at him.

"That really works?"

"Yes." Anders moved his head left to right, scanning the

property. "I'm not picking up anything. But let's just finish our tour."

They continued through the house, exploring two bedrooms, a lounge, a kitchen, and a bathroom. The decor was all very dated.

"Rubbish in the bin, seems recent," Anders noted.

"I noticed a cup in the sink too. It has been occupied," Maya added.

"I've not seen anything like it. How unusual. This is like the house time forgot," Anders said.

They finished their sweep of the building and returned back to the front door.

"Do you think he just left? Or has been gone for a while?" Maya said.

"I think he was here, and he disappeared the moment we were detected. The place feels lived in. Don't worry, we'll find another way to track him." Anders put the goggles away and started to walk out of the building.

"Do we leave a note?" Maya followed him and they walked alongside each other, their footsteps crunching on the dry ground beneath their feet.

"If you want, there's a pen in the van," Anders said.

"I guess I shouldn't have gotten my hopes up." Maya walked a little slower, losing the excitement that had fueled her before.

"Well, it was a bit of a long shot," Anders said. "But he's definitely been there recently. We're on the right track."

They could still see quite clearly with all the floodlights, and there was no trouble making their way back toward the van.

"Well, it's not done yet," Maya said. "We can keep looking for him. I do need a proper teacher."

Maya kicked a pebble in front of her and it rolled away into some nearby brush.

"I promise we'll find him, and we'll do whatever it takes to get his help," Anders said. "Just keep your mind on the possibilities we have here.

"You're right. Once I can master this, I can go anywhere. I mean, there's gonna be some limitations. But...wow. I'm excited. This is the kind of stuff that just doesn't happen."

Anders gave a broad smile.

"That's it. That's the right attitude. We focus on what we can do, and Kora and I will help with the nitty-gritty of how to get there."

They continued trudging along the dusty ground. As they left the well-lit areas, Anders pulled out his torch again, shining the way for them. They didn't talk anymore. Maya instead let her mind wander again, thinking about how she was going to get better at teleporting, but also worrying about the Master Sage.

What if he comes to me now? I'm completely defenseless. I... I can't do anything yet. Gotta get better. And fast.

They reached the van soon enough. Anders lit it up with his torch and unlocked the doors. He opened Maya's door and waited for her to get in before he closed it.

Maya sat in the van, staring out into the darkness. Anders got in the driver's seat and started the van. As Maya turned to look at him, something caught her attention in the rearview mirror. She turned and gasped.

There was a man sitting in the back of the van, lounging on the seat. He had black curly hair, thin-rimmed glasses, and a thick bushy beard. He was dressed all in black.

"Who might you be paying me a visit so late at night?" the man said, his voice had an amused tone to it.

"Who are you, sneaking into our van?" Maya said in response. Anders looked like he was reaching for something. The man held out his hand.

"Stop. Don't do anything rash. You know who I am, but I don't know who you are," he said.

"Are you Eduardo?" Maya said. He held out his hands in a grand gesture, displaying himself.

"The one and only," Eduardo said. "And you are?"

"I'm Maya, and this is Anders. How'd you get in here?" she said. Eduardo scoffed at that.

"I teleported, of course. Isn't that why you came to find me?"

9

THE TELEPORTATION MASTER

"How did you find me?" Eduardo asked, looking from Maya to Anders.

"It's a bit of a long story," Maya said. "But we found another teleport user called Georgia." Maya paused and looked for Eduardo's reaction.

"Oh yes, yeah, I know her," Eduardo said. "But she didn't know enough about me to find where I am. I kept a lot from her. What else did you have?"

"You're right. She only had your first name, which put us on the trail. Another contact of mine gave me your full name and mentioned that you were still in the city," Maya said quickly. Eduardo nodded along, stroking his chin thoughtfully.

"This colleague of yours. A Speedster?" he asked.

"Yes," Maya said. "Once we had your name, I had some help canvassing the city. Anders, do you want to talk about that?"

"Sure. A mutual friend of ours helped me run some searches based on your name, any identifying photos, satellite imagery, and so on. It was a pretty comprehensive search."

"Are you worried?" Maya said.

"No," Eduardo said. "I like to think that I keep a low profile, so I'm always interested to hear how someone tracks me down. It's been a while since the last person. So now that we've figured that out, why are you here?"

"I need your help," Maya said. "I have the teleportation power, and I don't know how to use it. Georgia gave me a few tips, but she's very limited in her ability." Eduardo leaned forward in the chair, staring at Maya, studying her.

"Well, it's always good to master a skill that you have. But why do you need to learn?" he said. Maya took a breath before responding.

"I, uh... I need to increase my power. I have unlocked this power and it's of no use to me right now. I can't move forward until I learn how to master it," Maya said cautiously. Eduardo kept peering into her, tilting his head slightly, as if thinking of something.

"You look familiar," he said, gesturing with his hand. "There's something about you. I've seen your face...somewhere." Eduardo trailed off, lost in the thought. Maya cleared her throat.

"There's no point pretending. There's been a video released recently about a woman—" Maya said, before Eduardo interrupted.

"That's you!" he said excitedly, clicking his fingers. "I saw you on the news. You're a multi-blood, aren't you? You've got the LifeDeath and the Chakra bloodlines already mastered." Eduardo then clapped his hands in delight. "Oh, this is interesting. Really interesting. So, you've activated the Haste bloodline, and now you're powerless."

"I wouldn't put it in those words, but...yes," Maya said slowly. Anders reached into his coat.

"Slow down there," Eduardo said. "Like I mentioned before, don't do anything rash. We're just talking here. I'm not trying to scare you. I apologize. Now I understand your urgency in learning. That's a useful thing to have in your pocket."

"What is? Maya said.

"The need for urgency, the desire to get stronger faster. It's a good way to inspire the tremendous effort you'll need to get better at this," he said, leaning back in the seat. "Well, it was nice to meet you. I think I'll be going now."

"Wait!" Maya cried. "Why won't you help me?"

Eduardo looked thoughtful. "You are a walking problem. Everyone's looking for you, and I bet the Master Sage is as well. That's not the kind of heat that I'm looking for right now. No offense." He turned to open the van door to leave.

"You have to help me, please. I'll do whatever it takes," Maya said. She reached down and grabbed his hand, pleading with him. Eduardo shook her hand away from him.

"I'm sorry. Those are forces that I'm not willing to get tangled up with. Good luck, Maya. It was nice meeting you." Eduardo bowed his head and then—vanished. Maya stared in disbelief at the space in front of her.

"That didn't go well. At all," she said.

"Well, we did find him, and he is a teleport expert. You know, that's something," Anders said, trying to remain hopeful.

"That just makes it even more depressing." Maya turned to sit back in her chair. "He was right here, and now he's gone. Who's gonna help me now?" Maya sighed, staring off into the darkness.

"This isn't over," Anders said. "He just popped away somewhere. We'll find him tomorrow. Next time, he'll say yes." Anders gave her a reassuring look, and Maya gave him a brief smile in response.

"You're right. Let's regroup and have another try," she said.

*

Maya shuffled her weight, leaning awkwardly as she balanced a tray of coffees in one hand and knocked on the door with the other.

"Come in, it's open!" Kora called out from inside the suite.

Maya twisted the handle and leaned into the door, walking backward through it, and turning to avoid spilling the tray. Kora and Anders were hunched over a computer, talking quietly amongst themselves.

"I'm here with coffee," Maya announced, walking into the room. She handed Kora and Anders their coffees. They accepted them without even looking up. Maya sat down nearby, taking a sip of her coffee, and listening in.

"I'm running my program now," Kora said, gesturing at the screen. "You'll see in a minute all the facial recognition hits."

"Good. We can track his movements," Anders said. He took a sip of his coffee and turned to look at Maya. "This is good coffee, thank you."

"Anytime. Where are we up to with Eduardo?" Maya said.

"Anders managed to get a few decent snaps of his face during your conversation last night." Kora brought up images on the monitor. "These, combined with the photos already around, have been enough for me to build a face to pattern-match against." Kora brought up some more screens on the monitor and nodded.

"We're using a blend of satellite imagery and video feeds from across the city. Kora has managed to access a surprising number," Anders said slowly.

"I see. So, do we have any locations? Do we have an idea of where he's going to be?" Maya asked.

"That's all we're waiting for now," Anders said. "How long, Kora?"

"A matter of seconds. Oh, here we go. Let's have a look." Kora hit a few more keys, and then a map was shown on the screen. There were five red points marked on the map. Kora zoomed in, reading off the locations.

"Hmm. This looks like the tech markets. Over here it's vehicle workshops. This is a museum. This is a library. And this...aha!" Kora pointed at the last point on the map and turned to look at Maya.

"This is your mysterious facility."

"What?" Maya said. "He's inside there? He's also interested in that place?"

"That's not inside," Anders said, interrupting. "But it's very close. Maybe he's scoping it out."

"You're right. This is a nearby building. Let me bring up the specs. It's quite a tall one. Probably has a good vantage point over that Haste facility," Kora said. She started drumming her fingers on the table.

"We've got a good idea of what this guy's up to, I think. He's interested in the same things you are. Is that an angle you can follow up on?"

"I think so. We've got something to negotiate with, but now we just need to figure out where he's going to be next," Maya said.

"Where can we find him?" Anders said.

"Let me think a minute." Kora stretched her neck and rested her hand on the back of her head, looking around at nothing in particular.

"There has to be a pattern here," she said. "Where's he going to go next?"

"Can you plot all these points in relation to the house we visited last night?" Maya asked. Kora leapt into action, and soon there was a network of lines connecting all the locations.

"Hmm...nothing much is popping out just yet, but I think we can start to see his comfortable teleport radius," Kora said. She tapped a few more keys, and then a circle appeared on the map, enclosing all of the locations she'd selected. The house they'd visited last night was at one end of the circle.

"So, this is his maximum range, we think," Anders said staring at the screen.

"I think so. Or at least it's the maximum range he's willing to share with us. You already mentioned how you tracked him so far. He might be playing games with us," Kora said.

"Is he still at that building with the vantage point?" Maya pointed at the location on the screen.

"That was the last location. We haven't had updates since," Kora said.

"Let's go there. Maybe he's waiting for us," Maya said. Anders shrugged.

"It's as good an idea as any. Let's go, Maya."

"Kora, can you call us if you have any updates?" Maya stood and took her coffee with her.

"I always do. Good luck," Kora said, turning her attention back to the screen. Anders followed Maya toward the door. Kora didn't even notice them leave.

ANDERS PARKED the van around the corner from the destination.

"Second time's a charm," he said.

"I hope so. I'm not sure we'll get a third," Maya replied. They left the van and walked along the street. There wasn't a lot of foot traffic. And barely any cars. It looked like the same kind of industrial area they'd already explored. But most of the buildings seemed closed or inactive.

"You would probably pick this area because it's quiet and hard to get spotted," Anders said.

"I hope so. Maybe he'll feel safe and wait for us. Or at least we can surprise him," Maya said.

"I'm not sure if he's going to let us surprise him at all. But let's at least check out the location." Anders led them down a narrow alley into an emergency staircase at the back of the building. He pulled out a grappling hook and threw it toward a metal ladder, hooking it on the top rung.

He dislodged the ladder from its resting place, and it slid down, giving access to the fire escape. "Ladies first," Anders said, gesturing toward the ladder. Maya started climbing, rung by rung, and once she reached the catwalk, she continued ascending the metal fire stairs at the back of the building.

"It's going to be pretty exposed up on this roof. Are we sure he's up here?" Maya said, as they walked.

"It's our best guess. At the very least we can always use the roof as an entry point to the rest of the building," Anders replied. Maya kept walking, trying to balance speed against making a lot of noise.

Maya crested the top of the building, looking out over the empty roof. It was all made of concrete, with some air conditioning ducts and other small structures. Toward the back, Maya saw a man sitting on a deck chair, relaxed, and facing away from them. It was Eduardo.

Maya stepped aside to give Anders space to come up and she pointed out Eduardo.

"It's him. It looks like he's waiting for us," Maya said.

"You were right. Well, let's go see what he has to say." Anders took off, and Maya walked with him. They picked their way across the roof, weaving in between the different structures. As they walked, Eduardo didn't stir. He remained seated, waiting.

Once they were closer, Maya noticed that Eduardo's eyes were closed.

"We meet again," Maya said. Eduardo opened his eyes and turned his head to look at them.

"You finally found me. I got a nice nap in before you did, at least."

"So, you were waiting for us?" Maya said, watching his reaction.

"Of course. I wanted to see how resourceful you were." Eduardo looked at Anders. "You talked a big game last night about how sophisticated your search was."

"Well, we found you," Maya said. "What are you doing up here?"

"Waiting for you," Eduardo said. "I think we have something in common." He pointed at the Haste facility over the road and around the corner.

"I did my research, and you were spotted fleeing from this facility. I don't think you were just there to get trained, but that's just a guess." Eduardo paused, waiting for Maya to reply.

"I might have some business there. Perhaps we might be able to work together," Maya said slowly.

"I'm not sure," Eduardo said. "Again, there's too much attention on you. You'd have to be really good to make it worth the risk."

"I can be. I just need someone to train me," Maya said. She stared at Eduardo defiantly, challenging him.

"Against my better judgment, I'm thinking about it. How about this? If you can teleport to that building next to us, we'll talk, and I'll take you on as a student," Eduardo said with a sly look on his face. Maya turned and looked at the building.

"No way," she breathed.

LEAP OF FAITH

Maya walked up to the edge, peering over at the other building. She couldn't help but notice the large drop in between the buildings.

I really don't want to fall down there.

She turned back to look at Eduardo.

"You want me to teleport over there?"

"Yes. If we work together, I'll be expecting much more from you. It's not that far. What, five to ten yards?" Eduardo stood up and wandered over until he was next to her.

"It's easy. Look," he said. And with that, he clicked his fingers, smiled, and then vanished. He appeared on the other building, facing Maya.

"See? That wasn't so hard," Eduardo said. A few seconds later, he reappeared next to Maya.

"There you go. Now it's your turn," Eduardo said. Maya stood there with a stunned look on her face.

I guess this is what I imagined, but just seeing it is incredible. It feels impossible.

Maya regarded the gap again, assessing the distance she

had to move. She tried to study the other building and its features.

"I'm not sure I can do this. I've only teleported a short distance and it required a lot of practice and study," Maya said.

"Here's one thing I'll teach you for free. The unconscious mind is so much more powerful than the conscious mind. All the things you've been trying sounds like how Georgia approaches teleportation."

"Well, she's the one that's taught me so far," Maya said. Eduardo laughed.

"She has no talent. Unfortunately, she has to scramble and scrap for every inch of her power. And that's why she needs to study a location in such fine and concentrated detail. But her lack of imagination is holding her back."

Maya looked over at Eduardo and then back at the building opposite her.

"Are you saying it's easier to imagine the location than what I've been doing?"

"Yes," Eduardo said. "It's the difference between thinking you know something and knowing it. If you can know the place, then you can be there when you need to be. That's all I'm going to say. The rest is up to you." Eduardo walked back to his deck chair, turned it to face Maya and the edge of the building, and sat back with his legs crossed.

"I'll let you try as much as you want, but you have till the end of the day." Eduardo settled into his chair. Anders walked over, close to Maya.

"Are you going to try?" he said, looking worried.

"Yeah, I have to try. This is our best shot."

"Well, that's fine. I know you can do it. But this is a big leap, isn't it?" He looked conflicted between trying to be supportive and also concerned.

"I think leaps are how you make progress. Leaps of faith," Maya said.

At least I sound more confident than I feel.

Maya turned to face the gap again. She looked over at the other building, trying to take in the location without studying it the way she had before. She tried to imagine what it felt like standing on the other building, the way that Eduardo had just done.

Seeing it was possible made her feel like it had to be possible.

If he can do it, I can do it. I've mastered two bloodlines already. I can do this too.

Maya closed her eyes and tried to imagine willing herself over. She focused, slowed her breathing, and began the same process she'd been practicing the previous day. She felt the power surge and fall away.

Maya let out a frustrated breath, composed herself, and tried again. It didn't work. She felt the power building, and it just kept fizzling out.

"Having trouble, are we?" Eduardo called out from his chair. Maya tried to ignore him.

"How do you think you're going to make any progress if you can't see where you're going?" Eduardo called out again. Maya opened her eyes and glanced over at him.

I think he's trying to help. Maybe I should try it, doing it differently.

Maya looked over at the edge. A chill went down her spine. She raised her gaze, focusing only on the building.

You just have to get over there. Just do that, and he'll train you. And we'll figure out everything else.

Maya took another breath, slowly, in and out. This time, she blocked out all distractions, all thinking. She stopped focusing the way that she was before. And her entire thought was just being somewhere else. Not willing herself there, not teleporting, not leaping. Just being there.

In one moment, she was where she was, and in the next

moment, she would be there. And with that, there was a sudden shift.

Light and sound flashed around Maya. She was completely disorientated. Swirls of color filled her vision. Strange spirals and other patterns emerged around her. There was a sensation of moving almost like swimming through space.

She felt almost like she was underwater trying to stay afloat. Suddenly everything solidified. Her feet were on the ground. She let go of a deep breath that felt like it'd been trapped in her lungs. Looking around, Maya saw herself on the other side of the building. She was facing back toward Anders. The look on his face was priceless. After an initial pause, Maya burst out laughing. "I can't believe I just did that."

Anders's jaw was still dropped, and he looked completely stunned.

"What did you think, Anders? Not bad, huh?" Maya said.

Anders visibly tried to shake himself out of whatever trance he was in. "Uh, yeah, great."

I don't think he can say anything else right now.

Maya turned her attention over to Eduardo. He was regarding her with curiosity. He stood up from the chair and walked over next to Anders.

"The results speak for themselves," he said. "Can you make it back?"

Panic set in, and Maya felt a shiver down her spine. Her legs trembled a little.

"I don't see why not," she said.

You can do it. You did it one time. You can do it again.

Maya stretched and relaxed her limbs, preparing herself for another teleport. Eduardo looked amused, and Anders looked panicked.

You'll be fine. Just do it again. You'll be okay.

Maya tried to remember what she had done the last time, but her mind was a blank. She remembered focusing on the location, but the exact train of thought, the emotions, and feelings she had were not accessible. It was like her head was stuffed with cotton wool.

You're just gonna have to trust in yourself and figure it out again.

Maya looked over where she was standing before. She picked a spot in between Anders and Eduardo. That's where she was standing before. It wouldn't take that long to get it back there. She just had to make it happen again.

Maya was about to close her eyes and she stopped herself.

Remember, eyes open. Feel your way through.

She focused again, knowing that she was somewhere different and was going back to where she had come from. She focused her energy. She felt something building and shifting. And with a deep breath, she stepped out through nothing.

The sea of colors and shapes was there again, only this time she felt more in control. Less drowning, more gliding through. Whatever she was passing through, she didn't let the sensation bog her down. She just focused on being where she needed to be.

Suddenly, she was back on the original building. Her legs a little unsteady, she wobbled backward, and Eduardo reached out to grab her by the arm.

"Stay there. Don't want to undo all that good work you just did," he said. Anders reached out too, and the two of them pulled her away from the edge.

"Would you like a chair?" Eduardo offered and guided her over to where he'd been sitting. Maya sat down, more like fell into the chair. Her legs felt loose, and her strength drained out of her.

"Why am I so exhausted?" she said, looking at her body with confusion.

"You've got quite a lot of power there, but you pushed your body a lot for one day," Eduardo said. He looked her up and down.

"I think you'll recover quickly, but you shouldn't push it more today. You've shown you've got determination and potential. We'll work together."

"Great," Maya said weakly. She forced a small smile, but she didn't have the energy for anything else.

"Since I'm so wonderful, why don't you tell us a bit about what you're trying to do?" Maya said. She inclined her head toward the Haste facility that they'd been looking at before.

"Well, I guess you've earned a bit of information," Eduardo said. "I'm planning a bit of a heist, as it turns out. There's something in that facility that I need. They've taken precautions against teleporters like me. But if I had an accomplice, the plan is foolproof." Eduardo looked at her with determination. Maya nodded slowly.

"I think we can help each other," she said.

"If you don't mind me asking, what business do you have with that facility? I know you weren't trying to get in just for training," Eduardo said.

Maya paused before she responded. "We're on the trail of something. Something big. And all the clues point to that location. Part of what we need is information. But I know there's something else there I need, and we must get in. That's where all the answers lie." Maya spoke slowly and deliberately, and she could see the understanding on Eduardo's face.

He nodded. "That is no ordinary facility. Things of great value are stored there and kept secure. Once we get in, who knows what else we'll find." Eduardo's face lit up with a mischievous grin.

"Here's hoping," Anders chimed in.

"What part do you play in this?" Eduardo said, looking over at Anders.

"I'm the hired help," Anders said, mysteriously.

Maya tried to laugh, but she just coughed instead. After she recovered, she spoke again. Softer this time.

"It's true, Anders is the hired help. I need a lot of help these days, especially now that I'm an internationally wanted fugitive. But in all seriousness, he's a good friend and I wouldn't have gotten this far without him." Maya looked over at Anders and gave him a kind smile. He returned it.

"Very well. As long as we're all close friends, there's going to be a lot of trust required to pull this off." Eduardo said.

"We can work on that. Plus, we have someone else to help us who's pretty extraordinary," Anders said.

"Oh, I'm intrigued. Who is she?"

"Maybe you should meet her," Maya said.

"ARE YOU SURE ABOUT THIS?" Anders whispered to Maya as they walked out of the elevator doors and approached their suite in the hotel.

"Yes," she hissed at him under her breath. They walked past their door and instead knocked on Kora's door.

"Come in!" she shouted. Maya opened the door. Anders entered first, and then Eduardo. Maya entered last, watching the scene play out before her. Kora stood instantly and observed Eduardo. "This is the great Eduardo Estevez, huh?" Kora said.

"Yes, indeed. I believe you have me at a disadvantage. And you are?" Eduardo said.

"Kora. Nice to make your acquaintance. I take it you've joined the team?" she said.

"Or perhaps you've joined my team?" Eduardo countered.

Kora laughed. "I like your style, but I think you'll find you're on our team." She winked at Maya.

Eduardo looked confused for a moment, then regained his composure.

Did she use her power of persuasion on him?

"I see you're a woman of many talents," Eduardo said carefully. "You don't have to worry about me. I'll do my part."

"I'm sure you will," Kora said. "So, what's the plan?"

"I've been working on it for a while and it's gonna be a little tricky to pull off. But we're going to break into that facility, and once we're in they'll never be able to keep us out."

11

THE GLASS WALL

Eduardo walked Anders and Maya through an old, abandoned train station. There were grimy white tiles all over the walls, with faded peach tiles on the ground. They walked through some broken turnstiles, down some stairs onto an empty platform, and continued on to a small door at the end near the tunnel.

"This place is just left like this?" Maya said. She couldn't seem to make sense of it.

"Yes, there's a project to revitalize the train network, but it always keeps being pushed another year or two down the road. I've taken the liberty of setting up in the meantime." Eduardo stopped and pulled out a key for the door before them.

"Normally I wouldn't use a key, or even walk down here," he explained. "But for today, I need to introduce you to the location, and also Anders needs to be able to come and go freely." Eduardo unlocked the door, opened it, and ushered Maya and Anders in first.

They walked down a narrow, dimly lit tunnel. The floor was concrete, and the walls had faded white paint on them. It was clearly some kind of service tunnel. They continued along until the tunnel ended at another door.

"Allow me," Eduardo said. He unlocked this door as well and entered first. As Maya entered the room, she was astonished.

What is this place? How much money has he poured into this?

The room before them was unlike anything they had seen on their way down. It was all black and grey with polished stone, pieces of technology, monitors and towers, and glass rooms in odd locations.

"This is our training and operations center," Eduardo said with a grand flourish.

"It's incredible," Anders said, walking around, peering at some of the different gadgets on display. He found himself at a glass cabinet full of devices.

"I am somewhat of a collector," Eduardo said, walking through the space. "Some of these things have been liberated, some commissioned, and others merely purchased." He led them through to one of the glass rooms. He walked outside and slid the wooden door to the side.

In the room there was a single terminal with a keyboard and mouse. Eduardo brought up a video feed on the screen.

"I've shared this with our associate, Kora, but I thought I'd also set it up here so we can routinely have a look."

"What are we looking at?" Anders said.

"This is probably my greatest accomplishment in penetrating the facility so far," Eduardo explained. "This is a video feed of one of their internal training rooms."

"Which of the buildings is this in?" Maya said.

"Oh, the main one. The secret one," Eduardo said, with a sparkle in his eye.

"Wow, how did you manage that?" Anders said.

"Oh, a bit of luck and some careful planning. Bit by bit, we'll strip away all their layers of protection and get to the jewels inside."

"What have you learned from this so far," Maya asked.

"Not a lot yet, but it's been helpful in recording all the regular visitors and deducing who are staff at the location and who are just passing through."

"That would be very helpful," Maya said. She was about to make another comment when she just gaped and pointed at the screen.

"That's Valerie!" Maya cried, astonished.

"Oh, I've seen her a lot. Do you know this woman?" Eduardo said.

"Yeah, we've run into her a few times." Maya looked over at Anders as if to get some sort of agreement from him. Anders nodded at her.

"One thing we can share," Maya said, "is that Valerie has the Haste bloodline. She's a Speedster."

Eduardo looked at her with a questioning look. "Not from what I've seen. She's doing LifeDeath training, but she's deep in a Haste Clan facility. It's been bugging me to no end."

"That we can explain," Maya said. "The thing is, the Master Sage has been doing experiments, and has successfully granted new bloodlines to test subjects. Valerie is a new recipient of the LifeDeath bloodline."

"What?" Eduardo said, his cool and calm demeanor vanishing in an instant.

"We've got the data to back it up, and the data has led us here." Anders pointed at the monitor.

"Hmm. This place is even bigger than I realized." Eduardo tipped his head, deep in thought. "This puts a new perspective on things. We're going to have to be even more careful. And even more thorough with your training," he said, looking at Maya.

"Maybe we should get started," Maya said.

"Certainly," Eduardo said. He guided Maya out of the room and over to a separate glass room. This one had a clear door and all the walls were completely clear glass.

"Looks like a fishbowl," Maya said.

"That's the idea." Eduardo opened the door and walked through it. Maya joined him inside. "Stay outside for this one," Eduardo said to Anders. "Why don't you stand over there?" Eduardo pointed to a spot outside the room that was clearly visible through one of the main walls.

"Okay, so, so far, you've managed to teleport a short distance with no barriers. And a small distance over a dangerous gap. What you haven't done is teleported through a wall. You haven't actually passed through solid matter."

"What do you mean pass through?"

I hope he's not going to explain that I'm somehow going to move through material.

Eduardo laughed.

"It's not quite how you think it is. But teleporting through solid objects, solid spaces, is harder than just through the air. It's not because your body has to become like a gas or anything like that. It's just a function of the magic. You have to skip over these physical barriers."

"I think I get it," Maya said, allowing Eduardo to continue.

"Look at Anders through the glass. He's right there. But you can't walk to him because the glass is in the way. This is the first level of training because you can see the target from where you're standing, and I find that when we're starting out, it's easier to be targeting a person rather than just a location."

"That's good to know." Maya waved at Anders, and he waved back, unsure of what they were saying from outside the room.

"Now, we're going to do the same thing we did yesterday. The only difference is that there's a wall between you and the location you're teleporting to. You can still see the destination, it's probably around about the same distance. Should be easy," Eduardo said.

"Alright. Let's give it a go. Should I..."

"Just from where you're standing is fine." Eduardo stepped back and observed. Maya recalled the focus, attention, and mindset she had used the day before to teleport between the two buildings. She went through the same internal routine, summoned the power, and focused on being at the destination.

Then she pushed and slammed right into the glass, falling back dazed on the floor.

"Not bad for a first attempt." Eduardo walked over and helped her up. Maya was a bit groggy and rubbed her forehead.

"What happened?"

"Oh, so your mind saw the wall as an obstacle and therefore it stopped you."

"Hang on," Maya said, scratching her head she looked at Anders who had a mixture of confusion and amusement on his face, and back at Eduardo. Maya touched the glass with her hand, feeling the surface.

"So, because I know the wall is here, my brain is stopping me from getting past it because it expects that I have to bump into it," she said slowly, gathering her thoughts.

"Exactly right. You have to free your mind to get past the wall. It's like a mental wall is standing in for the physical wall. It's quite philosophical if you think about it," Eduardo said with an amused look on his face.

Maya sighed. She gathered herself and walked back to her original starting position. "Alright, I get it. Let's try this again." Maya resumed her focus. She went through the same preparation. She focused on the location where Anders was, so she would be standing right next to him. And she tried to ignore the fact that there was a wall in between them.

Her power built up, she focused, and she pushed. Slam.

Into the wall again, this time with maybe even more speed than before. Maya lay on the ground, just staring at the ceiling.

"Well, that was another good try," Eduardo said diplomatically. He offered her a hand again, and she stood up groggily, as before.

"I'm taking this to mean that it's not going to be an easy process," Maya said.

"I think so. It's hard for me to judge. I haven't really had a lot of other people to compare myself against. It's a pretty rare talent," Eduardo said.

Maya dusted herself off and wandered back to the starting position.

"Do you have any tips?"

"Not yet. I really don't know how your mind works, unfortunately. I think this is one of those things where you need to figure out how to overcome this block."

"Alright, well usually, I keep trying until I have the breakthrough."

"Or break yourself," Eduardo offered. He didn't laugh, but Maya could see the twinkle in his eyes.

"I'm sure the glass will break before I break, but let's hope it doesn't get to that." Maya concentrated and launched itself again.

Eduardo helped Maya up and held her hand as she steadied herself again.

I'm not strong enough for this.

"Maybe we should take a break," Eduardo said. "I have something important to discuss with you anyway." He let Maya out of the room and waited for Anders to come and join them. Once Anders walked over, the three of them navigated through the room into a special door at the far end of the space.

This metallic door had a retinal scanner that Eduardo peered into before the door unlocked. "This is the inner sanctum," Eduardo said before taking them inside. It looked like a command center. There were lots of computer monitors and keyboards and other equipment all around the room. Workstations were set up on multiple desks with multiple chairs. Eduardo sat down at one.

"Make yourselves comfortable," he said. Maya and Anders each found a chair and Eduardo sat up the front.

"This is a lot of kit. Were you expecting us?" Anders commented, looking around the room.

"I had grand plans of having a team but turns out I work better alone." Eduardo quickly brought up a screen on his monitor, and it was suddenly duplicated to the rest of the monitors.

"Okay, this item here, this is what we're going after tomorrow. It's a garden variety security pass."

"Looks easy enough," Anders said.

"Precisely, that's why we're starting with this. Now, based on my research, the security staff that work in this facility also have access at another facility across town. Luckily for us, they use the same system."

"Go on," Anders said, leaning forward.

"So, the plan is to swipe a security pass from the other facility of someone who has access to this one."

"I see."

"And that way, we won't be seen skulking around the location we want to break into, and instead, piecing it together," Anders said. Eduardo clapped once.

"Very good. I'm glad you're on the same page. There's obviously more to the plan, but this is the start. You know, we will have precious little time once this heist is initiated to get what we need. We have to raise as few alarm bells as possible. Tomorrow, you and I are doing this, Maya."

"You want me to go?" Maya said, completely surprised.

Anders looked at Eduardo with confusion.

"I'm probably a bit better equipped at this stage to assist," Anders said diplomatically. Eduardo shook his head emphatically.

"This is probably normally your area of expertise, I understand, Anders," Eduardo began. "But it is critical that only Maya and myself are on this particular mission."

"Why?" Anders asked.

"Two reasons. The first one is that the stakes of this mission and the importance of it will help push Maya's training ahead much faster than these repetitive exercises." Eduardo gestured away from them, seemingly toward the room that Maya had been training in during the day.

"But I barely made it," Maya interjected.

"What you're going to understand, is that progress is more of a mindset, than physical experience. Unless you're ready to call it quits?"

"And the second reason?" Maya asked in a soft voice.

"The second reason is probably even more important. We have to work together like a team. This heist has to go off perfectly, and we each need to know every aspect backward and fully trust each other. That trust has to be real, and it starts with successful missions." Eduardo paused and looked at the two of them. Anders nodded along and then so did Maya.

"Alright, we'll make it work. Like you said, we have to start somewhere. Will there be a lot of teleporting?" Maya asked.

"As much as we can, without being spotted," Eduardo said with a grin.

12

A THICK CONCRETE WALL

Maya was jolted around in her seat as Anders took a corner too hard. She bumped up against Eduardo, who seemed unfazed by the driving.

"Does he always drive like this?" Eduardo said.

"Yeah, but it's usually more fun in a sports car," Maya said.

"Hey, no backseat driving!" Anders called out. Maya shrugged and settled back into the chair.

"I hope this is not too bumpy for you, I know it's not your regular mode of transport," Maya said. Eduardo looked unfazed.

"Normally I wouldn't even bother with transport, but we start with small steps and at least this way we can all go together. We can go over the briefing again."

"I understand why we need a security pass. But what are we going to do with it? Surely, it's linked to an identity already. We don't look like the person that's using it," Maya said, trying to explain herself.

"That's a fair question, all will be explained in the next step. This is the foundational piece that we need, so let's make sure we get it today."

"Anything else I should know?" Maya said.

"Not a lot of people we can target. They need to have the right access and ideally be on leave."

"Right, so they won't notice that the pass is missing," Maya said, filling in the blanks.

"Correct. Don't worry, we'll return the pass when we're done with it." Eduardo gave her a mysterious look and then remained silent.

"And you're going to fill us in at some point? Seems like you've been planning this for a while," Maya said.

"Sorry. This is...important to me so I'm a little cautious. Had some bad experiences in the past. But I'll be more forthcoming soon." Eduardo looked into Maya's eyes and she saw the truth in his words. She nodded.

A few jolts later, the van came to a stop.

"We're here," Anders called out. He turned off the van, and Maya heard his footsteps as he walked around. Then he threw open the side door. Maya left first, and Eduardo appeared next to her.

"Too good for climbing out of the van, huh?" Maya said.

"Just warming up." Eduardo smiled and then reappeared behind Anders.

"Show off," Maya said under her breath. Eduardo winked at her, and she realized he must have heard her.

Anders rifled through his coat and thrust a few gadgets at Maya.

"Here's some stuff just in case."

"I know, I know." Maya accepted the items and stashed them in her pockets. She was wearing a black outfit similar to the ninja suit she'd been using on missions with Mikael back in Atlantis.

"From here on in, you pull down the masks. We need to be unidentifiable," Eduardo said.

"No need to explain that one," Maya said. She pulled down the visor on her mask. Anders checked the outfit.

"Okay, it looks good. Good luck. I will be nearby. You just have to call for help or pick up."

"We got it. Don't get too bored," Maya said. Anders went back to the car and Maya and Eduardo jogged off toward the facility.

Anders had dropped them off a block away. They were in winding, lush countryside. The facility stuck out as being odd, a monolithic concrete structure did seem out of place in rolling green hills. The lighting was minimal, only a few strong lamps to illuminate the entry gate. Eduardo and Maya went around the back and soon had to switch to headlamps to see where they were going.

"Based on the technical specs, there's a rear entry for emergencies. Well, evacuations really. But that'll be our point of access."

"How do we get past the gate? And the walls?" Maya pointed to the gigantic concrete walls. They were sheer with no handholds and the top was covered with barbed wire. "That wire looks nasty."

"Nasty and electrified," Eduardo corrected her.

"How are we going to get past?" Maya said.

"Well, it's easy. Just watch." Eduardo stood in front of a section of wall. He tapped it a few times with his hands, nodded, and then vanished. Maya looked around and couldn't see him anywhere.

"Where are you?" she said.

"I'm on the other side of the wall. Are you going to join me?"

"But how? I can't see the other side of the wall," Maya said, panicking.

"I don't need to. We saw it from a distance. I don't know

roughly how thick it is, the grounds all the same here you know just feel it out," Eduardo said.

"Just feel it out?" Maya said, almost yelling over the radio.

"I couldn't teleport through an incredibly thin glass partition even after hours of trying. You think I can do this? Teleport through thick concrete walls in the pitch black in a location I've never visited before."

"Yes. Otherwise, you're being left behind and there's no way you'll make it to the real heist," Eduardo said.

Maya leaned her head against the concrete wall.

This can't be happening. You have to figure this out.

She banged her head against the wall three times, then leaned against it. Her frustration seeped through her entire body, filling her limbs with an energy that just wanted to break out.

"Do hurry along, Maya. I think I'll need some help at some stage," Eduardo said through the radio link. Maya kicked the wall with her toe, wincing in pain and just trying to relax. All the tension and frustration she'd felt from failing the training was coming back tenfold.

Look at you, you're on this mission. You've gotta get better. You've gotta make this leap. Keep up with him. Or you'll be left behind.

Maya knew that Eduardo wouldn't wait. He had a mission to get on with. He'd already left Georgia behind. And she would be next. She took a moment to pause and reflect, trying to push away the extreme feelings.

She stepped back, looked at the wall, went closer again, knocked it a few times to understand and get a sense of the thickness. She focused on the ground with her headlamp, understanding the nature of the dirt, noticing the tufts of grass sparsely poking through.

Okay, just don't get in your own way. Don't have to figure it all out now. Just get yourself past the wall so you can move on.

Maya nodded, steeled herself, and just pushed through. She

stumbled and fell onto the ground, eating some dust and launching into a coughing fit for thirty seconds.

She pulled herself together, stood up, leaned forward to lean on the wall, and fell over again.

"I think we need some classes on stealth if this is how you think you should comport yourself," Eduardo said, looking down over her. Maya quickly stood up and looked around.

"Where are we?" she said. "Did you rescue me?"

"No, I just found you on the other side of the wall, making a bit of a scene," Eduardo said. Maya looked around, half-fully turned, and saw the rather thick, imposingly tall wall.

"What's behind here? Oh, I did it. Nice job."

"We're very lucky that I patrolled this area. Come on, let's go find the emergency exit." Eduardo jogged off and Maya followed him happily.

You actually did it! I don't know if I can do that again but doesn't matter. It worked once. Let's just move on.

It didn't take long for them to reach the massive structure. It was made from a dark grainy stonelike substance with no markings or features whatsoever. Eduardo seemed to know what he was looking for, so once they reached the building itself, they ran around the perimeter until he paused at what seemed like an arbitrary location.

"It should be around here. It's well concealed."

"What is?" Maya said, looking at the wall.

"The emergency exit. There is a way to trigger it from the outside in case they get stuck. And it's around here somewhere. Come and help!"

Eduardo was feeling along the wall with his hands, pressing occasionally, and peering with his headlamp. Maya picked another section nearby and did the same thing. She ran her hands over the featureless stone, feeling nothing.

"Well, at least if we find something it'll be obvious because there's nothing here otherwise," Maya said.

"I certainly hope so," Eduardo commented. They continued like this for a few minutes in silence. Maya was just pulling her hand off the stone when she brushed something. Panicking, she put her hand back on the stone and carefully felt around where she had been, trying to get that same spot. After a few goes, she found it.

There was a tiny raised surface, like a mini dome. She pressed it and nothing happened, but she applied a little bit of extra force and she felt it push into the building. Next, she heard a sound like a distant clank.

"I think I found something," Maya said. She kept her hand in place, and Eduardo darted over.

"You pressed something?" he asked, peering at her hand.

"Yes, I found a button of some kind, and when I pressed it, I heard a noise. Hopefully, this is going to open up." Maya waited a few more seconds. She started to peer around. She noticed in the corner of her eye that a section of wall was shifting and soon enough there was now an opening where there had been none before.

She carefully stepped back from the wall.

"This is it, ladies first. Here we go." Maya ducked over to the opening and peered inside with her headlamp. The passage was lit with amber lighting strips at the top and bottom of the corridor.

"Let's get a move on," Eduardo said. Maya took off on her jog, trying to reduce the sound from her footsteps through this concrete passage. After a minute or so of jogging, they started to descend, and then they found a stairwell. Down they went: one, two, three flights of stairs before finally reaching a large metal door with a keypad.

Eduardo plugged in a device and started it off. Within a few seconds, he discovered the code and the massive metal doors unlocked with a hiss and swept aside to reveal a room.

"This is hopefully the server room," Eduardo said. He

found a light switch, and racks and rows of computer equipment confirmed his theory.

"There must be some good stuff in here," Maya said.

"I'll bet on that. But we have another mission, and we cannot risk it." Eduardo led her down a row and around the perimeter of the room. They went through another door, through another corridor.

This part of the facility looked completely different. It was all-white corridors, identical doors, and different branches.

"This is a maze. Do you know exactly where to go?" Maya said.

"Not exactly, but I've got a pretty good indication. From here on in, we will probably start to bump into people, so let's keep it quiet. No more coughing fits."

"I promise," Maya said and navigated down a corridor through another junction.

Eduardo stopped before a door. "I'm going to open this door —be ready."

"Okay, on your mark."

"Going in." Eduardo opened the door. A security guard, clad entirely in black with a helmet, spun around to look at them. As Maya processed the man's presence, Eduardo appeared behind the man and knocked him out with a single blow.

The guard crumpled to the ground and lay still.

"Impressive," Maya said.

Eduardo didn't acknowledge the comment. Instead, he was rushing around the room. It looked similar to Eduardo's command center with an array of monitors and a few workstations.

"Is this like a security room, reviewing video cameras?" Maya said thinking out loud.

"That's exactly it. It could probably produce and store ID passes here as well. Start looking, I'll check the database."

Eduardo fired up one of the computers and was busy paging through.

Maya noticed some filing cabinets along the side, and she started rifling through them. They were mostly empty. But she did find lanyards and security card holders and other accessories.

"Everything's here for security passes. We just need to find the actual passes," Maya said. She ran over to the other end of the room and found a locked drawer.

"Here's hoping." She fished into her pocket and pulled out an electronic lockpick that Anders had given her. She put it in the lock and jiggled around. It made a small buzzing sound and the drawer opened.

Maya dug through the drawer and found what looked like spare security passes.

"These must be the passes. I think we've got it."

"Good, good, I just need to find the right person." Eduardo was busy on the computer.

"I think we need to hurry up," Maya said, pointing at the monitors. There was a security attachment of four guards hurrying down.

"Are they coming here?" Maya said.

"We should expect so," Eduardo countered. "I can't find the information we need. I think we will have to grab one?"

"What do I get?"

"Just pick one so we can get out of here."

He's got a point. We're out of time.

Maya searched through the passes not knowing what to pick. She quickly settled on two women who looked roughly her age and she shoved them into her pocket.

"Okay, I got it. Let's move." As Maya turned, she saw a security team waiting outside in the corridor.

13

———

STUNNING EXIT

"Follow my lead," Eduardo said. He walked out of the door. The security team focused their weapons on him, and he held out his hands.

"Hey, boys. Let's keep this nice and civilized, why don't we? We're just gonna leave, and you can leave us alone. Everyone wins."

The lead security guard thrust his weapon into Eduardo's face as a response.

Eduardo moved too quickly to register, appearing behind the guard in no time and knocking him out in a single blow. As the other guards opened fire, Eduardo scooped up the fallen weapon and took shelter behind the door.

"How'd you do that?" Maya said.

"I'll explain later. You got any tricks in that bag that Anders gave you?"

"I've got something. Get ready to move again," Maya said. She reached into her pockets and pulled out a metallic ball. She hit a button on it and rolled it through the doorway.

It beeped once and then a massive bright light flooded the corridor, dazzling the security team. Maya ran out with her stun wand, discharging both charges and taking out two security guards. The third was disabled by Eduardo with no effort at all.

He retrieved the guard's weapon and threw it to Maya.

"Keep this on you. It'll come in handy."

"What does it do?" Maya said.

"Oh, it shoots tranquilizer darts. They don't like to kill people around here. They prefer to keep them as test subjects."

"Okay, I'm definitely not getting shot while we're here," Maya said.

"That would be best. Let's go." Eduardo ran off down the corridor, and Maya stayed close behind him.

"How'd you move so fast? That was incredible," Maya said.

"Well, I can't move that fast. It was just a lot of teleporting. But if you do it fast enough, people think you're just moving very quickly."

"That sounds really useful."

"Oh, it is. But the thing is, the most important part is this. The more you can fool people into thinking that you're just a vanilla Speedster, the better off you're going to be. As soon as they figure out you can teleport, it's a whole new game. One that you do not want to be playing."

"Yeah, I get it. I'm with you on this one."

"Good. Let's keep it moving." They continued down the corridor at breakneck speed with Eduardo leading the way. They came to a branch in the corridor and there was another team waiting for them.

Without even skipping a beat Eduardo fired his weapon. A strange projectile twirled out, hitting a guard in the neck, and he crumpled to the floor. Shots were fired toward them, and Maya and Eduardo hid behind opposite walls.

"Have you got a shot?" Eduardo said.

"I can try." Maya leaned out and aimed the weapon, firing at one of the guards. The recoil shocked her, and it bumped her aim slightly. As they returned fire, she disappeared behind the wall again.

Eduardo used that distraction to fire his weapon, disabling two more guards.

"Let's move." Eduardo charged out, and Maya followed quickly behind. They reached the final corridor before the stairwell. Standing before the large doors was a single woman.

She had short black hair and a tightly fitted black outfit. She was wearing red gauntlets and her hands curled into fists. Without even speaking, she charged ahead.

Oh wow, she's fast.

Before she could even finish the thought, the female Speedster was at Eduardo, swinging her fist. Yet, Eduardo appeared to move faster, getting behind the Speedster, and firing at her point-blank with the tranquilizer gun. She collapsed to the floor in no time.

"That was incredible," Maya said.

"Thanks. I'd love it if you saved the adoration for when we're back to base." Eduardo tore off toward the doors, and Maya ran as fast as she could to keep up. They burst through the main doors, hustling up the steps to reach the exit.

As they reached the end of the tunnel, Eduardo stuck his head outside.

"Looks quiet. I think we've got a window. Come with me." He led Maya across the ground until they found a section of wall. Eduardo crouched down beside it, pulling out a tool. With a flick of a button, a tiny laser popped out and he started cutting a section of the wall away.

"Do we really have time for this? Should we just teleport out and be gone?" Maya said, looking around.

"That would be ideal, but then they'll start asking questions about how we got in and how we got out. It's better to leave this little piece of evidence to answer those questions and not make them think of more creative answers."

"Got it." Maya looked around, trying to see if there were any guards. She couldn't spot any.

"No sign of them. Maybe they're heading to the main gate."

"I sincerely hope so."

"How long are you going to need for that?" Maya asked.

"Probably thirty seconds. Hopefully no less. Hopefully no more."

"Unfortunately, I'm not sure we're going to have thirty seconds." Maya noticed a shape flying at them at great speed. It wasn't fast enough to be a Speedster. As the shape grew closer, Maya understood.

"It's Valerie," she said.

"Oh, our friend. LifeDeath powers, right?"

"Yeah, don't let her hit you."

"I can manage that. Do you want to swap places?" Eduardo said.

"Gladly." Maya grabbed the laser cutting tool and resumed the work on the wall. She heard a scuffle behind her as Eduardo and Valerie started fighting.

"I'm going to enjoy interrogating you two. I'd like to know who's dumb enough to try and rob us," Valerie said. Eduardo said nothing in response and Maya kept her mouth shut.

I don't want her to recognize my voice. I'm just gonna finish cutting this wall.

As Maya was cutting, she heard the sounds of a scuffle behind her. Shifting ground, strikes, grunts. And then a cry of triumph. A woman's cry. Maya turned back and saw Valerie standing over Eduardo's body. Victorious.

Without thinking, Maya grabbed the tranquilizer weapon and fired at Valerie. She scored a hit in Valerie's neck and the woman staggered back, trying to fight whatever was being injected into her body.

The cutting tool was not quite finished, but Maya stashed it in her pocket and kicked at the wall as hard as she could, drawing on all her force. It must have been enough, because the mostly cut piece tumbled out of the way. Maya grabbed Eduardo under his arms and crouch-dragged him through the hole she had cut as Valerie slowly, slowly sank to the ground on her knees.

"You won't get away with this," she croaked, before finally succumbing to the dart. Maya didn't look back. She kept dragging Eduardo and continued making her way away from the facility.

In no time, they're going to find Valerie and the hole, and they'll be onto us.

Once they were a little bit further away from the walls, Maya, activated her radio earpiece.

"Anders, we need an evac. They're onto us and Eduardo is paralyzed. What can you do?"

"Hang on, I've got your location. There's a ridge not far away. Get over to that ridge and wait for me there."

"Got it." Maya shifted Eduardo and tried to carry him, but she wasn't strong enough.

It would be really nice to have that extra strength right about now.

But she was strong enough to drag him. So, she found a more comfortable position, slumped him over, and continued dragging him away from the walls. There was a bush nearby that she dragged him through.

"Sorry Eduardo, I've got to get to cover," she said.

I'm not sure whether he can hear me or not.

After dragging Eduardo through the bush, she saw the ridge that Anders had mentioned. She paused for a few seconds to gather her breath, and continued dragging Eduardo until they crested the ridge. Almost falling down the other side, Maya stumbled and found a safe spot to rest.

Anders, you better get here quick.

Maya leaned over and checked on Eduardo.

"Eduardo, you okay? Can you talk? Is it wearing off?" Maya said with concern. Eduardo blinked at her a few times. She turned her headlamp on, and he shied away from the light.

"Oh, good. You're getting some movement back."

"Almost there," he said, with some effort. "Haste recovers quick."

"I get it. The body is working faster."

"Yes," Eduardo answered. With Maya's help, he reached a sitting position.

"Anders is coming for us. He's going to help me get you to the van."

"Good." Eduardo seemed content with one-word answers. Maya turned off her headlamp and looked over the ridge. She noticed there were search parties out, but none were anywhere near her yet.

It's only a matter of time.

"Anders, how far out are you?"

"I can see you now. Just hold on." Maya heard footsteps approaching, and Anders appeared before them.

"Looks like you had some adventures. Let's get back to the van."

"Gladly," Maya said. They each took one arm and helped Eduardo down the ridge. Here and there he could hold his weight and take a step. The three of them moved fairly steadily along the ground, down the ridge, and followed a meandering path to the van.

Maya looked back and could see some lights in the distance, but they still had some time.

"Where are we?" she asked.

"Somewhere else. I had to drive the van as close as I could to get here faster. If we make a move now, I think we're home. Home free," Anders said. Maya supported Eduardo, and Anders opened the van. They both managed to push him inside and steady him.

Maya sat with Eduardo while Anders got in the front. Anders turned on the van, screeched away, and after a tense minute they were on the main highway, trouble getting further and further behind them.

"Well, we made it," Maya said. "And I got these." She held out the two security passes. "I got two in case we needed a spare."

"Considering how fast they were on us, we should have taken a whole fistful," Anders said with a chuckle.

"This will have to do."

"All right, well done. We've got to get cracking," Anders said as they continued into the night.

BACK IN THE COMMAND CENTER, Eduardo was his normal self. He inserted one of the security passes into a special machine.

"Good job, Maya, on fetching these. We're going to have to analyze the format, download the access, and essentially make our own version of them."

"Awesome. So, what's the next step?" Maya said.

"Tomorrow, I'll brief you on the next item, which we can discuss then. For now, you can have a hard-earned rest."

"Great," Maya said, leaning back into her chair.

"After I show you your next training exercise." Eduardo led Maya out of the room. They headed to a corner of the space they hadn't visited before. There was a long black mat and three white steps equally spread along the mat.

"This is pretty simple. All you have to do is teleport to each step," Eduardo explained.

"That doesn't sound too bad," Maya said.

"You see these posts on either side?" Eduardo pointed with his right hand. Maya looked over and noticed a white post at each end of the course. Atop the white post was a red buzzer.

"You hit the buzzer to start, and you hit the far buzzer to finish."

"Sounds easy enough," Maya said.

"You should be able to teleport between all the steps and hit both buzzers within a second."

"One second!" Maya blurted out.

"That's right. This is a quick multi-teleport challenge. You're going to need to be faster on your feet. You can start whenever you want but you need to master this as soon as possible." Eduardo gave Maya a serious look.

"All right, I'll give it a go. Tonight," Maya said.

"One other thing," Eduardo said as he turned away. "From now on when you're down here, no walking. Only teleporting."

"Isn't that going to wear me out?"

"Yes, and then you'll get stronger. This has to be as natural and as easy as breathing. Okay?"

"All right, I got it."

"Thanks for the assist back there. Have a good night." Eduardo waved and then vanished.

"I see he's taking his own advice," Anders said after Eduardo had left.

"Yeah, he's right. It just feels like this is a lot."

"It is," Anders said. "But that was a close call tonight. He's not wrong. You need to get faster. That's your way of fighting back right now."

"Well, I'm going to start this training, and I would prefer it if you weren't looking over my shoulder as I do this."

"Understood. I'll be in the command center, reviewing material," Anders said. He walked off, and Maya waited for him to disappear around the corner before she went to start the course.

Okay, step one. Finish the course.

She hit the buzzer and it lit up immediately. Focusing, she

teleported to the first step. She landed relatively easily but with a bit of a wobble and almost fell onto the mat.

That's one.

She stayed herself and did it again.

That's two.

Or it would have been two, if she hadn't fallen off the step and landed on the mat. Maya stood up and went back to the start of the course. The starter button had already been switched off.

Hmm. Let me test something.

Maya hit the button and waited for three seconds. And then the course powered down.

Great. So, it won't even record a time over three seconds. This is gonna be a long night.

14

BALCONY ENTRY

Maya stumbled into a chair in the command center. "Alright, I'm a captive audience now. Tell me whatever you need to tell me," she said. Anders looked over, amused.

Eduardo stood before them. "Glad you could join us, Maya. How'd you go with the training course last night? Did you manage to complete it?"

"Not yet," Maya said with a groan.

"Oh well, you'll get there. It's all about practice, practice, practice." Eduardo paused and then moved on.

"Time for a bit of a recap. Last night we retrieved these two security passes from the alternate Haste facility. We encountered some resistance and they're now doing an investigation. But the good news is they didn't see our faces." Eduardo paused to bring up some images on the monitor.

"We've pulled the security profiles off the access cards. Thankfully, one of them had access to the main Haste facility, which is what we need."

"Awesome. Glad I got two," Maya said with relief.

"Yes, that was quick thinking. Obviously, we can't just rely on the person's access that we stole. It'll be recognized. But I already planned for this anyway. I didn't want our whole mission to ride on the identity of one employee." Eduardo looked around the room, Maya nodded, and he continued.

"That brings us to the next part of the heist. We need to get an identity kit."

"What's that?" Maya asked, her gaze fixed on Eduardo as he leant over one of the terminals. He tapped away at the keyboard before something appeared on the screen.

"This is an identity kit," Eduardo explained. "It lets us build an identity using all the elements that we need: photos, voice signatures, and biometrics. We're going to use that in conjunction with the security pass to create our own access pass."

Maya nodded.

"What if they change the system access and it locks us out?"

"We'll keep an eye out for that," Eduardo said. "It is definitely a risk, but these things take time. And while they know there's a pass out there, they're not going to expect that we'll be able to create and use an identity with it fast enough. The protocol for these things is just to lock away the compromised account."

"Okay, so we're good so far," Maya said, "but they'll change things eventually?"

"Correct," Eduardo replied. "So, there is a timeline now. They're alert, they're investigating. They will be increasing their security. But that's to be expected."

"So where do we get one of these identity kits?" Maya asked.

"In the city, there's a manufacturing facility dead in the middle of the commercial zone. It's used by lots and lots of different companies, so we're just going to break in and steal one. Then we can use that to create new identities for the infiltration."

"Okay, so we steal this kit, then we use that to make new

identities and access passes to get into the facility?” Maya asked slowly, checking her thinking.

“Correct. That's not going to be enough, but it just means that we'll be able to get initial access without raising alarms.”

“Won't we need to get these accounts on the system?” Anders asked.

“Absolutely. And Kora will do that for us, at the appropriate time. Doing it now would be way too suspicious.”

“Sounds solid. Let's just figure out what prep we need to do.”

“Anders, I'll work with you. Maya, you need to rest a bit.”

“Agreed,” Maya said with a sigh. She couldn't even get out of the chair.

“Don't worry,” Anders said. “We're gonna run the operation in the evening, so we've got time.”

EDUARDO APPEARED in the room and Maya's eyes snapped open.

“Ah, Maya, you're awake. Wonderful.”

“I wasn't sleeping, I was doing a meditation. So, what are we doing now? Are you all ready?” Maya sat up in her chair.

“Mostly. We're gonna do the operation. I don't want you to do any more training because you need to save your energy for the mission,” Eduardo said.

“Sounds good to me,” Maya said, leaning back in the chair.

“Before we go, I need to ask you about Valerie,” Eduardo said.

“What about her?” Maya asked. Eduardo leaned in.

“Is this personal? I need to know what's at stake here.”

“It is,” Maya said with a sigh. “I've beaten her in every encounter so far, and she's very driven. Despite what it sounds like, she's actually very dangerous.”

“Oh, I can see that. I pulled her file. She is quite the operative and has been very active. When she masters the LifeDeath bloodline, she's going to be real trouble. Super speed, combat experience, Special ops, and LifeDeath powers. She would be very hard to stop. I'd say almost unstoppable." Eduardo's face showed his concern.

"Oh, I understand completely," Maya said. "That was me until a few days ago." Eduardo looked at Maya's arm thoughtfully.

"So glad you brought that up." Eduardo walked around and sat next to Maya.

"Now that we're a bit more comfortable with each other, can you just fill me in a little bit? I've seen the video, I made a lot of assumptions, shared a few things, but can you just give it to me straight?"

Maya took a long, slow breath and exhaled.

"Okay. I'll give you the summary for now."

"Let's hear it," Eduardo said.

"All right, so I have all the bloodlines just like the Master Sage."

"Okay," Eduardo said, not giving anything away.

"I have activated and mastered both the LifeDeath and Chakra bloodlines." Maya paused and Eduardo nodded.

"When I activate a new bloodline, I lose access to most of the power from the other bloodlines, but I keep some of it passively. Right now, as you've seen, I'm not at my best. But when I master this one, I will get all of my power back. And then some. So, you see, it's critical that I master this power."

"And you have mastery marks?" Eduardo focused his gaze on her arm again.

"I do. We've concealed them for now."

"That's prudent," Eduardo said. He looked away for a moment, deep in thought. "You're not the first person I've met with multiple bloodlines."

"Oh really? You knew someone else?"

"I did. He's gone now. The limelight was too much for him. He's gone. But I'm worried about Valerie. She knows you. And it sounds like she's got a bone to pick with you and she's all over this now. We have to be very careful."

"I agree," Anders said. "Let's keep communication on each mission to a minimum."

"Lovely chat, let's get ready." Eduardo stood up and disappeared from the room.

MAYA AWOKE with a start to find herself in a pitch-black room, illuminated only by the twinkling light of monitors around her.

Mission time. Hope I didn't miss it.

She headed out of the room, looking for Anders and Eduardo. Anders was lounging on a nearby couch.

"Oh hey, how'd you go?" he said, his gaze on Maya.

"Uh, good," she replied. "I feel much better. How long was I out?"

"Hours," he said. "I was gonna come and get you in a minute, but it's probably better you woke up on your own." He reached for a coffee cup and handed it to her. She took a sip and sighed contentedly.

"Okay, now I'm ready."

"Let's head out, Eduardo's going to meet us at the location."

Anders and Maya exited the training center, heading up the stairs, through the abandoned station, and eventually up to the street where Anders's van was parked nearby. They jumped in and soon they were driving through the streets toward the commercial district.

"What's your take on Eduardo?" Maya asked as Anders slowed for a red traffic light.

"I think he's a good guy," Anders replied, quickly adding, "There's a lot he's not telling us, but I trust him."

"What do you think he's holding back?" Maya queried.

"I'm not sure," Anders responded slowly. "I think it's just about his past. I don't think it's about us." Anders took off again, taking his time, driving through the city.

Maya considered him as he nodded.

"I know, I know. Not my usual driving style. I'm trying not to draw attention."

"I appreciate it." Maya looked out the window at the city. It was a lot more built up than she expected, with plenty of high rises and neon lights everywhere. It was bustling, even at this late hour.

"The area's a bit busier than I expected. We're gonna have to be careful with this one," Anders said. He found a dark alley and parked the van.

"We're a few blocks away, but you can approach from here. It's safer. Radio check?" Anders said. Maya put the earpiece in and pressed it twice.

"Test-ing, test-ing," she said.

"Sounds good. As usual, I'll be in the van. Here is a selection of gadgets." Anders handed her a few things, which she quickly pocketed.

"Take care and, um... Call me if you need help. I'll be listening out for any radio chatter."

"Thanks Anders. I promise you won't be the man in the van forever."

"That's okay. I can help you from here, and I can't teleport, so I'd probably slow you guys down. Probably. Have fun in there." Anders smiled and Maya waved, stepping out of the van, and closing the door behind her.

She walked slowly down the street. This time she was wearing normal clothes with a jacket over the top. She didn't want to draw too much attention with a full stealth suit. She had the hood of the jacket pulled down over her face, obscuring her looks. She turned into a side alley and walked through the darkness.

There were no lights over there, but her eyes quickly adjusted to the dark. Once she reached the end of the alley, she spotted Eduardo on a nearby building, standing on a balcony. He motioned for her to join him.

You've been training for this, just get up there.

Maya focused on Eduardo, took in the location around him, and pushed. She stumbled into him but was otherwise pretty stable. Maya looked down to see how far she'd come.

"That was pretty good," she said, complimenting herself.

"Yeah, I'll give that a B," Eduardo said. "It's getting better. Definitely getting better. Look at the rear of the building." He pointed out the commercial building in front of them. "What do you see?"

"I see a lot of floor-to-ceiling glass windows without any openings. Some structures on the roof, maybe roof access. And I see a balcony over there with an open door."

"Bingo," Eduardo said. "Care to join me?" He disappeared, then reappeared on the balcony Maya had just described.

He's really testing me. Alright, here goes.

Maya repeated what she'd done moments before. Focus, attention on Eduardo and the surrounding area, and pushing, but harder this time. She arrived at her destination at a run. Eduardo quickly reached out and grabbed her, slowing her down.

"You're getting the hang of this, but you're still lacking some finesse," he said.

"That's fair." Maya steadied herself and looked around the balcony. There was a table and chairs made out of some kind of wicker material. Otherwise, the balcony was empty. The door was shifting with the wind.

"Lucky someone left this open, otherwise we would have had to be more creative on our way in," Eduardo said. He was wearing a similar outfit to Maya. Casual streetwear. Jeans and a hoodie with the hood pulled over his face.

"Yeah," Maya said, agreeing.

"Take this." Eduardo handed Maya a face mask. She put it on, covering her nose and lower face. Eduardo did the same.

"This should scramble any facial recognition from the cameras. Let's go." Eduardo entered the building through the open door and Maya was only a step behind.

15

THE GREY BOX

Eduardo held Maya back as she entered the building.

"Careful," he whispered, pointing ahead. The room beyond was pitch black except for an array of red lasers moving through the room in odd patterns.

"You cross a beam, you trip an alarm," Eduardo said.

"I figured that. I've seen the movies."

"What movies?" Eduardo said.

"Never mind." Maya focused on the pattern, looking for a place of safety.

"That corner of the room looks safe," Maya said, directing Eduardo away to look. He studied the pattern for a few moments.

"Agreed. We should teleport there and take the next step. I'll go first." Eduardo stared at the area in concentration, and then he appeared right on the spot that Maya had pointed out. One of the red beams moved very close to Eduardo's position and Maya froze, watching it happen.

But the laser continued on its path and Eduardo was safe. She could hear his voice over the radio in her ear.

"Maya, this spot is not big enough for two people. Wait for me to move to the next before you follow. Please confirm."

"I heard you. I'll wait," Maya said. She kept watching the beams, checking on Eduardo's position.

"Okay, now," he said and was gone.

All right, now you've got to do it. No margin for error. No stumbling ahead.

Maya focused and pushed. She arrived almost perfectly still, teetering a little on her feet. She focused her weight back against the wall behind her and watched the array of laser beams moving through the space.

I wonder if a Speedster could just do cool moves around all this stuff. Oh well. Teleporting's cooler anyway.

Maya spotted Eduardo further down the corridor. He waved to get her attention and held his hand out for her to pause. He pointed to the next spot, which was conveniently right next to the door out of this section.

"That's the destination. Follow me after I move." With those words, Eduardo disappeared and reappeared next to the doorway. Maya paused and followed in his footsteps. She almost lost her balance when reaching the next spot but regained it just in time for a beam to narrowly pass where her head had been.

"Going through the door now. Follow me as soon as you can," Eduardo said. He opened the door and stepped through. Maya quickly teleported to the location he had been in and peered through the doorway to the next room. Eduardo was standing in the middle of the room and Maya couldn't see anywhere that there were signs of danger.

She paused to orient herself and then teleported next to him.

"Well done, this is the only safe spot in the room," Eduardo said. He pulled out a little torch and shone it on the ground around them. There were metal plates surrounding them with holes in them.

"Pressure plates where I presume little spikes will jump out. I don't want to prove my theory in case that also trips an alarm somewhere," Eduardo said.

"I'll take your word for it," Maya said, not wanting to try it either. Eduardo teleported to the end of the room, pausing in front of the next doorway.

"There's enough space here. Come immediately," he said over the radio. Maya concentrated and teleported again. It was becoming a bit more natural now, and not quite as tiresome. But she still felt the fatigue building up.

"I'm not sure if I'm going to be able to retrace our steps," Maya said.

"It's okay. We've got a contingency for that."

The next room didn't have the same kind of security measures. There was only a simple camera that panned across the room.

"Just try and time your run with this one. Teleport as backup. I want you to save some of your strength for when you really need it." Eduardo studied the pattern, and then he ran along one wall, pausing halfway. Then resuming his run until he was under the security camera and in safety.

Maya watched the camera do an extra rotation before she tried the same thing. She was able to match his speed, pause at the same spot, and reach his final position without any issues.

"Good I think we're here," Eduardo said.

The door before them had a keypad lock with an access card reader. Eduardo pulled out an access card and tried presenting it to the reader. It beeped with a green light and the door unlocked.

"Nice!" he said, pushing the door open and holding it for Maya. The room they stepped into was a tiny warehouse, full of racks and shelves.

"This is the one. Here we go." Eduardo walked along the racks, carefully looking over all the numbered black boxes.

"We're looking for part number 347B," he said to Maya. She scanned the boxes as she walked, picking a different row to search.

Maya noticed part numbers with a three in front of them.

I think you're close. Slow down.

She took more care in looking at the next numbers, trying to figure out if they were getting smaller or larger.

Larger. Okay, now do I go up high or down low?

She carefully searched the shelves, picking out numbers. She found 347, not B.

B, B, B, maybe it's bottom?

Maya checked the bottom shelf in the same location, and she saw the box.

"I think I've got it," she said and Eduardo rushed over.

"Okay, let's open it," he said, impatiently. Maya pulled out the box and lifted the lid. The metal slid back, and she saw three grey, featureless boxes inside.

"Well, this is definitely it," Eduardo said. He grabbed one and stashed it in his pocket. Maya closed the lid and put the box back in the location where she'd found it.

"Is that it?" she said.

"Yes. Now, we use the access card to get into this door and hopefully use it to get out." Eduardo led Maya to the other end of the room with another security card reader. He presented the access card and the door unlocked.

They stepped out into a poorly lit corridor. At the end of which, Maya spotted an elevator.

"Do you know where that goes?" she said, pointing it out to Eduardo.

"Oh, reasonably confident. Let's give it a go." With no cameras in sight, they walked casually over to the elevator. Eduardo called the elevator, and it opened instantaneously.

They entered and he pressed the 'G' button, swiping the card again. The lift doors closed, and the elevator rumbled to life, descending to the ground floor. The doors opened with a 'ding' sound into an empty lobby.

"There's a side door out here without cameras," Eduardo said, pointing. Maya could see three other cameras trained at the main doors of the lobby, the security desk, and the passageway which had a sign showing that there were toilets.

"After you," she said. They stuck very close to the wall outside the lift, edging around the perimeter until they found a fire escape.

"Is this exit door alarmed?" Maya asked.

"According to Kora, no."

"She's usually right," Maya said. They unlocked the door. Eduardo turned the handle and pushed the door open slowly. There were no alarms. They both rushed through, closing the door behind them silently.

Maya ran down a flight of stairs and came to the last door.

"Here we go." Eduardo turned the handle and pulled the door open. Cool night air swept in, and no alarm sounded. They quickly headed into another alley, unsure of their exact position.

"Okay, masks off and let's just casually walk around till we find Anders," Eduardo said.

"Agreed." Maya spoke into the radio.

"Anders, we're out of the building at a different location. We're coming around to find you. Please stay put."

"Confirmed. I'll see you soon." After traversing two very dark alleys, they found themselves back on a main road. Maya checked the map on her phone.

"Oh, just one more left and we're back on track," she said.

"After you," Eduardo said. Maya walked ahead, looking around, and noticing that there were few people on the streets, which was a bit of a relief. She took the turn and spotted the alley she was after. It took a lot of willpower not to just sprint to the alley to get to the van as quickly as possible.

But she kept her cool, with Eduardo close behind her. Whenever Maya checked back, she could see Eduardo looking around cautiously, assessing for danger. They returned to the van without incident, Anders waiting for them outside.

"Did you get it?" he said.

"This one?" Eduardo held up the grey box. He had taken it from his pocket. "Here it is," he said handing it over to Anders.

"Nice work, team. I've been monitoring the radio and all the other channels. No hint of an alarm. I think we got away with this one."

"Here's hoping," Eduardo said as he stepped into the van.

VALERIE SLAMMED her fist into the concrete slab one more time. It finally cracked and with a kick she shattered it.

That's more like it.

She stretched her back, cracked her neck, and swept the sweat out of her eyes.

You're not strong enough yet. You have to beat her. She cannot beat you again.

An annoying beep broke her out of her focus. Valerie looked over and saw her phone ringing. "What is it?" she answered.

"Uh, Valerie, you asked us to call you about anything unusual," a man said on the phone, very unsure of himself.

"Yes, now spit it out. What is it?"

"One of our partner companies had an unusual event. An employee was accessing secure areas in a strange pattern late at night."

"What kind of facility is this?"

"They do security tech. Should I ask them to do an inventory?"

"Yes. You should. Find out if anything's missing and brief

me in the morning." Valerie hung up before the man could respond. She tossed the phone back to the table where it had been sitting before.

She's up to something. I'm gonna figure it out. And she's gonna pay.

~

MAYA HANDED the grey box to Kora.

"This, I'm told, is an identity kit," Maya said. Kora's eyes lit up.

"You got your hands on one of these? Ooh. Well done." The admiration in Kora's voice was unmistakable.

"Well, it was Eduardo's operation I just tagged along."

"I don't care who orchestrated this. A box like this unlocks many wonders. Have Eduardo send me the specs that he wants. I'm going to have a bit of a play." Kora pulled out some cables and plugged the device into her computer. Without so much as another word, she was deeply focused on the monitor in front of her.

"Okay, you're welcome. Great chat. I'll see you later," Maya said. She walked away without a response.

The next morning, Eduardo was waiting for them in the command center.

"Good job last night. I take it you delivered the box to Kora?" Eduardo said.

"She started playing with it immediately. You just gotta let her know what spec you need."

"Thank you. Before you start your training today, Maya, I want to brief the two of you on our next item."

"What is it?" Anders said.

"This is a really fun one. The other two, you know, are necessities. This one is starting to feel more like a heist."

"Don't keep us in suspense. What's the third thing we need?" Maya said.

"A vault hacker. And it's just as cool as it sounds," Eduardo said with a wink.

16

A SMALL VICTORY

"A vault hacker sounds interesting, but what does it actually do? I mean in detail," Maya said.

"Well, it's quite a broad-acting tool. It has a drill component, a PIN cracking component, and also a diagnostic component for older style vault mechanisms."

"Sounds like quite a comprehensive tool. I can't imagine these are commercially available," Anders said, looking at Eduardo with skepticism.

"You're absolutely right. However, there are some enterprising people who create these and sell them on the black market to freedom-loving individuals such as ourselves."

"Are we gonna buy it or steal it?" Maya said.

"My preferred method is to buy it and not create any bad blood amongst those who have similar interests," Eduardo said carefully.

"I'm fine with that. What have you lined up?" Anders said, curious.

"The purchase is tonight. Maya, I want you to come with me as usual. Anders can do monitoring and backup."

"And if it's a buy, I guess I need less powers, so more training today," Maya suggested.

"Correct. You've still got that quick teleport challenge to complete, don't you?" Eduardo said gently. Maya sighed.

"Yes, yes I do."

"I will leave you to it. I've got some of my own preparations to make." Eduardo turned and disappeared from the room.

"If it's all the same, I'll do that as well. Good luck with your training and let's catch up a bit later," Anders said.

"Bye." Maya waved him off. She stood up from the chair and was about to walk away when she remembered.

Don't walk. Teleport.

She teleported out of the command center to the space just outside.

It's getting easier and easier to do with repetition. I think. Maybe this location is becoming easier to teleport as well.

Maya teleported herself over to the kitchenette and prepared a coffee. Once it was ready, she teleported herself to a soft armchair and sat down, enjoying her coffee and the quiet. Her eyes kept darting over to look at the teleport course that she had yet to complete.

You'll get it today, don't worry.

When Maya finished her coffee, she found herself staring at the bottom of the cup and noticing there were no more drops.

You really drank it. There's nothing left. It's time to train. No more putting it off.

Maya teleported back to the kitchenette, replaced her cup, then teleported to the start of the course.

It's okay. You can do this. Step one is to smoothly complete the course. And then we'll go for speed. Am I ready for this?

She teleported to the first step and landed comfortably. The next step Maya almost overshot but was still comfortable. She teleported to the third step.

Okay, that wasn't so bad.

She teleported back to the start.

Let's try again.

Maya hit the buzzer, teleporting straight to the first step. Took it on the edge. Rather than recover, she teleported to the second step. Almost fell off but teleported to the third step.

Maya went to hit the buzzer, but it just turned off.

Alright, here's something we can work with.

She teleported back to the start and tried again.

HOURS LATER, Maya was a little bit wobbly on her feet.

You're probably past the point of this being effective training anymore. Maybe you should stop.

She steeled her resolve and looked over the course one more time.

One last try. One last try.

She prepared herself, reaching out to smash the start button and teleporting. As soon as she noticed her feet on the first step, she teleported again. Onto the second step, just as she was feeling contact, she prepared the next one, teleporting again.

Maya reached out with her hand and smashed the buzzer.

"1.8 seconds," a robotic voice said. Maya sighed with relief.

You did it. Beat the course. That's pretty good. You should feel proud of yourself.

Maya looked around the room. She was too tired to walk anywhere. She teleported to the comfortable armchair and settled in for a little rest. Maya awoke to her phone ringing. She answered quickly.

"Uh, yes?"

"Hey, come up to Kora's suite. We're gonna review a few things before we go and complete the buy," Anders said over the phone.

"Can you get me some food? I'm starving," Maya said.

"We'll sort it out. Just get yourself here as soon as possible."

"Thanks, bye," Maya said and hung up the phone. She looked around and realized that quite a long time had passed. She turned to walk out and remembered. Instead, she teleported straight to the exit and walked out through the corridor.

Maybe you can teleport out of the station. Nah, you'll exhaust yourself even more. Just walk.

After exiting she took a cab back to the hotel, playing on her phone rather than talking to the AI driver, and soon found herself at Kora's suite. Without knocking, she just opened the door and walked in. Anders was lounging on the couch and Kora was on the computer as usual.

"Any updates?" Maya said as she walked in.

"Just the one. I'm fairly confident that the Master Sage is not the person behind the viral video," Kora said, looking up at Maya.

"Even though he can shape-shift and become anyone?"

"Precisely," Kora said. "We've done some voice analysis, and he doesn't speak like that. It's very unlikely that it's him."

"Okay, so do we have any other suspects?"

"Not yet. Have a think about it though. Is there someone you've been working with that would want to out you? Someone from your past perhaps who's recognized you and put the pieces together?" Kora said. Maya paused before responding.

"I don't think so. I got on well with people who knew, and that person on the video definitely wasn't Valerie. People in my past, I don't know where they are." Maya shrugged her shoulders and collapsed onto the couch.

"Well, I have the list of people you gave me that you wanted to search through the LifeDeath database for. If I had more information on them, I could run their profiles against this video."

"Hang on." Maya tapped her arm and thought. "Why don't you run the list of people I'm trying to find against all the test subject data we've been pulling from the facility records? Maybe people in my past have been targeted and tested upon." Maya looked up excited. "And that would be why we can't find them and why they haven't contacted me."

"It's a long shot, but I have the data. I can cross-reference it," Kora said. She looked back at the computer and started working on something.

"Thanks, Kora. I know it's a long shot. I appreciate your help, just in case."

"No problem. I'll do it in spare moments when I'm not working on other things. Are you two ready for the buy tonight?" Kora asked.

"I think so. Do you agree?" Maya asked Anders.

"Absolutely. You should eat and then we'll go." Anders pointed to a dish in the kitchenette. Maya teleported over. She inhaled the fragrance coming off it.

"Mmm. Teriyaki tofu if I am not mistaken. How'd you get this in Spain? Wow."

"I found a place. I hope it's alright."

"If it tastes anything like it smells, you did well." Maya opened the lid and dove in.

"How was the training?" Anders asked while they were driving through the city.

"It was good. Pretty tough, but I beat the course finally."

"That's a win. Well done. Took a lot, didn't it?"

"Yeah, it was a real slog, but not harder than any of the other things I've done. I think I'm gonna get really used to this teleporting around business. I'm gonna miss it whenever I lose it again." Maya sighed wistfully.

"You're already looking to that next bloodline, huh?" Anders slowed the van for a traffic light. "Go live in a cave somewhere and ignore everything. You can get off the bloodline treadmill."

"I know what you mean. But we've seen too much to just walk away."

"Do you still think about family and friends, Maya?" Anders's eyes remained focused on the road, navigating through the streets.

"Every day. I know my parents are gone. And that's still not easy. But what's harder is everyone else. I've made the news not always for good reasons. But I haven't heard from or seen anybody from my old life. I just don't get it."

"It must feel strange. Disconnected."

"It is. Where are they? I don't know, I mean maybe they saw enough and are hiding in a cave somewhere."

"Yeah, maybe. That's my advice," Anders said, forcing a chuckle.

"At least I'm making new friends."

"Yeah, everywhere you go. You know, you made those friends at the academy. Mikael was a big help. Derek. Kora. Kora's your friend now, not just someone helping me out," Anders said with enthusiasm.

"No, you're right, I shouldn't... I shouldn't take for granted the group that I've got. Including you. You've all been very good to me. And now we're adding Eduardo."

"He's a good guy. You're right. Focus on what you have, not what you've lost. It will help," Anders said.

"Okay, I'll try to remember how good I've got it when I start dwelling about the past."

"Good. Sounds like a nice plan. And speaking of plans, we're here." Anders parked the van and stepped out of the driver's seat. He walked around and opened up the back of the van. Maya left too and looked around.

"So where do I meet Eduardo?" Maya looked up at the buildings surrounding them.

"Just go around that corner. There's a nightclub called The Golden Crow. He's gonna be inside and that's where you're gonna meet the seller." Anders handed her an earpiece.

"As per usual, take this and I'll be listening in."

"If it's really a nightclub, I don't think you're gonna hear much."

"Well, I'll be able to enjoy some good music." Anders smiled and returned to the van.

Maya went around the corner and saw a line of people waiting to get into The Golden Crow. She walked past the whole line and stood in front of the bouncer.

"Can I get in? I'm meeting someone," Maya said. He looked at her and sneered. The heavyset man brushed a hand through his short, peroxide-blond hair and then showed her a toothy grin.

"That's what everyone says, love. Why should I give you special treatment?" he said, challenging her. Maya shrugged and looked past the bodyguard at the area behind him, taking in more detail.

"Can I at least go around the side here and use the bathroom?" she asked.

"No. Back of the line for you."

"Alright." Maya walked back past the line, noticing a dark corner with an alley nearby.

Worth a try.

She wandered past the end of the line, stepped into the alley, and looked around. There was nobody watching. She turned to roughly orient herself to where she thought the inside of the club was.

Well, you know where you're heading to. Give it a go.

She readied herself, focused the image in her mind, and

pushed. Maya bumped into someone and apologized, stepping aside quickly.

Lucky it's dark in this section.

She had teleported a little bit past where she was hoping to go, inside a dark corridor that led from the entry into the main club. She shoved open the double doors and stepped into a mixture of music, light, and lots of people. She didn't recognize the music, but it had a pumping beat.

Everyone was dancing, dressed in brightly colored clothing, and gyrating furiously to the frenetic beat. Maya looked around, noticing there was a bar at one end and a limited area for seating in the corner. She struggled through the sea of dancing people making her way toward the seating area.

Hopefully, I'll find Eduardo at a table somewhere. Not dancing in this crowd.

17

VAULT HACKER 101

Maya made her way through the crowd ever so slowly, getting shoved, pushed, and bumped all the way through by the throng of energetic dancers. On the other side, there was a little bit of breathing room, but not much. She peeked over the tables and booths that were for sitting and lounging and could not see Eduardo anywhere.

She turned her gaze over to the bar and couldn't see him there either. Something was coming through the radio earpiece, but the music was so loud that she couldn't really hear. She inched her way around the crowd, past the sitting area, and found a quieter nook near the bathrooms.

"Please repeat. What are you trying to say it's too noisy?" Maya said over the radio. There was a garbled response. She couldn't tell whether it was from Anders or Eduardo. But she could make out the word 'stairs'.

"Go downstairs?" Maya suggested. The response was unintelligible, but it felt like confirmation. She searched the room for a staircase and spotted one down by the side of the bar. Fighting her way back through the crowd, Maya moved closer to the bar, pausing briefly to admire the pure glass cabinetry and the hundreds of different liquor bottles arranged behind it.

Approaching the stairs, she noticed there was a single, heavyset, bald man in an impeccable suit, blocking the way with his arms crossed. Maya walked up to him.

"I'm going downstairs," she said, pointing. The man just stared at her. She leaned in close.

"I'm with Eduardo," she said. The man nodded and stepped aside. Maya walked past him and descended the creaky wooden stairs one at a time.

She reached the bottom and it looked very different, like a historic building. Before her was a wood-paneled corridor with a few rooms on either side and a large door at the end. Maya slowly shuffled along the hallway, listening for signs of a meeting or even trouble. She couldn't really hear anything and didn't want to try opening doors.

Instead, she headed straight for the big doors at the end of the corridor.

If I know Eduardo, there'll be some kind of meeting in there, and it'll be very grand.

She continued down the corridor, pausing in front of the large doors. She leaned in to try and listen when the doors were suddenly pulled open.

"Ah, this is her now," Eduardo said, smiling at Maya, and ushering her inside the room. It was a grand wooden sitting room with velvet armchairs, a library around the edges of the room, and a fireplace on one wall, not currently in use. Two other people were seated across a wooden coffee table. Eduardo walked over and sat down, offering Maya the seat next to him.

"This is Maya, my associate," said Eduardo. The two strangers looked her up and down, taking stock of her. One was an older woman with short red hair and piercing blue eyes. She was wearing a business suit. Next to her was a man of similar age with shaggy blond hair and glasses wearing a leather jacket, T-shirt, and jeans.

That's an odd couple.

"The lovely lady over here is Erica, and her partner is Stephen," Eduardo said.

"Pleased to meet you," Erica said.

"Likewise," Maya replied.

"The pleasure is all mine," said Stephen, and did a tiny mock bow. Maya looked down next to Stephen and noticed a rather large black case with a handle.

That must be the device, the vault hacker.

"So, we've discussed price. Are we agreed on that?" Eduardo said, looking at the two. Steve looked over at Erica. She nodded.

"We're good on price," Erica said.

"We'd like to get some publicity around this," Stephen said.

"I don't think that will be possible. This is a delicate operation," Eduardo said.

"I don't know. We completely appreciate that. The thing is, this is our prototype. We're supposed to be using it to get investment. If we sell it to you, then we've got no prototype and a generous cash injection, but it's not enough. We need to get some buzz around this. You know, get people excited, get the orders flowing in." Stephen looked at Erica.

"What he said. My money's all tied up in this. I want a proper return," Erica said. Eduardo looked at Maya.

"So, we could offer another twenty percent on top?" Eduardo said. Maya leaned in and whispered to Eduardo.

"I don't even know how much we're paying."

"Don't worry, you're good for it," Eduardo said quietly.

"Twenty percent extra is fine by me if we can make a deal tonight," Maya said.

"We'll find a way to drum up business ourselves," Erica said to Stephen.

"Alright, we have a deal. And let me just give you the

payment details." Stephen pulled out his phone and set up his account details. Maya paid with her phone without even checking the amount.

I don't want to know. It's better if I don't know. Now it's paid for.

"Pleasure doing business with you," Maya said. "Is that the device there?"

"It sure is. Let me just give you a quick tour." Stephen excitedly grabbed the case but set it down very carefully on the coffee table.

"This is the unlocking code for the case. One, two, three, four," Stephen said it with a smile.

"Oh, that's very, very secure," Maya said, putting on a smile.

"It's configurable. The idea is that you don't get locked out of your new purchase," Erica said.

"Very good feature," Eduardo said, looking at Maya and encouraging her to be more positive. Stephen punched in the code and opened the lid of the case.

"This is the unit here. You can see this module over here is the drilling section. Over here is the keypad hacker and over here is the diagnostic suite. You'll also notice this data drive, it has schematics, instructions, demonstrations, and so on."

"Will this require a lot of training and practice to use," Maya said.

"It's pretty pick up and play, I would say, but like any tool, it's worth testing it before you use it in a critical job," Stephen said carefully.

"What kind of warranty do we have?" Eduardo said.

"I'll answer that." Erica shuffled a little closer in her chair. "If used in the correct manner, we will do a free assessment of any issues and agree on a mutually beneficial repair cost."

"I think that's reasonable. What do you think, Maya?" Eduardo said.

"It is a prototype, so I agree there is some flexibility here. However, I do think since we're buying it without a true demonstration, there should be a little bit of leeway on ensuring it's functional."

"All good, I have complete confidence in the product," Stephen said. "I think you'll find it's up to the task, but I must stress you do a test to both demonstrate to yourselves that it is working correctly as per the instructional videos and also to reduce the likelihood of misusing the tools and then damaging them by mistake." Stephen closed the lid, locked the latch, and slid it over toward Maya.

"Take good care of it. It took me way too long to develop it, and I'm hoping the next one is a lot faster."

"Me too," Maya said. "It looks fantastic and, you know, I'm sure we'd like to have a spare, wouldn't we, Eduardo?"

"Absolutely. You couldn't have too many of these," he said with a smile. "Well, I think that's our cue to leave." Eduardo stood up and Maya stood as well, grabbing the case off the table.

"Lovely to meet you both in person and we'll be in touch," Eduardo said. He shook Erica's hand and then Stephen's hand.

"Likewise, it was lovely to meet you both. And we'll take good care of this," Maya said, shaking both their hands as well.

"The old vault hacker will not let you down. Good luck and happy hacking," Stephen said with a grin. Maya waved goodbye and they turned to leave, walking at a normal pace out of the room. Eduardo opened the door, held it for Maya, and she walked through.

They continued on in silence until they reached the staircase.

"Well, we got it," Maya said as they started to ascend the wooden stairs.

"We did indeed."

"I think the overarching theme I'm getting from that is we need to test it," Maya said with a chuckle.

"Absolutely. We just need to find some vaults to test it on. Feels like a job for Anders, doesn't it," Eduardo said with a grin.

"I think so." Maya pressed her radio earpiece.

"Anders, we have the package, and also you just got a new job."

"Can't wait. Fill me in when you get here," Anders said over the radio. They made their way up the stairs. Eduardo went ahead and forged a path through the sea of dancing, sweaty bodies.

It was a relief when they finally emerged into the night air. Walking quickly, they turned the corner and made their way over to the van. Anders was lounging around outside, playing on his phone. As soon as he saw them, he opened the van doors and ushered them in.

Within moments, the van was on, and they were driving away.

"So, you got the item? Does it look alright?" Anders said.

"I don't know what it's supposed to look like, but I think so," Maya said.

"It's as we agreed. It doesn't look like there's any surprises, but we need to make sure it's working properly before we use it," Eduardo said.

"I can help with that if you'd like," Anders offered with surprising enthusiasm.

"Sure. Since you've been volunteered to procure us a whole bunch of vaults to test this thing on," Maya said.

"Okay, that's not something I've had to do before. This actually sounds pretty fun."

"See, I told you he'd love it," Maya said to Eduardo.

"I never doubted you." Eduardo chuckled as they sped along through the night.

~

The next day, Maya was taking the case through the training area to the command center when she received a call from Kora.

"Hi Kora, do you have good news for me? Did you find anything?"

"I'm sorry, Maya, this is not good news. So, you procured yourself a vault hacker last night, correct?"

"That's right. It looks fine. We're going to test it out today and Anders is going to secure us some vaults to test it on."

"Well, it seems like the folks you bought it off got a little bit too excited."

"What did they do?" Maya said with a sigh.

"They basically spammed all the black-market boards, distribution lists, and channels, that they've sold their proto-type to a lucky buyer and they're ready to go into mass production."

"So what, anybody with a pulse and an ear to the ground now knows there's a vault hacker out there ready to be used?"

"Precisely. At least they didn't say who it was, but did you guys use your real names?"

"Yeah, we did. Eduardo set it up."

"Okay, well, hopefully, people don't track these guys down and get your names. Sorry to be the bearer of bad news, but I guess what's done is done."

"Thanks, Kora, at least we know." Maya hung up the phone and let out a deep sigh.

"Eduardo where are you?" she called out.

18

FAMILY CONNECTION

"Have you seen this message?" Maya said, pulling out her phone.

"About the vault hacker?" Eduardo said, a disappointed look on his face.

"I guess you have. Is that trouble for us?"

"It could be. As much as they're trying to drum up business, I don't think it'll come back to us. For now, all we can do is focus on the next mission."

"Let's do that. What's the next thing?" Maya said, curious.

"It's a very cool device called a WallSpy."

"A WallSpy? What is it?"

"It's what you think it is. It lets you look through a wall," Eduardo said with a laugh.

"Oh. I can see the benefits of this one."

"I'll save the full explanation for Anders. Let's go into the command center." Eduardo disappeared and Maya followed him, teleporting to her usual chair in the command center. This time she managed to be sitting on it.

I feel like I've achieved something. I teleported from a standing to a seated position.

Eduardo noticed Maya's teleport location.

"Nice one. I've got some special training for you after this," he said. Anders was lounging in another chair, playing on his phone.

"Oh, were you ready to start?" he said.

"Yes, we are. Anders, I assume by now you've heard about the vault hacker announcement?"

Anders nodded.

"Good, we can move on. Anders, as discussed, it's going to be your job to set up a test facility with the top five most secure vaults that we can test the hack on."

"Already working on it," Anders said.

"Good, because we're going to need to do a full simulation pretty soon, I think. Our timeline keeps moving with all this attention." Eduardo brought up some images on the monitors.

"This is our next target, our WallSpy. It lets us see through walls, which as you're beginning to appreciate, has two wonderful benefits." Eduardo brought up an image on the screen. A mockup of a wall becoming transparent, highlighting items in the other room.

"First, great for spotting traps, dangers, or even security presence on the other side of a wall."

"That's a lot of applications right there," Anders commented.

"Exactly. The second particularly useful benefit is scoping out suitable teleport locations."

"Oh, this is going to be really handy," Maya said, thinking back to her experience teleporting through the concrete wall.

"Exactly. Which is why we need to get our hands on this. It's critical to the plan."

"Where do we start," Anders said.

"I've got a lead on the device. Again, it's a prototype. This time I think we might just have to liberate it."

"No question," Maya said.

"If word gets around town that someone's buying all the prototypes up, it's basically a giant neon sign saying, 'Heist in progress'," Anders said.

"Well, more appropriately, 'Heist about to be in progress'," Eduardo said, correcting him.

"True, true. Where do I start?" Anders said.

Eduardo typed a few keys on the keyboard. "The information's on its way to you both. You can start exploring what I've already discovered, and then we'll liaise a bit later to work out a plan."

"What about me?" Maya said.

"You have a very important training challenge. Come this way. Or should I say, meet me out by the couches." Eduardo vanished, and Maya teleported after him.

"I'm going to go to the far room in that corner." Eduardo inclined his head in that direction. Before Maya could clarify, he disappeared.

I'm pretty sure I know where he's going.

Maya concentrated and teleported. She arrived, landed just outside the room, and could see Eduardo inside. After a brief pause, she teleported herself inside as well.

Eduardo was standing in an otherwise empty room. There was a single circular table about waist height in the middle of the room with only one object on it. A black rectangular metallic case.

"This looks like the vault hacker," Maya said.

"It's a copy. A non-functioning copy, but it's the right size and weight and overall structure. And why is that?" He rapped it two times with his knuckle so that Maya could hear the sound.

"Sounds solid, I'm curious," Maya said.

"As you're probably realizing, teleporting is easier when it's just yourself that's being moved. And your clothing."

"So, it's even easier without clothing?" Maya blurted out, surprised.

"It is, but there's no point starting there because then you're just adding more mental blocks for your brain to have to work around. Better to just make the assumption that you need your clothes and start from there, like you did."

"Agreed," Maya said with a laugh. "You want me to teleport with the vault hacker?"

"Yes. With teleportation you have, let's call them freebies. You can take some equipment in your clothing, and it tends to just come with us without a noticeable burden." Eduardo paused and Maya nodded along.

"However, carrying another physical object, especially a heavy and bulky one like this, is something extra."

"Can you carry a person?" Maya said.

"I think, technically, yes, but I've not seen it work, and I'm not really in the business of experimenting with that." Eduardo had a very serious look on his face. A stern one.

"Okay, I'm not going to try that."

"Good. Thank you. So, your challenge will be to teleport from here to the command center with the vault hacker," Eduardo said without fanfare. Maya turned to look in the general direction of the command center.

"That's a fair jump," she said.

"It is. I would recommend just teleporting outside the room as a starting point."

"Alright. That sounds like a smart idea. I can do that."

I'm really not sure about this. That box is heavy.

"Great, well, I've got a few things to plan for tonight's mission. I will leave you to it." Eduardo turned to leave.

"Wait, wait, before you go, do you have any tips?"

"Yeah, I've got a really good one. Make this work. Good luck and bye." Eduardo smiled and vanished.

I guess it's back to me again.

Maya leaned over and grabbed the metal case by its handle. *Heavier than it looks.*

She lifted it off the table and held it in one hand, dangling it.

Hmm. Let's just see if I can move a tiny bit.

Maya picked a spot a few feet away and teleported. She arrived, but the metal case swung wildly, and she almost dropped it.

Okay, short distance, mostly under control. Time to practice.

REPETITION ISN'T DOING ENOUGH. *I need to change my approach.*

Maya changed her grip, hugging the case close to her chest before teleporting. She tried returning to the same spot.

It worked a little better, although she almost unbalanced herself with the additional weight.

So far, so good.

Next, Maya picked a spot just outside the room, cradling the case like the last time. She paused, focused her energy, and teleported. At least she tried to. It felt like there was a barrier, something holding her back.

Oh no, not again.

She was running into the same problem again. The wall. Or she was creating it again. Maya turned around and noticed that this particular room had no door, just a doorway.

Aha! This is a good trick.

Maya turned and picked a spot just outside the room, but through the doorway. Clutching the case carefully, she prepared and teleported. It worked, but she almost toppled over.

This weight is really unstable. Let's try something else.

Next, she crouched down and placed the case on the ground in front of her, just holding it by the handle.

Let's see how this goes.

Maya tried teleporting again. She blinked and realized she was now in the room.

Oh. That was much better.

The case and her had traveled safely and she hadn't lost her balance or been at risk of dropping anything.

So all I did was hold the handle with the intent of holding the case and bringing it with me. That's cool.

Maintaining her position, Maya selected a spot on the other side of the glass wall in front of her.

Here's the real test.

She focused her energy, pushed, and felt a resistance. But for some reason, time and energy slowed, and she had a moment just to consider the blockage. She thought back to all of her time mastering the Chakra bloodline, surpassing her limits. Being strong but flexible, being like the water. With that, her mindset changed, and she was outside the room, with the case.

Yes! You've got this!

Without even turning around, Maya teleported back into the room. It was still hard, but easier than before.

Alright, now it's time for distance.

Maya appeared in the command center, seated on her chair with the metal case in front of her.

"That looks awfully comfortable. Well done," Eduardo said. Maya leaned back in the chair and put her feet on top of the case.

"All in a good day's work," she said. "Have you finished your job today?" Maya said to Eduardo, feeling quite pleased with herself.

"We have indeed. We have located the WallSpy and we have a plan. I'm just waiting on Anders to come back with the final element."

"Great. I guess we just kick back and have a bit of a rest." Maya paused, waiting for Eduardo to respond.

Is this where he says I need more training?

"Well, rest is good while we have the time. I'm quite impressed, Maya. You've come a long way in a short time."

"Thank you. I should stop being so surprised when this happens. That's the last thing my last mentor said, and the one before that."

"So, you're a bit of a quick learner, huh?"

"Not as quick as I'd like, but I'm stubborn enough to make improvements." Maya laughed. Eduardo smiled back at her and chuckled.

"You remind me of someone, actually. An old friend who's since disappeared." Eduardo's smile faded away.

"The multi-blood user you mentioned?"

"Yeah, him. He was my teleport mentor."

"Oh. Multiple bloodlines and teleport? That's really rare." Maya sat up in her chair, leaning forward.

"It is rare. He had more power than most, and he wanted to make a difference. And he had the means to do so, or so we all thought."

"What do you mean?"

"He started to collect like-minded people from different clans."

"Oh, I see where this is going," Maya said softly.

"Yes. The Master Sage did not take kindly to this, as he called it, insurrection." Eduardo shook his head.

"Oh, I bet."

"And so, just as my mentor was building stability and an alternative home for people who didn't want to buy into the factional fighting and discord sold by the Master Sage. It was all gone. He soundly beat my mentor and stole from him his most precious possession."

"Is that what you're going for? In this facility?" Maya said.

"It is. It's very special to me too."

"What was the name of your mentor? I'd love to find out more about him."

"His name? His name is Alastair Mills."

"Alastair Mills? What a weird coincidence. That's my uncle's name," Maya said, astonished.

"Quite so. I've done my homework. He is your uncle. I don't think it's a coincidence that we found each other, Maya."

"You have to tell me more about him. I haven't seen him since I was a kid. He lived overseas. How did this all happen?" Maya was struggling to form a sentence and her mind was racing.

"There's a lot we need to talk about. I will find time to talk to you about this. There's so much I need to pass on."

"He's still alive, right? Where was he last spotted? Do you know where he is?"

"He was in Spain. That's where it all happened. I think he got away, but at great cost to himself and everyone around him."

"Were you there?"

"I was there, and I was a coward. I could have done more, should have done more. But, in the face of that monster..." Eduardo sighed and looked away.

"You don't have to blame yourself. I've faced him. It's... I didn't even know what to say. It's overwhelming."

"It is." Eduardo turned and saw Anders walking in.

"It's also a tale for another time. Anders, are we ready?"

"We're ready. This time, I am leading the mission."

19

WALLSPYING

nders parked the van and quickly left the vehicle. Maya and Eduardo left as well, making sure they didn't fall behind.

"Okay, radios on," Anders said. Maya popped an earpiece into her right ear and tapped it twice.

"Remember, the target is in the penthouse apartment. The WallSpy is in a lockbox. Follow my lead and we'll be in and out in no time."

"You're the boss," Eduardo said.

"Let's go." Anders led them around to the rear of a very tall apartment building.

"How many floors is that?" Maya asked.

"Eighteen," Anders quickly responded. Around the back was a loading dock, Anders walked up to the yellow and black roller door and attached a device to the control panel next to it. Within seconds the roller door started opening.

"A bit noisy, I know," Anders said. Eduardo had no reply. Anders led them into the dimly lit loading dock and car park. It was empty, with white paint markings on the ground showing the appropriate locations to unload and what were valid parking spots.

They walked through the still, quiet space and went up a ramp to a raised platform next to an elevator.

"This is a service elevator. No security cameras, provided we can get in." Anders called the elevator, and when it opened, he stepped inside. Maya and Eduardo followed close behind. Anders waved a key card over the reader and hit the button for the penthouse.

The doors closed immediately and the lift ascended very fast.

"Good preparation, I like it," Eduardo said."

"You shouldn't sound so surprised," Anders said with a grin. The lift opened and they stepped out onto a plush purple carpet. They were in a narrow corridor with another lift next to them and a door at the far end of the corridor.

"This way. Keep it quiet," Anders said. They padded down the hallway and Anders used the access card to open the door to the penthouse suite. He carefully pushed it open, stepping into the lavish suite.

"Looks better than ours. We need an upgrade," Anders said. Eduardo went through second, and Maya passed through last, taking additional care to close the door quietly. It was an open-plan suite with huge floor-to-ceiling windows showcasing the sparkling city view.

They were standing in a bar area with a kitchen nearby, a pool table just beyond, and another lounge off to their right. Anders signed for them to follow. They walked through the lounge, and he stopped at a large cabinet.

Anders pointed to Maya and then pointed to a nearby corridor.

"Be the look out," he whispered.

She nodded. Maya carefully walked over to the corridor, and she could see there was a bedroom at the end of the corridor with the door closed. She padded closer, listening for any signs of anyone awake. She couldn't hear anything. Maya retreated until she was back in the lounge area, but kept an eye on the door.

She looked over to see what Anders was doing. He had managed to unlock the cabinet, and in the bottom section was a heavy metal safe. Anders placed another gadget on the safe and it started humming away. He turned, stood up, and looked over at Maya.

"All clear?" he whispered. She nodded. He looked at Eduardo, who just shrugged and waited. Maya noticed movement up ahead. The bedroom door was opening. She stepped back and quickly ran to Anders tapping him on the shoulder.

She pointed in the direction of the bedroom, and he understood. Eduardo put his hand on Anders's shoulder and nodded. Anders went back to monitoring his gadget, and Eduardo carefully walked over to the corridor. Seconds later, Maya heard a thump.

She ran over to check and saw a man with long blond hair, lying asleep on the ground.

"Hopefully he thinks that he'd just had a rough night," Eduardo said.

"Is no one else here?" Maya asked.

"No, I checked the bedroom. It was empty." Seconds later, they heard a beep and a small cheer from Anders. He swung the safe door open and pulled out a pair of goggles.

"This is it," he said. He handed them to Maya. "Try them on." Maya put the goggles on, adjusting the strap.

Great, it's pitch black. Good for sleeping, I guess.

"There should be an on switch on the side," Anders said. Maya reached up with her right hand, feeling around for some controls. She found a switch and clicked it on. After an initial surge of light, she could see.

"It looks...normal. I can't see through anything."

"Try this wall over here, Maya." Anders pointed to a wall separating the kitchen and dining area. Maya walked behind it and stared at the wall while Anders put everything back where it was, to begin with.

"It looks like a wall."

"There must be another control to switch on the WallSpy feature. You wouldn't want to see through all the walls all the time," Anders said.

"Right." Maya felt around with her left hand, and after exploring the strap she found a separate button. She tried clicking it on.

Wow, that's something. There's Anders walking around over there.

"I can see you Anders. These are incredible."

"Okay, shut it off." Eduardo came over and took the goggles off Maya.

"We need to study these. We don't know how the battery works, what the limitations are. We can't ruin them on the first day."

"You're right. Also, we probably better get out of here before that guy wakes up," Maya said. Anders led the way back to the door of the suite. Before he left, he went into the fridge and took out a bottle of gin. He mixed a gin and tonic, poured some down the sink, walked over to where the man had fallen down, poured the rest on the floor, and placed it artistically near the man.

"Full points for effort. But I'm not sure he's gonna buy it," Eduardo said.

"A little bit of confusion will help us all the same." Anders wandered over to the front door, opened it, and strolled out.

MAYA HURRIED through the doorway into the underground training area. She immediately teleported to the middle of the room, looking around for Eduardo.

"Over here, Maya." Eduardo popped his head out of a glass-walled room, and Maya teleported over to his location.

"Great, you're here. I've just been playing around with the WallSpy."

"How is it working? Do you like it?" Maya asked.

"I do. I think it's going to do what we need. Which is a relief because the plan kind of hinges on it. Let's teleport over to that far corner." Eduardo pointed with his hand and then disappeared. Maya glanced over where he was pointing, brought the location into her mind, and then teleported as well.

"Okay, this is where it gets interesting. There is a utility room behind this wall, but the doorway is somewhere else. Let's see how we go." Eduardo put on the goggles, switched them on, and then hit the other switch to activate the WallSpy.

Maya watched him moving his head around, looking carefully.

"Here we go. First test," Eduardo said. He waved at Maya, and then he vanished.

I guess it worked.

A few seconds later, Eduardo appeared next to Maya, holding the goggles in his hand.

"Excellent. Worked as intended. Now the real trick is, can I go back?" Eduardo handed Maya the WallSpy, and then he disappeared.

I'm going to assume that's a yes.

Maya put on the goggles, switched on the unit, and then activated the WallSpy function. She peered through the wall, and she saw a mostly empty space, with cabinets around the walls, and right in the middle of the room was Eduardo waving.

That's cute.

Maya picked the spot next to Eduardo and teleported. It felt a little strange, the transition, but she noticed she was in the room with him. Maya took off the goggles immediately and looked around with her own eyes.

"Wow, this really works."

"It sure does. We do have to test the thickness of how much it can see through though."

"Do we have specs on how thick the walls are in the facility?" Maya asked.

"Let's check in with Kora. I sent her the specs for the facility and she can tell us what we need. Now that we're here, can you teleport back to where we were?" Eduardo asked. Maya nodded. She held the location in her mind and teleported back.

It felt the same as anything else. She noticed Eduardo popping in next to her.

"We learned quite a few things just now," he said. "First, that your understanding of a location from the WallSpy imagery is good enough. You can teleport with the WallSpy on, and you can teleport with it in your hands."

"And it's easy to return to the location," Maya added.

"Actually, now that you've been in that room, go back there," Eduardo said. Maya shrugged, imagined where she wanted to be and teleported.

She passed into the room without the strange feeling that had accompanied her the time that she'd never been there before. Maya teleported back and saw Eduardo looking thoughtful.

"That was fine. I did notice a difference when I teleported the first time, with just the goggles showing me the location."

"I did as well. I think it's a virtual leap of faith, but the goggles work well enough to trick your brain into being able to go there."

"Do you think it's really a trick or are our minds somehow

interpreting the spatial information that we're seeing?" Maya asked. Eduardo adjusted his glasses.

"I'm not sure of the answer for that one. Both are equally likely, but it doesn't really matter as long as it works."

"If one of us has this, how do we use it together?" Maya said.

"I have a plan for that, but there's also a better version of the plan if Kora can replicate the device." Eduardo gave Maya a knowing smile.

"I will be testing this a little bit further, and I need you to do some basic training."

"Any suggestions or just whatever comes to mind?"

"Actually, how about you do the speed teleportation course with the metal case," Eduardo said, excited. Maya groaned.

"I can see how that's gonna go. But I agree. It's good training."

"Happy trails! I think you'll find the metal case for testing is in the command center." Eduardo waved and disappeared.

"Here we go." Maya teleported into the command center, located the metal case, and teleported back to the start area of the timer challenge. She stared at the three steps and looked down at the metal case in her hand and sighed.

All right, let's make this work.

Hours later Maya was snacking on some sushi on the couch when Eduardo teleported back in.

"Ah, lunchtime, does that mean you're ready for a bit of a test?" Eduardo said.

"Actually, yes," Maya said, popping the last piece into her mouth. Eduardo continued his explanation.

"Well, for testing purposes, I have a second device with me." Eduardo pulled out the original WallSpy and another one that was a little bit more patchwork.

"How did we get a second one?" Maya said, looking at the new prototype.

"Well, Kora is quite resourceful. I already had her working on what a WallSpy might work or look like if she were to build one herself, and once I could take a real one over, it didn't take her long to reverse engineer what was special about it and integrate that into her prototype."

"That's pretty cool. So does it work?" Maya said eagerly.

"Let's find out." Eduardo tossed the prototype over to Maya. She put it on and felt around for the switches.

"Don't worry, they're in the same location," Eduardo said. Maya switched on the unit and her vision returned.

"Should we try the same spot or a different one?"

"Different one. There's an area in here that I haven't visited yet. Go into that far corner and I want you to pick a location through the wall and teleport over."

"Alright," Maya said. She teleported to the corner Eduardo had specified. Switching the WallSpy function on, which thankfully worked, she peered through the wall and looked at what was an old, abandoned locker room.

This'll do.

She picked a spot in the middle of the room and teleported.

"Are you there now?" Eduardo said. Maya heard his voice coming from the unit somewhere.

"Uh, yes?" she said, unsure if Eduardo could hear her. The next moment, Eduardo appeared next to her. Maya took off the goggles.

"What? How did you get here?" she said.

"Well, that's the fun bit. See, what's the point of having two goggles if you can't communicate?" Eduardo had a twinkle in his eye.

"Oh right, so there's a radio. That makes sense," Maya said, nodding along.

"Better yet, there's a video feed. I could see what you could see, and then I could teleport there."

"Oh," Maya said slowly, her mind running away with the possibilities.

20

DRY RUN

Maya handed her WallSpy unit over to Anders and Eduardo did the same.

"We've done enough testing for now. Do you reckon you could work with Kora on finalizing these units?" Eduardo said.

"Happy to. I bet the tech in here is awesome. Very keen to get stuck into it, get my hands on it in more detail." Maya could see Anders's eyes lighting up with the thought.

"Go enjoy," she said. Anders waved and jogged off out of the training area.

"Come grab a coffee." Eduardo teleported over to the kitchenette and started making coffee. Maya joined him.

"Well, how do you think things are going?" Eduardo said, putting the coffee beans into the grinder.

Maya waited for the sound of the grinding to die down before she responded. "I think it's going well. I mean, we haven't really tested the vault hacking yet, but you know, the identity kits are there. The security pass access is there as well. The WallSpy is going to be really handy for approaching the heists from multiple locations. And also being able to teleport to each other."

"Good summary. And next?" Eduardo prompted.

"I think now we need a dry run," Maya said.

Eduardo nodded. He turned on the coffee machine and watched the coffee extracting as he spoke. "Yes, that is the right thinking. We're on the same page there. I think we'll be able to do that tomorrow. The location that Anders has set up with the practice vaults should be a good testing ground."

"Great. I think after we do that, we'll know if we're ready."

"I think we're ready, but a bit more practice in a real scenario wouldn't hurt." Eduardo handed Maya her coffee and started making his own. She took a sip and closed her eyes. The wonderful smell and taste moved through her like a wave of happiness.

"I just hope we find what we need. There's a lot riding on this place," Maya said.

"I hope so too." Eduardo took a sip of his coffee and then pointed at the couches in the middle of the room. "Let's sit there." He teleported over, as did Maya.

"Oh, great. I didn't spill my coffee." Maya sat on the couch next to Eduardo and took another long sip of her coffee.

"The item I'm looking for is a relic. It's a very special item from ancient times."

"Oh, ancient? What is it?" Maya said, perking up.

"It's an amulet, made out of who knows what, some kind of ancient ore. But what it does is actually incredible."

"I'm listening," Maya said, leaning forward.

"It removes the distance limitations of teleportation," Eduardo said. His voice had a reverence to it and passion that Maya hadn't heard from him before.

"Really?" she blurted out. "That sounds impossible."

"Any more impossible than the actual ability to teleport in the first place?" Eduardo said, smiling.

Maya shook her head. "Incredible. No wonder you want that. Did my uncle have it?"

"He did. He never shared with me where he got it from, or how, but that was what kept him safe. Initially, it helped when he was jumping around trying to hide his presence and location. But also in the end when the Master Sage decided to teach him a lesson."

Eduardo paused before continuing. "The Master Sage didn't kill Alastair. But broke his organization, scattered his people, and took the item which gave him his safety and freedom away. And then hid it so no one else could have it."

"And you tied it back to this facility?" Maya said.

"Yes, with a great deal of trouble. I'm certain it's there. And I have to get it. Not just for the promise of freedom it provides. But it means a lot to me."

"Well, my reason isn't anywhere near as good as that, but I'll make sure you get that relic back. And while we're there, I can help myself to a few things as well." Maya took another long sip of her coffee.

"Well, this mission has to help you too. But I'm afraid I won't be sharing the relic."

"Oh no, no, no. That's fine. You do that, it'll be wasted on me anyway."

"How so?" Eduardo said, curious.

"Well, the thing is... I don't know what the future holds, but it seems pretty clear I'm going to be mastering bloodlines for a while. I would only be able to use the relic for certain periods where I have all my power at my disposal."

"You said you had all of them," Eduardo said.

"That's right. I've been tested on those machines and they all light up like a Christmas tree," Maya said. Eduardo laughed.

"You're gonna need all the help you can get. How is the Master Sage not on your trail right now?" Eduardo said, jokingly but with a serious expression.

"Oh, he is. I mean he's the one behind Valerie. And I think it's been three times he's captured me. No wait. Four times he's captured me and I've escaped."

"Sounds like he's toying with you," Eduardo said, leaning back into the seat.

"He has to be. I mean, with that much power, there's something he's playing at. Maybe it's the control. Maybe he's trying to build me up before he takes me down. I don't know what it is exactly."

"I think that you'll have to understand him before this is all over," Eduardo said.

"That's good advice. Do you have a place that you're gonna go? Where you can go anywhere?" Maya said. Eduardo scratched his chin.

"Actually, yes. Australia."

"Really?" Maya laughed. "Why there?"

"It's just so far away from everything. I feel like it would be a good place to get lost in."

"It definitely is. I should know, I grew up there."

"Maybe you can give me a tour?"

"I'd love to! But, you know, we just have this small problem of an un-break-in-able facility to break into."

"Yes, that is a small problem, but we're close to a solution." Eduardo finished off the rest of his coffee, disappeared, and then reappeared.

"Oh, sorry, I forgot your cup. Where's my manners?" He accepted Maya's cup, disappeared, and reappeared again.

"How about we run over everything with the rest of the team and get ready for our dry run tomorrow?" Eduardo said.

ANDERS WALKED them down the laneway toward a big concrete building. He was practically rubbing his hands in excitement.

"Alright, so we've got three of the top vaults installed here. Temporarily, of course. The building has multiple entrances, a maze of useless rooms, and I've also managed to put a rudimentary security system in."

"That's quite an achievement," Maya said. "Did you expect all this, Eduardo?"

"I did. In fact, if Anders didn't bring it, I was going to insist on him doing it properly. But this looks good."

"Okay, great. What is our plan then?" Maya said. "I mean, I know the plan, but how am I going to play this today?"

"There are multiple entrances, so we're going to take one each. Anders is going to wait outside as support and come in when required."

"Okay. Got it.

"Now every second teleport we should cross teleport to anchor the locations. That way we will increase our ability to adapt to the situation, but also return to specific points in the future as required."

"Awesome. What else?"

"Anders, are you able to simulate some kind of alarm or security breach halfway through?"

"I could do something." Anders looked like he was concentrating. "Yeah, I can make something up. I mean, with what we already have in the building."

"Great. Maya, we're going to both meet at the vaults for the vault hacking. So we both get experience with the tool, but in the real heist we may not do that at the same time as a security precaution."

"I understand, there's going to be a few differences to the final heist." Maya slowed, as they were now in front of the building.

"It's dark enough. Everyone's gone home in the area, and we have the building to ourselves. Let's give this a go. I will take the rear of the building and Maya can take the closer door. And we'll be in touch over the radio."

"Good luck," Maya said.

"You too." Eduardo disappeared. Maya spotted him reappear alongside the building and disappear again.

"How's your teleportation going? Are you gonna forgo walking soon?" Anders said.

"Not that soon, but I can see it as a possibility in the future, if I really want to."

"I think you'll miss walking too much."

"I guess we'll have to see."

"The door you want to attempt to access is down there. You've got the security pass and you can call me on the radio."

"Thanks, Anders. Let's see how we go." Maya waved and then teleported down to the door Anders had pointed out.

There was a nondescript door with a security card reader. Maya fished out the security pass and waved it over the reader. The door unlocked and she slipped inside, closing it carefully behind her. Once inside, she put the WallSpy goggles on, activating the unit so she could see normally.

She was in a large, cavernous space with a few doors along a wall to her right. She looked around for any security and then walked carefully over to the three doors.

"Trying doors," she said over the radio. The first one she attempted to open was locked. The second one she tried to open was also locked. The third door opened easily.

"Starting with the unlocked door," Maya said. She pushed the door open and stepped inside the room. It looked like a meeting room, with a table and chairs, a teleconference unit, and a whiteboard. Nothing else.

"It's just a meeting room," Maya said.

"Sounds like a good safe room," Eduardo said over the radio. "I'll teleport to your location." Moments later, Eduardo appeared in the room with Maya.

"Hello. This is a good one to retreat to if we needed some breathing room. There's a second switch on the left-hand side of the unit. If you activate that one, it'll switch your video feed over to my video feed if you want to try the same thing."

"Okay, I will," Maya said. Eduardo disappeared, and then she switched her unit over, so she was watching his video feed.

"Okay. You're in a break room with a vending machine?" Maya said.

"Correct. See if you can come over here." Maya held the location in her mind and teleported. It felt like a bit of a strain, but she arrived without too much trouble, shaking off some discomfort. She looked around the room.

"Okay, this is also a pretty good... safe room as you said."

"Exactly, we need to use this approach in the real heist, because being able to retreat to different spaces alone or together could mean the difference between getting out or not."

"I agree. Once we're inside we need to do whatever it takes to make it work."

"Go back to your room and we'll continue," Eduardo said. Maya teleported back to her boring meeting room, paused to catch her breath, and then walked around to try the next door.

She pulled out a lock-picking tool from Anders's supply kit and it made short work of the door lock. She pushed this door open and stepped inside.

Another corridor.

"Second door is a corridor. I'm going to explore," Maya said over the radio.

"Confirmed. I'm exploring a dining hall," Eduardo said.

"Any good food?" Maya said.

"Remember, this is a practice run of the real mission. Keep your focus."

"Sorry."

No more chitchat. Gotta treat it like the real deal. Focus.

21

INSIDE THE VAULTS

Maya kept exploring rooms. She found lots of useless meeting rooms, empty rooms, corridors, and also bathrooms. Eduardo called her to teleport on occasion, so they would exchange locations to improve their teleport options.

Finally, Eduardo called her over the radio with some good news.

"I found the vaults. Come meet me," he said, excited. Maya's vision switched over to what Eduardo was looking at. Three vaults, side by side.

"On my way." Maya pictured the location as before and teleported. As soon as she arrived, her vision switched over to what was in front of her. She looked over the room. It was a large space. Probably originally a basketball court. The three vaults were lined up one by one. Each were massive structures.

"How did Anders even get them in here?" Maya breathed.

"I'm not sure. You'll have to ask him after this. I'm quite impressed. Now that we're here, time to fetch the vault hacker."

"Mind if I do the honors, Eduardo?" Maya said.

"Feel free," he said. Maya teleported back to Anders who was waiting outside with the equipment.

"Good luck in there," Anders said, pointing at the vault hacker. Maya walked over, crouched before it, and held the handle like she had practiced.

The teleport back was smooth. She was right in front of the first vault.

"Okay, so let's give it a go." Maya opened the case and took out the vault hacker. She peered at the locking mechanism before her, unsure of which option to use.

"Try the diagnostic tool first," Eduardo offered. Maya retrieved the diagnostic tool from the hacking kit and placed it on the front of the lock. It was circular with no other markings.

The machine whirred away, and then it displayed a message on a screen.

"Hmm. This one has a complex key mechanism. The drill is recommended."

"Good. I guess one of them had to be the drill," Eduardo said. He walked over and helped Maya pull out and assemble the drill, clipping it onto the locking mechanism. Once it was deployed, Maya pushed the on button. The drill whirled into life.

"We're going to stand back," Eduardo said. As it burrowed away into the lock, it gave off light, heat, and smoke.

"While that's going, I guess we should investigate the next vault," Maya said.

"We should." Eduardo walked over and examined it.

"This one has a keypad."

"Well then let's try the keypad tool," Maya said. She went and retrieved the keypad hacking tool and brought it back, clipping it onto the vault door. It took a few moments to get it in the right position. Once it was there, she activated it and it started cycling through key combinations to determine which was the right one.

"I guess it's important to figure out how long these are going to take, so we know how much time we need in the real heist," Eduardo said.

"Makes sense to me. One thing I don't get though. I thought the space that we were trying to get into was gigantic. It wouldn't fit in a vault," Maya said, looking over the vaults.

"I'm not sure, but all the intel suggests that the vault is the way in, or it contains something that we need."

"Alright, well, we should make sure we're experts on vaults." Maya wandered over to the third vault and examined it.

"Looks like a combination. There's a keypad but also... oh, look at this. It's one of those old-school turning dials," Maya said with delight.

"I didn't know they still made these." Eduardo leaned in to have a closer look.

"Well, maybe the diagnostic tool can help us here. It's supposed to help with these older style mechanisms, correct?"

"That's the idea." Maya fetched the diagnostic tool and clipped it onto the vault lock, near the combination selector. It began scanning.

"I've seen movies where the people breaking into a vault would use a stethoscope to listen and understand when they'd triggered one of the right combinations," Maya said.

"I don't think we have that with us. You didn't pack one, did you?" Eduardo said with a grin.

"No, but maybe the diagnostic machine is sensitive to that." Maya started turning the knob slowly to see if there was any change in the diagnostic tool. As she passed the number twenty-three, the value was locked in on the screen.

"I think twenty-three is the first number," Maya said.

"Keep going," Eduardo said. She kept going with no results and continued to do another rotation. Six was the second number.

"Trying again." Maya went again. The next numbers were

forty-five, seventy-three, and nineteen. An audible unlocking sound emanated from the vault door.

"I think we've half unlocked it. Why don't we try pulling it open?" Maya reached out and grabbed the giant cross-shaped handle. She tried pulling it, but it didn't budge. She tried turning it, but it didn't budge.

"Worth a try. I think we'll need to do the keypad as well. How's it going over there?" Maya went to check on the keypad on the second vault. There was a six-digit number flashing on the screen. Maya tried punching in the code, and she heard a hiss as the seal was released from the door.

Here we go.

Maya unclipped the keypad cracker and connected it to the third vault. Once it was running, she went back to the second vault and tried opening the door.

"It's coming, it's just a little stiff." She turned it harder, and the door swung open.

"Success!" Maya looked over at Eduardo and he nodded with approval. Eduardo walked into the vault and looked around.

"Anders could have at least stocked it with something," Eduardo said, disappointed. He wandered out of the vault. "Doesn't feel good in there. Feels very closed in."

"Yeah, I don't feel like going in myself," Maya said.

"Well, let's hope that we don't need a drill to get into the real vault because this is a very slow process." Eduardo and Maya walked back to investigate the third vault. There was a keycode already decoded.

"Here we go." Maya punched in the code and heard an audible clunk as what she assumed was a secondary lock was released. She tried spinning the cross-shaped handle and it turned easily, the vault door starting to open.

"I knew it was you," a female voice said from behind them. Maya quickly spun to confirm who it was.

Valerie.

What are you doing here?" Maya said.

"Catching you, of course. There were so many breadcrumbs left over the city, I had a wonderful time following them here." Valerie was almost cackling with delight. She advanced upon them.

"You may be powerful, but you're no match for both of us," Eduardo said. He stared her down, readying himself.

"I'm not so sure about that," she said, looking between the two of them. "Maya here is defenseless. She's activated a new power and not mastered it yet. Her mobility will be worthless. And you? You're just good at running away. So I've read." Valerie stepped closer. Maya could see her preparing some kind of skill.

Her right hand flashed with dark energy.

"Be careful, she's preparing a curse." She activated her radio. "Valerie's here. Change of plans," Maya said over the radio.

"Acknowledged. I'm coming in," Anders said. Maya realized that she could escape at any moment, and Eduardo too.

If we leave, we lose the vault hacker. There's no way they could pack it up with Valerie here.

Maya advanced toward Eduardo.

"Don't let her hit you," she said.

"I'm well ahead of you there." Eduardo started walking backward, keeping his distance from Valerie.

"You don't have to play coy with me, Eduardo. I know you can teleport. I've read your file. In fact, I'm wondering why you haven't run away already."

"Bullies like you need to be confronted," Eduardo said. He looked like he was preparing to fight. Valerie lunged at him with surprising speed, trying to connect with her curse. Eduardo vanished, appearing behind Valerie, and attacking in that same moment.

As the hit connected, he dropped to the floor. Maya was shocked.

What happened to him?

Valerie whirled around and struck Eduardo with the curse. He was now completely paralyzed.

"What'd you do to him?" Maya asked him.

"Once I figured out it was you two that I met the other night, and that Eduardo could teleport, I knew he'd try and get me from behind again because he had the upper hand. So, I developed some countermeasures."

Valerie turned her back slightly, showing Maya.

"What's on your back?"

"It's a stun pack. He activated it himself when he attacked, and then all I had to do was finish the job." Valerie left Eduardo on the floor and moved on Maya instead.

"I'm not sure what tricks you've got there. Looking at your friend, I'm guessing you can pop around to different places. But the same tricks are not going to work on me," Valerie said with a grin. Maya wracked her brain.

You need something to get out of this. With Eduardo. Something. Anything.

She backed away, nervously.

"You can't run forever. I'll just find you," Valerie said, preparing another curse. This one was a Dante Sphere.

"You shouldn't use those. They're too destructive," Maya said. Valerie laughed.

"They sound good to me. They get the job done right. I'm really enjoying this new power. And once I master it, no one's going to stop me."

"Well, except the Master Sage. He'll just toss you aside when he's done with you," Maya said, trying to buy some time. Valerie kept advancing.

"I'm pretty sure this curse won't even kill you. Your body's too hard for that. But it'll take you down enough that we can hand you back to the Master Sage on a silver platter and he can do whatever he wants in his next round of tests. You liked being a lab rat, didn't you?" Valerie laughed and Maya shuddered. She stepped back again.

Unfortunately, she wasn't aware of her surroundings and tripped on the edge of the vault door, tumbling back into the vault. Valerie laughed and slammed the vault door shut.

Maya was in pitch black. She remembered she still had the WallSpy hanging around her neck. She slipped it back on, activating the WallSpy function. She could see through the front of the vault door.

Valerie was approaching Eduardo.

There's no time. What have you got on you?

Maya wracked her brain. She had a stun wand. But only one shot left. There was a stun grenade. And the goo. Maya pulled out the stun wand.

Okay, it's got one shot.

She focused her mind and then teleported right in front of Valerie. As Valerie attacked Eduardo, Maya hit her with the stun wand. It connected and Valerie dropped to one knee, convulsing, but not down completely.

Eduardo looked worse for wear. Maya scooped him up, but he was too heavy.

Try and teleport. It's worth the risk.

Maya sunk to her knees, supporting Eduardo like she had with the metal case. She pictured the van in her mind, and pushed hard to get away. She felt a wave of resistance and almost passed out.

Stay with it. There must be another way to help.

Maya tried dragging him away, with minimal success. In that instant, Anders burst through the door. He saw what was happening and threw some kind of grenade. Smoke and light burst out in an explosion behind them, and Anders helped her drag Eduardo out.

As they passed through the next door, Anders threw something else behind them.

"Keep going," he said. "I'm just buying us time. Just follow my lead, I know the best way out of the building." Anders led Maya through the maze, room by room.

Finally, they burst through the security door and out of the building.

"The van is around the corner. Let's keep going." Anders hurried on, but Maya was starting to tire.

Don't let them down now. Keep pushing hard. You can do this.

They reached the van. Maya flung the door open. They got Eduardo in, and Anders slammed the door shut, running around to the driver's seat. He kicked the van into gear and sped away. There was movement back in the building. The screen door flung open, but Valerie was too far behind.

"I think we got away. Well, probably," Maya said.

"She was too arrogant to bring back up," Anders said.

"Here's hoping. We've got to ditch this van as soon as possible," Maya said.

"No arguments over here." Anders kept speeding away, nervously looking into the rearview mirror. Maya looked over at Eduardo. His face was ashen.

"Oh no," Maya said. "He's been hit by the Dante Sphere."

22

THE AFTERMATH

Maya checked all over Eduardo's body. "That's definitely it. A direct hit and his body is failing."

"That sounds bad. How do we fix it? How do you reverse it?" Anders said, panicked.

"I can't fix it. If I had my power, I could stop this. I could save him. But I can't. Nobody can."

"This is a pretty connected city. They've got people. This has to be fixed. Just think. How can we solve this?"

"Anders, listen. I'm a wanted fugitive. The Master Sage owns everyone. We don't have anyone to turn to. We don't have time. He's not going to make it."

"Look, let's just get him back to the base. Do what we can. Let me make a call."

"Kora, are you there?" Anders said over the phone. "Drop whatever you're doing and find us a way to stop and reverse a Dante Sphere in the city. Whatever it takes, Eduardo has been hit. Okay, thanks. Call me back." Anders hung up the phone. "She's onto it."

Maya looked at Eduardo again. He was dropping in and out of consciousness.

"Maya," he said, faintly.

"Eduardo, we'll figure it out. I'm so sorry. It's my fault. I couldn't help you in time. If I had my power, I could save you."

"It's okay, Maya," Eduardo said again, softly. He seemed to lose focus for a moment before regaining it.

"This was always a long shot. There were red flags everywhere, but I had to help."

"Just save your energy, we're going to fix this. We don't need to have this conversation now," Maya said.

"But we do. My time is up. Search my left pocket." Eduardo leaned back, his eyes vacantly staring in the distance. Maya quickly searched the pocket and found a data drive.

"That's the key to all I've got. Use it to finish your mission."

"Eduardo, I'll hold onto this, but I'm just going to give it back to you. We're going to solve this, okay? I'm really sorry, but I'm going to fix it."

"Maya, stop lying to both of us. My time is up. Just promise me you'll do the right thing. Don't run like I did," Eduardo said, his voice barely a whisper. Maya nodded, tears streaming down her face. She tried to say something back, but her voice was all choked up.

She could see in his face, Eduardo was slipping away, very fast. He couldn't speak anymore. Even breathing seemed hard. And by the time they reached the base, he was gone.

Anders stopped the car. He came round to the back. Maya didn't need to say anything. Anders just gave her a hug.

"Let me take care of this," he said. "I'll do everything properly."

Maya nodded. Everything else was now a blur.

MAYA AWOKE on the couch in the underground training area. Eduardo's face flashed through her mind, and she sat up quickly. Looking around, she teleported to the command center, but it was unmanned and empty. She pulled out her phone and called Anders.

"How are you feeling?" he asked.

"I'm awake. What happened?"

"You were kind of out of it, so I left you there to rest. It seemed like the safest location."

"What about Eduardo?" Maya said.

"I made preparations. As per his wishes, which he had recorded in the drive, he will be cremated."

"Oh. I see."

"He has no living relatives, so he left everything to you."

"Where are you?" Maya said.

"I'm coming back now. I'll be there soon."

Maya hung up the phone and just stared at the screens.

This can't be happening. This can't be real.

True to his word, Anders was soon there, carrying a metal box with him. Just seeing the box, Maya burst into tears. Anders set the box on the table and came over to give her a hug.

"I'm sorry we couldn't do more. He didn't deserve this."

"Valerie's gonna pay. I swear, I'm going to kill her."

"Maya, that's just the anger talking. Eduardo wouldn't want that."

Maya pushed Anders away.

"Who knows what he wanted? It wasn't death. He wanted to live. Everything he did was so meticulous. Until he met us. And we just ran around town all gung-ho until we got caught and he paid the price. I should be the one paying the price, not him."

"He's given us an opportunity and it's not clear right now, but we'll find a way through this." Anders walked over to the chest and opened it. Inside was another wooden box and other effects. A phone, some drives, some keys.

"He left instructions on what to do. But some things will have to wait till our mission is over," Anders said gently.

"What mission?"

"He thought this might happen, or at least he prepared, just in case. You've got to finish the mission. You have to get what he could not."

"The amulet," Maya whispered.

"I'm not sure what that is, but yeah." They heard a door opening and Maya and Anders turned to look. It was Kora. She walked through the room, her usual energy gone. She just looked flat. Without a word, she walked over and gave Maya a hug.

"I'm so sorry," Kora said. "This should never have happened. I just wish we could do more. I wish we could go back and fix it. We can't do that, but we can do something worthy of his name."

Maya stepped back from the hug and nodded.

"When you are willing to look at it, I found something." Kora handed a drive to Maya.

"What is it?" Maya asked.

"It's the test data from one of your friends. She was a test subject." Maya looked at Kora in amazement.

"Which friend? Who?"

"Nadia Hunt. I think she was an old friend of yours?"

"I can't believe it. I haven't seen her since the day I disappeared. Could you search for her, please? I know it's probably pointless, but I need to find her."

"Of course I will." Kora stepped back and looked at the two of them.

"I did some exploratory hacking after what happened. I'm really sorry we couldn't save Eduardo. The Haste facility is on full alert and has been for probably a week. When you do want to go ahead, I'll let you guys know when I find out something else." Kora waved and left.

Anders stepped away from the box.

"I'll leave you these things. I need to investigate a few leads. Are you gonna be okay, Maya?"

"Yeah, I'll be fine. Somehow. I think I'll train."

"That's probably the best way to start. You should read through the stuff too. I haven't looked at all of it. There's probably something helpful in there. Not just about the mission, but about Eduardo. Just, just read it." Anders gave her a long, sad look before he turned to leave.

Maya watched him go. Once he had finally left, she let out all the tension and just held her head in her hands.

What are you going to do now? It's hopeless.

Maya walked over to the speed teleporting training course.

How am I supposed to master this power without you, Eduardo?

Maya punched the nearest wall, not sure how to deal with all the feelings. She pushed them all aside.

I'll train. It's all I can do right now.

She focused her will on the course, hit the starting buzzer, and teleported.

One, two, three, and then hit the final buzzer.

"1.2 seconds," a voice announced.

That's pretty good, but not good enough.

Maya went back, so she could train over and over again.

MAYA SMASHED the buzzer and then collapsed on the ground.

"0.9 seconds," the voice announced.

Under a second. That's pretty good.

Maya pulled herself up into a seated position and then dragged herself over to lean against a nearby wall.

That's got to count for something, but who knows how long this road is? I'm not even sure if Eduardo was a master. We never talked about that yet. But it must be in his notes.

Maya lurched to her feet and teleported to the command center. She slowly stumbled her way toward the middle of the room with all of Eduardo's things. She closed the metal box and carefully set it up on the front table where Eduardo liked to work. She threw it open and sat in his chair.

First, she grabbed the drive that Eduardo had given her himself and plugged it into the computer. It was full of files, documents, plans. There was one video. Maya played it. It was Eduardo filming himself.

"Hello, Maya. If you're watching this, then I've met an untimely end. Hopefully after successful completion of the mission. But there's a fifty-fifty chance it would have happened earlier. And for that, I'm sorry. You're probably not in a good frame of mind right now, but I need to reassure you. I have to admit, this time with you has been exciting.

"So long ago, when everything happened, and my mentor died. I just, I wasn't the same. I wasn't living my life. I was just hiding. Scurrying around the shadows. Pretending to have a life. But this, this felt like living again. Thank you for that. You have to promise me you'll watch this again later, when the mission is done so we can have a virtual celebration across time.

"But, for now, I'll just say I've left everything here to you. Everything I've built up. Find a way to use it. Find that spark inside. And just go for it. Don't slink away in the shadows. I've done enough of that for both of us. It's not a satisfying life, and you deserve better. So please, do what you have to do.

"But don't run away. Come back and finish what we started. I'm hoping that when the mission is done, I can show you this video and we can have a good laugh together. But if I'm not here to watch it with you, then it was my honor to meet you and I wish I could see all the great things you're going to do next."

Maya closed the video and wept. The tears just wouldn't stop flowing. All of the emotion just became raw again. She was filled with this raw energy. Too much emotion, too many feelings trying to get out. She teleported to the training area. Then around the room. Then through the challenge course. Over and over and over, trying to exhaust herself as much as possible.

The more tired she felt, the more she kept teleporting, just hoping to crash. Begging that her body would let her rest from the agony of what she was feeling and thinking. She pushed herself harder than any of the training she had done. As soon as she arrived in a location, she would teleport again.

Short, medium, long distances, bouncing around the room and picking locations at random. Just pushing and pushing and pushing. And finally, she stopped, staggered, and fell to the ground. The sweet gentle embrace of sleep swept over her and she didn't have to think anymore.

MAYA AWOKE SLOWLY, stretching her arms. She sat up, confused by where she was. She was in a bed. Her bed. She looked around the room and it was pitch black, but it was definitely her room. She scrambled around on the bedside table, finding her phone, looking at the time. It was afternoon.

Maya tried to rouse herself, sitting up straighter. There was a glass of water on the bedside table. She picked it up and drank it greedily. She stood up slowly, then wavered slightly on her legs. There was immense exhaustion through everything.

Maya walked over to the door of her room, opened it, and stepped into the common area of their suite. She saw Anders over on the computer, tapping away. He looked up.

"Good afternoon," he said. "Coffee?"

"Yes," was all Maya could manage to say. She walked over and plonked herself down on the couch. Anders stood up and wordlessly walked over to the kitchenette, making coffee. Maya could hear the grinding of the beans, the running of the machine. But it all felt distant, like somewhere else.

Anders brought her over a cup of steaming coffee. At first, she just held the mug, appreciating the warmth. She took a sip, and it was like heaven. She drank it in and then took another sip.

"Things will get better, and when you're ready, I've got a proposal for you," Anders said.

23

THE LAB

Maya and Anders were sitting in a dingy, tiny, poorly lit restaurant. There was a series of small plates on the table with a variety of food. Some meat, some vegetables, some mixtures of both.

"So, what do you call this again?" Maya said.

"Tapas. It's Spanish style, good for sharing and trying lots of different foods. It's very popular. I'm surprised you haven't had it before."

"I guess I didn't really come across it." Maya poked at her food, not really feeling an appetite but mechanically tried some.

"I'm not ready, but at least tell me your proposal," Maya said, looking over at Anders.

He'd been vibrating with excitement just waiting for an opportunity to tell her.

I have to at least let him get it out, even if I'm not interested in doing anything about it.

Anders nodded excitedly, then composed himself. "Look, there's no rush. I just found something that I think will really solve our problems."

"Well, what is it?"

"I don't want to go into too many details just yet, but it'll be a device that will help us bypass all security. It should make it as easy as walking through the door." Anders grinned before shoving some pork into his mouth.

"Okay, well that certainly sounds interesting. But what's the catch?" Maya scooped some buttered vegetables into her mouth and started chewing.

"Well, the device is highly theoretical, and we'd have to steal the blueprints." Anders paused, waiting for Maya's reaction.

"Another prototype device? I sort of understand, considering we're trying to push the boundaries of what's possible. But this one hasn't even been fabricated yet?"

"No, no, it's a design concept that looks fantastic and it needs to get built. Luckily, we have the brilliant Kora, your bags of money, and of course my resourcefulness at securing parts and expertise." Anders watched Maya expectantly, looking for any hint of what she was thinking.

"I'm not too keen on breaking into another place and stealing something else after what just happened."

"I understand, and as I said, there's no pressure. I think we've got some time to think about it. It doesn't seem like this device is going to get built without someone like us intervening."

"All right, well, I'll think about it. You do whatever research you have to do in case we go ahead with it."

"That's fair, I'll keep advancing the plan, and so we'll be ready." Anders pulled over a plate with steak and started carefully cutting into it. The rest of the dinner passed with minimal conversation. They paid the bill and hailed a taxi to get back to the hotel.

As they got out of the taxi, Maya turned to Anders.

"We seem to be going through vehicles a lot. At least we've

tried a few things. Would you prefer more of the sports cars or the van?"

Anders paused, looking very surprised. "I hadn't really thought about it. Probably the van was more useful and less recognizable. Well, until it became a getaway vehicle."

They walked through the main doors of the hotel, passing through the empty lobby with its fading carpet, and directly over to the elevators.

Anders called the elevator.

"We probably need another vehicle. Unless you think it's better to get taxis everywhere?" Maya said.

"No, we do need something we can rely on. I'll figure something out," Anders said quickly. The elevator arrived, and they stepped in.

"Any updates from Kora?" Maya asked.

Anders shook his head and pressed the button for their floor. "Nothing, I'm afraid. She is researching your friend, but as expected, there's no public data on her. It's like she vanished." Anders held the doors open, waiting for Maya to exit first.

"She probably did." Maya swiped her access key, opened the door to their suite, walked over, and collapsed onto the couch.

"Plans for tomorrow?" Anders said.

"More training."

"Sounds good. At least you're moving forward," Anders said. Maya nodded, her attention starting to fade.

"I'll get back to work then." Anders wandered over to the computer and buried himself in some research. Maya stared at the ceiling and continued to drift away.

THE NEXT MORNING, Maya walked all the way down to the training center. Once she was through the main doors, she teleported over to the command center, her hand hovering over the mouse of the computer that Eduardo usually used. All of his data was there, waiting to be accessed.

She stopped and withdrew her hand.

Not ready yet.

Maya teleported to the main room and then to a series of training stations she'd used before. Starting with the clear walled room made out of glass. She made a circuit, teleporting through one panel and back, then the other, rotating around to make sure that she did all four walls in the room. And then did different orders and diagonals and other combinations, quickly changing direction and aspect.

She moved on to the room with regular walls, practicing the same routine. Then she repeated all those while holding heavy items. One time she carried a chair around. She ran the speed course, furiously trying to get a better time than 0.9 seconds but failing to do so.

They still had a functioning WallSpy, so Maya trained with that too. Getting used to using it in different scenarios. She pushed herself to teleport everywhere in that safe space. As much as possible. Doing strange leaps to places that she didn't know well.

All in an attempt to exercise her power and push its limits. And while she seemed to be getting better at the routine of it all, she couldn't seem to take the next step.

Why aren't I getting better? I can't beat my time. What do I have to do more of?

After a long and frustrating day, Maya threw in the towel and called Anders.

"Okay, I'm looking to the future, and I cannot handle this training over and over with no chance of improving. Tell me more about your plan."

MAYA STEPPED out on the street, her lab coat blowing around with the wind. She adjusted her glasses and looked over at Anders.

"You're sure these will help us blend in," she said.

"Absolutely. It's a research lab. Everyone's wearing this. We'll just fit right in."

"If you say so." Maya followed Anders along the busy street. It was dusk and many people were heading home after a day of work. They were in an industrial area with lots of traffic. A bus zoomed by so close that Maya had to step back for fear of getting hit.

They came to a large building complex. It boasted a massive driveway, and parking was set back from the road. A large neon sign on the building said, "Cybertech Español".

"So, is this a company or what?" Maya walked through the main gate and along the driveway.

"It's a private company that subleases its labs to other companies, and also individuals."

"So, we're just going to go in and swipe something from one of the labs?"

"That's the plan. It's all different groups, so we don't have to worry about not being recognized. We pretend that we belong here and be on our merry way."

"I'll follow your lead then," Maya said, dubiously.

"It'll be fine. Don't worry about it." Anders led the way along the drive, stepping aside as some cars were leaving the premises. The main revolving doors were locked, but there was a steady stream of people leaving via a side door.

Anders and Maya paused to let people leave, slipping in after them before the side door closed. They walked through the lobby and Maya looked around. It was all shiny tiled floors and polished metal accents.

Feels expensive and pristine.

Maya stopped staring and focused on the mission. Anders headed over to the lift and pressed the call button. The doors opened immediately. They stepped in and he pressed number five. The lift zoomed away without any hesitation.

"So, there's no security here?" Maya said.

How'd we get so far without a single challenge?

"There is, but because so many groups frequent this space, the security is all at the lab level. Not so much on the building level. I mean, the doors are locked, but we got in easily enough."

"Sounds good so far," Maya said.

The doors opened and Anders stepped out, looking left and right for landmarks. He turned right, and soon they passed by a series of labs, all with clear glass instead of regular walls.

Maya could see in each lab. Some were just rows of computers, others had animal cages, which were empty. Others had robotic equipment, or robots roaming around. Every second lab had a person in it working, and the others were empty.

"The diehards work around the clock, but many people just go home, end of the day, and come back the next," Anders said.

"Yeah, I never really had a job like that. Probably never will now," Maya said.

"I've done some like that. If you ever want one, you can be my office administrator. I promise you, it's a regular boring job. Every day is the same. Always the same hours. Nothing exciting happening."

"A girl can dream," Maya said.

Anders shook his head and continued on down the hallway. They rounded a corner and Maya noticed a new type of lab coming up. All of them had closed walls with only a small window in the doorway to look into.

"Are these more private labs?" Maya asked.

"Yes, these are the ones that are generally used by third

parties, or individuals. They want a little more protection over their work, which is understandable. Good for us too. Less likely to get spotted."

"That would be helpful. I'd like a simple job, thanks," Maya said. They continued down the corridor, Maya looking around. She noticed some security cameras but no other security features. They arrived at a door with a key card reader and Anders stood over it.

He swiped a key card on the door reader, but it didn't work. Next, he retrieved something from his pocket and clipped it over the reader. After a few moments, the door unlocked and he retrieved his device and pushed open the door, Maya following behind and closing it.

The lab was surprisingly small. There was only a long metal bench top and a few computers and monitors. There was a metal cabinet at the back which was locked. But nothing else. Anders checked his phone.

"This is the right one. I won't take long, I don't think." Anders first tried the thick metal cabinet, and the door was locked. He pulled out a lock-picking tool, and within moments it was open. As he rifled through the cabinet, Maya kept looking around the room.

"Anything in particular you need me for?" she said.

"No, just keep an eye on the door. If you stand by it, you should hopefully notice any passersby, and if any of them stop to take interest in this lab."

"I can do that." Maya wandered over to the door and sidled up to it. She peered through the tiny porthole.

Can't really see anyone walking around. I don't even remember passing anyone in this section.

She heard Anders slam the cabinet closed.

"Nothing in there." He turned his attention to the computer next, tapping away at the keys.

"Maybe you should have brought Kora. She's next level compared to you," Maya said.

"I can handle this. I did my homework. Ha! I'm in!" Anders grinned at her and then turned his attention to the monitor in front of him. With a few quick keystrokes, he seemed to find what he was looking for.

"Got it. Let me just download this." Anders inserted a data drive into the computer and downloaded the files. "Ah ha! Perfect." He pulled out the drive and pocketed it, shutting down the computer. "There you go. The perfect crime. Let's get out of here."

"Gladly." Maya pulled the door open, and a blaring alarm sounded through the entire facility.

24

A NEW TOY

Maya turned to Anders.

"Is that part of the plan?" she said.

"No, no it's not." Anders pulled out his phone and dialed a number.

"Kora, we need some assistance. We've tripped the alarm at Cybertech Español." Anders paused, listening intently. "Okay, thanks." Anders hung up the phone.

"Kora's gonna work some magic. She said we should aim for the back door."

"Good advice. She's a real pro. Do you know where that is?" Maya asked, looking left and right.

"More or less, but I think we need to get back down to the lobby." Anders sprinted off down the corridor and Maya hurried after him. The few people that were in labs were streaming out, racing for the exits.

Just before the lifts, there was a door that everyone was going through.

"It must be a fire escape or emergency exit," Anders said. He pulled at the door before it fully closed and reopened it. Before them was a pure white stairwell and the stomping sound of people's footsteps in the distance.

"Let's take the stairs."

"After you," Maya said. Anders charged down the stairs, and Maya kept up with him easily. Around and around they went. Floor after floor after floor. Maya occasionally looked behind her, but there was no one following.

"We must be the last ones on the floor to evacuate."

"That's okay. Let's just keep moving." They reached the lobby level, and it was filled with people. The front doors were locked, and there was a security team screening each person who tried to leave.

"And that's our cue to head this way," Anders said, starting down another corridor. They wound their way around the back of the building when suddenly the alarm stopped.

"Oh, she's good," Anders said.

"Of course she is. Kora's the best," Maya said. They slowed their run down to a relaxed walk, continuing around the perimeter of the building. They turned a corner and kept walking. A few people emerged from labs and walked in the opposite direction but didn't pay them any special attention.

"Okay, so the lab coats and the glasses should help us be hard to distinguish," Anders said as they passed another security camera. They came to a regular door with an exit sign above it.

Maya read aloud the sign next to the door. "This door is alarmed and for emergency use only. Do not open as it will set off an alarm and you'll be fined the emergency response costs. Good luck fining us." Maya laughed.

"I know, haha. I wonder if we were supposed to go through the door before Kora killed the alarm?" Anders said.

"Only one way to find out. After you."

Anders sighed, and tried the door handle, thrusting it open.

He paused, listening for a sound. There was no alarm. "Come on then."

They both rushed out the back door and found themselves in a tight alley. There were some garbage bins, but nothing else. They walked around the alley, stalking alongside the building and approaching some car parking spots.

"Okay, so we're just going to be really casual," Anders said. They wandered through the car park, spotting a security presence up ahead.

"They look like they're more focused on people leaving the lobby," Maya said.

"Agreed. Let's just keep to the fringes and idly pass by."

They picked their way through the cars, as if they were about to go into their car, but steadily making their way through the car park and down the long driveway.

The main gates were still open. Once they passed through the gates, Maya felt the tension start to dissolve. A huge wave of relief swept over her.

"Well...that was way more exciting than I expected. Perhaps I should have expected it. You know what, Anders, this is actually all your fault."

"How so?" he said, confused.

"Just before the alarm got tripped, you said it was 'the perfect crime.'" Maya shook her head with mock disapproval.

Anders chuckled. "You're right. There it is, in black and white. Completely my fault."

"Okay, drive us back, and then you can explain what it is we've just stolen."

"Happily." Anders unlocked their nondescript white van and drove them back to the hotel. Calmly and responsibly. He kept his cool, parked the van, and didn't let anything slip on the way up to the suite.

They headed straight for Kora's suite, not bothering to knock. As they walked through the door, Kora was standing and waiting for them. "You two need an escort wherever you go. It's like working with kids."

"Sorry, Mom," Anders said as a joke.

Kora shook her head and muttered under her breath. "Alright, come on over here. Show me what you swiped."

Anders handed her the drive he had downloaded the files onto.

"This is something pretty cool," he said.

"I'll be the judge of that." Kora started the drive and brought up the plans. "Hmm," studying it closer, "this is... next level."

"Mind telling me what it actually is?" Maya said, looking over Kora's shoulder and trying to make sense of the plans.

"It's a personal hologram device."

"That doesn't feel that new. Holograms have been around for years? We even had them," Maya said.

"No, no, no, it's better than that. It projects the hologram over your body, so you look like someone else."

"Like a shapeshifter," Maya said.

"Exactly," Anders said. "Exactly that. It's like being a shapeshifter, but with a hologram."

"But if anyone touches you the illusion is disturbed?" Maya asked.

"Correct. It's just visual. But I think it would be good enough to fool people at a distance and most security systems as well."

"What do you think, Kora?" Maya said, looking over at her friend.

"Actually, it's fascinating tech. It seems quite adaptive as well. I think Anders is onto something here," Kora said.

"Wow, huh. I didn't expect that," Maya said.

"I told you it was good." Anders's excitement was renewed by Kora's praise.

"It's not going to be easy to build this though. You do need me to build this don't you?" Kora said.

"Yes, please. I can't think of anyone better suited to build it."

"Your flattery is lost on me, but you're right. You need my skills on this. This is a work of art. I'm really quite impressed." Kora leaned in, studying the plans in more detail.

"I'm glad that we have such an interesting project to give you," Maya said, looking at Anders, shrugging her shoulders.

"Yeah, I guess this is our way of saying thank you for bailing us out," Anders said. "Call us even."

"Yeah, nice try. I'm still doing you a favor and you still owe me," Kora said without looking away from the monitor.

"Fine, fine. We'll figure it out. Just make a list of what you need, and I'll source it," Anders said.

"Alright. I will. It's not gonna be cheap."

"Well, Maya has some extra money lying around and why not spend it?" Anders winked at Maya.

"He's got me there. I'm kind of curious to see how this thing turns out. If you can build it."

"Not if. When I build it. If you can find the parts," Kora said.

"Leave it to me," Anders said with conviction.

MAYA WANDERED THROUGH THE STREETS, not in a rush to get back to training. She meandered along, peering into shop windows, and staring at video advertisements for an upcoming soccer game without actually paying any attention. Eventually, she found her way to the aged staircase and walked down to the abandoned train station.

Why does nobody else come down here? It's not even locked?

She let that thought sit and kept her pace through the station. For some reason it seemed emptier today. Creepier as well. Like there could be something hiding in the many shadows. A chill ran down her spine and she shook it off.

Don't start to imagine things. There's nothing.

Maya unlocked the door to the access passage and locked it behind her. Technically it wasn't required. She could have just as easily teleported from the platform itself. But it was a force of habit. Since she was already walking, she opted not to teleport over the final stretch.

Opening the door to the underground training area didn't just give her access to the facility. It also opened a wave of emotions. Many she wasn't quite ready to deal with. She teleported around the space, warming up. As usual it was almost effortless. But there was this wall looming ahead of her. She could almost sense it.

Don't start banging your head straight away. Try something else.

Maya teleported into the command center. She sat down at Eduardo's computer and started browsing. She took a deep breath, then opened up the files he had left for her.

First, she found properties. There were three other properties spread throughout the city in addition to the remote house they had originally tracked him to. One was a penthouse apartment, the others looked like warehouses or storage spaces.

I'll have to check those out. Let's have a look here.

Maya brought up the locations on the map. They looked to be within teleport distance. Well, at least Eduardo's range.

It's how he remained undetected. He just popped from place to place, staying out of the public eye. Until we made contact.

Maya pushed aside the feelings welling up. She kept searching. Amongst the other files she found some documents. Most were mundane records. But one was not.

Oh, now this is something. Notes for Maya.

Maya quickly opened the document and started reading. It was a training manual, of sorts. The beginning was a recap of all the things he had been training her on, and the rationale behind each one.

He was very methodical. I wonder if he designed this training himself, or if someone else taught him this way?

She skimmed through all the sections she had already covered. Eagerly she read the next section.

Pushing boundaries until perfect freedom is established. Hang on. That's it?

Maya looked up from the screen and tried to process it. It took a moment for the revelation to sink in.

There's no more training. I just have to get better now?

Maya pushed herself away from the desk and stood up. She swore under her breath.

There are no shortcuts.

She was about to teleport away when an idea popped into her head. She went back to the computer, pulling up the map again. This time she entered the address of their hotel suite. Studying the location, she looked up the distance. As her mind ticked over, she drummed her fingers on the desk.

Not that far at all. It's possible. Certainly not as far as Eduardo's properties.

Maya closed her eyes and pictured their suite. She focused on her bedroom, which would be empty. She summoned her power and went there in her mind.

Her power built up, and she felt pressure building with it. It increased and increased until she felt like she would burst. Then it all suddenly dissipated. Maya sank down, suddenly exhausted.

It's beyond my limit. Not quite productive enough for training right now.

After getting her breath, Maya went back to the map. She made a note of several locations on the way back to her hotel.

❧

MAYA SCOUTED out the first location. It was approximately a quarter of the way from the command center to her hotel. It was a busy street, with a convenience store on the corner and a row of tall office buildings.

Too much foot traffic and exposure.

Maya glanced around, searching for somewhere more discreet. She noticed a back alley and headed down it. The alley was mostly empty, with some large metal garbage bins. Behind the bins she found a nook that was not used for anything.

Perfect. Let's give this a go.

25

A HOME AWAY FROM HOME

Maya focused on the command center. She had teleported there countless times by now. It was easy to call up. But she had never tried this distance before. She steadied her breathing and used a mantra from her Chakra training.

My focus must be absolute. No excuses.

Everything calmed down. Peaceful and steady. She just had to shift herself there. Like a step between two places. As easy as walking. Maya focused and pushed herself there.

She collapsed into Eduardo's chair. The pressure hadn't built like before. But she couldn't move.

At least I landed on the chair.

Maya tried moving her arm. It was made of lead.

C'mon. You can do this.

Maya slowly inched her arm down to her pocket, searching for her phone. She could feel it inside her pocket. She grabbed at it with her fingers. It was frustratingly difficult, as she had no energy to force them to work as normal. After some steady coaxing, she dragged the phone out of her pocket. It clattered to the ground.

Awesome. So helpful.

Maya looked at the phone on the floor.

If you go down there, you aren't getting back up. Oh well.

She let herself slide off the chair, landing unceremoniously on the floor with a bump. Luckily, the phone wasn't too far away. She reached over slowly, unlocked it, and after a few attempts dialed Anders.

"Hey, how's training?" Anders said. There was a lot of background noise.

"Hey. Good mostly. But I need help," Maya said, forcing the words out.

"What happened? Where are you?" Anders sounded concerned.

"Just exhausted. Command center. Thanks." Maya hung up the call and found a way to awkwardly lie on the carpet. It wasn't comfortable, but she didn't care. Sleep was calling.

MAYA AWOKE IN HER BED, again. She sat up slowly, without any trouble.

Did I teleport here?

Confused, she paused and forced her mind back.

That's right, Anders came to help. I teleported back to the command center.

Maya swung her legs off the side and then stood up slowly. Everything seemed normal. She walked into the lounge area, seeing Anders bent over his laptop. Daylight was streaming in.

"Did I miss a meal or two?" Maya said.

"Yeah, it's practically lunchtime. You feeling okay?" Anders looked her up and down. Maya nodded.

"All good. Just needed a rest."

"I ordered food over to Kora's suite. Let's go eat and you can update me." Anders closed his laptop and headed for the front door. Maya teleported into Kora's suite instead.

"Woah, okay. Cool," Kora blurted out. She was standing right in front of Maya and quickly stepped back. The door opened behind Maya and Anders walked in.

"Right, should have expected that," Anders said slowly.

Maya stepped to the side. "Sorry, we need to establish some sort of protocol for this," Maya said sheepishly.

"Fine by me, provided there's no unfortunate accidents." Kora set down the food bag she was carrying on the tiny circular table in the middle of the room.

"I can't teleport in your personal space, so it's pretty safe. I didn't really think about it, I just came here. I think it's a good sign."

"Sounds like progress to me. Although you probably don't want to do that in a crowd." Kora started pulling out food. There were chorizo sausages, salads, and other delicious smelling dishes.

Maya and Anders pulled up a chair, and Kora handed them plates.

"Help yourself. How was your training?" Kora sat down and started serving herself some salad.

"Making progress. I calculated the distance from here to the training command center and picked a place a quarter of the way. I successfully teleported from that spot to the command center." Maya beamed a smile at them and then started getting some salad.

"That's impressive. Are you going to figure out some other waypoints so you can hop over?" Anders said. He started with the chorizo sausages.

"I hadn't planned on it but that's a great idea. Better than mine." Maya grabbed a forkful of salad and eagerly devoured it.

"As you get stronger you could try jumping halfway, then

three-quarters, then the whole distance," Anders said over a mouthful of sausage.

"Agreed. I'll work on that. I also discovered Eduardo's other properties. He's got a penthouse in the city, with a few storage locations."

"I bet he has some good stuff stashed away. Can you get me the locations?" Kora said.

Maya nodded. "I'll send them over today. How's the device going?"

"It's getting close. Anders just needs to get me a few more things."

"They're not exactly stocked at the local convenience store. And I'm trying to avoid any undue attention. We can't let ourselves get tracked again," Anders said rather quickly. He soon started on another sausage.

"Relax Anders. Maybe the two of you can check out Eduardo's storage rooms. He might have what you need, and there'll be no trace of it." Maya looked over and saw Kora's expression. She was calculating something. "It's worth the delay. Get back down there as soon as possible and call me. I'll walk you through the data transfer."

"Will do." Maya finished her bite and stood up. She looked wistfully over the rest of the food.

Later. There's a job to do first.

"Eat up, I'll be calling soon." Maya jogged over to the door and left immediately. She rushed over to the lift and called it.

I wonder how quickly I can get there by myself. If I rush over to my teleport spot, I can save some time.

Maya quickly left the hotel, efficiently making her way through the streets. She needed to check the directions a few times, as her usual route was different from the one she needed to take to the teleport spot. But in no time, she was there.

Maya ducked down the alley and looked around for any people. Nobody was in the alley or seemed to notice her presence. She continued past the bins and into the nook. Without a moment's delay she teleported to the command center.

Maya staggered, the wind taken out of her. But she kept her footing.

Need more practice. But at least I didn't collapse.

Maya sat down at the computer and immediately dialed Kora.

"Okay, I'm here. What do you need?"

"All right, pull out the drive I handed you and plug it in." Maya did as requested and plugged it into a free port on the computer.

"Okay, it's in."

"Run the file called Kora's Magic Box."

"Sure." Maya found the file and executed it. A little image of a box with a wizard's hat on top of it appeared and then quickly vanished.

"Give me a few moments. Alright, I'm in, I'll get what I need. Thanks, Maya."

"What should I do now?" Maya said.

"Oh, whatever you like. I'll work with Anders to collect what we need from these places if we think there's stock there. You just do what you do best and let me finish this device."

"Thanks, Kora. I'll do just that." Maya hung up and stared at the screen with a blank look.

What do I do now? More training? Unless...

Maya quickly grabbed her phone and dialed Anders.

"Anders, do you have a device that can crack Lift Access?"

"Of course I do. Do you need one now?"

"Yeah, I do. I'm gonna come over. Are you at the suite?"

"I am. I'm about to head out, but I'll wait for you before I leave."

"Thanks. See you soon." Maya hung up the phone and a smile crept onto her face.

This'll be fun.

MAYA STOOD outside a gigantic high-rise building. It was sleek, modern, and refined, with polished black stone gleaming in the sunlight.

This looks like the fanciest building in the whole city. Eduardo must have done well for himself.

Maya adjusted the strap on her backpack and walked through the lobby. It was magnificent. A dark stone, polished to perfection, served as the floor, with gold streaks running through it. Plush chairs and more stone and gold were everywhere.

Staff in black and gold designer uniforms flitted around, serving the elite. The lobby was bustling with a mix of both guests and what looked like tourists. Maya picked her way through the crowd and found the array of lifts.

There were three regular elevators and one special one at the end. She pressed the regular call button and stepped inside one of the three lifts. She let her eyes run over all of the floor numbers, but there was no penthouse button.

An older man with white hair and a bit of a stoop stepped into the elevator after her.

"Sorry, I forgot something," Maya said, stepping out while the man was trying to select his floor. She wandered over and reviewed the other elevator. She pressed the call button and it arrived promptly. She stepped inside and saw that there was only one button. The penthouse.

She let the doors close before pulling out the device Anders had given her. It was much smaller than the ones that he usually supplied, and she managed to attach it to the card reader. She pressed the penthouse button, and nothing happened, but the little device lit up.

The rectangular screen was flashing white, and a block of text scrolled along, but Maya couldn't quite catch what it said.

Finally, it flashed green, the penthouse light level button lit up, and the lift suddenly accelerated. Maya almost stumbled back, surprised by the sudden speed.

It took way longer than she expected to reach the penthouse, despite the extreme speed of the elevator. Maya carefully removed the hacking tool and stepped through the open doors onto a plush red carpet. There was nothing in the corridor except a single golden door at the end.

This is going to be pretty special.

Maya walked up to the door and paused in front of it.

Here we go.

She pulled out the WallSpy and put it over her eyes. First, activating the device and then switching on the WallSpy function. She could see through the door to a lovely but sparsely decorated foyer area. It looked similar to the lobby but had white stone for the floor instead of a dark stone. The threads of gold, however, were still through the stone, in the same signature style.

Effortlessly, Maya teleported into the room. She removed the WallSpy and stashed it in her backpack, wandering around the apartment. It was very minimally decorated. There was a little lounge and television, a dining table, a kitchen, what looked like an incredible balcony or terrace, and a single bedroom.

Maya walked into the bedroom and noticed an envelope sitting on the perfectly made bed. She wandered closer and picked it up, curious. It said "Maya" on the front. Maya turned it over and quickly opened it. She pulled out a letter and started to read it.

Maya, *you found your way here. I left you a list of some good places to visit - Eduardo.*

. . .

SHE PUT the letter aside and saw what else was in the envelope. Something was folded. She pulled it out and carefully unfolded it. It was a map of the city with eight spots marked on it.

I wonder what these are. I should investigate this. Maybe it's related to the training that I should be doing.

Maya pocketed the map, wandered around the penthouse, and opened the glass doors to the balcony terrace area. The view was incredible. She could see out and across the whole city.

No wonder you kept this place. You could come and go as you pleased, but still be at the heart of everything. Thank you, Eduardo.

Maya left and closed the balcony door.

26

MAMA'S PIZZERIA

Maya opened the door to Kora's suite and stopped suddenly. Kora was standing right in front of the door, waiting expectantly.

"Hi," Maya said, a little confused.

"We've been waiting. We've got something to show you."

"Or two things to show, if we're going to be more accurate," Anders said in the background.

"Okay, great." Maya closed the door behind her and walked into the suite proper. There was a new workbench set up in Kora's living area. On it sat two devices. One took up the majority of the bench and had camera-like adapters attached to it. The other was a belt.

"I take it you've finished with the hologram device?" Maya said slowly, looking at their expressions to gauge if she was correct.

"Absolutely correct. This is remarkable technology. I actually struggled to build it," Kora said, the admiration showing through in her voice.

Wow, that's high praise coming from Kora.

"So, it works?" Maya said.

"Well, we've only done limited testing. Now's the real test. Maya, would you mind standing over here, please?" Kora directed Maya to a spot on the floor. She stood there and stared ahead.

Kora went over to the workbench and pressed a few buttons on the side of the panel. "Okay, Anders, can you check the monitor, please?" Anders walked over to Kora's main monitor and started reviewing something.

"Maya, shuffle a bit to your left and look straight at that array of cameras," Anders said.

"Maya, you're moving around. Are you alright?"

"I feel a little bit self-conscious staring into all of the cameras." Maya remained still and waited.

"Starting the scan." Kora pressed a button and the machine in front of her suddenly came to life. The cameras started moving and Maya noticed lights appearing on her.

"Just stay as still as possible," Kora said.

"Now turn to the right," Anders said. Maya turned to the right and shuffled her feet so that she was standing side-on.

"Perfect. Stay there," Anders called out. Maya stood, waiting patiently.

"Now turn again so that your back is to the cameras," Anders said. Maya complied, trying to stay as still as possible.

"Now turn again so that we see your other profile," Anders said. Maya turned again. This time showing a different side of her to the cameras. Again, she waited, slowing her breathing down to be as still as possible.

"We got it," Anders said. "It will take a few minutes and then we will power down the machine."

Maya relaxed her muscles.

"Quick question. If this is the scanning process, how are we going to do this to someone without raising any suspicions?"

"That's the process, no way around it. We'll figure that out later. For now, this is a prototype," Kora said. She walked over and stood next to Anders. The two of them seemed deeply entranced by what was on the monitor.

Kora gently shoved Anders aside and took over the controls, adjusting something. "Here we are." Kora strode over to the workbench and picked up the belt. She clipped on the belt and turned to face Maya.

"Okay, Maya, time to look in the mirror." Kora pressed a button on the belt and her image shimmered. Suddenly, Maya was staring at herself.

"What?" Maya said in disbelief. Kora turned, looking from side to side. The image remained perfectly natural.

"This is creepy." Maya reached out to touch Kora. As her hand got closer, it passed through a net of light, piercing the illusion.

"This is pretty amazing. It's not until I actually come into contact with the hologram that I can even tell it's not real," Maya said. Anders walked over and inspected Kora from different angles.

"Yeah, the clothing is perfect. This is really impressive." Suddenly, Kora was back to normal. Maya had to blink and readjust.

"You outdid yourself this time," Maya said. "That was amazing."

"Yeah, looks like you had just the right parts to pull it off," Anders said with a grin.

Kora winked. Then she let out a deep sigh. "This is groundbreaking stuff. I haven't seen anything this sophisticated before. But this is the first time this machine was even built. It doesn't feel right." Kora wandered over to her desk and started working on the computer.

Maya wandered over to talk to her. "What's wrong? Kora, I can see something's affecting you."

"It's this device. We're not ripping off some corporation who's mass producing them. We're not buying a prototype from an entrepreneur who needs seed funding to build more of them. We stole someone's research and built it before they could even see it realized. It just doesn't sit well with me."

"Well, I mean, we could always drop the device off after we've used it. As a thank you? Anonymously, of course," Maya said.

"It needs more than that. It's fine. Let's not dwell on it, but it just doesn't sit well. I don't like it," Kora said, trailing off.

Anders cleared his throat. "So, Maya, did you have some news?"

"Yeah, I found and explored Eduardo's penthouse. He left me a list of locations in the city. I'm going to visit them all so that I can teleport to them later. I'm guessing they're probably good ways to get around the city quickly."

"That's really handy. Do you need someone to drive you around?" Anders said.

"No, I'll just make this a solo trip. I think you need to work on how to get all of this out of the lab and into a usable state." Maya gestured over at the workbench with the hologram equipment.

"Understood. It's definitely still very theoretical, even though it works."

"I will catch up with you a bit later. Great work, Kora." Maya waved and left the suite.

MAYA WANDERED through the city on foot, looking for the closest location marked on the map. She meandered along busy streets, regularly checking between her actual location and the map to make sure she was heading in the right direction. It was lunchtime, and the streets were full of people heading out to grab something to eat, office workers pouring out of the buildings like a swarm.

The first location looked like it was in a mall. Maya wandered inside. The pristine white tunnel she was in, wide enough to fit thirty people at a time, led down into an underground food court.

The smells wafted over, and Maya instantly felt hungry.

Just find the first place. You can eat after you find something.

Maya walked through the food court, steering past Japanese cuisine and classic Atlantis fare, and found herself in the shopping area of the mall. She missed the sights and smells of the food, but it made it a little bit easier to concentrate when she wasn't being tempted constantly.

Maya pulled out the map again, studying it. There was just something not right about the location.

If it was in the middle of this mall, there would be no way to find out what spot he meant. That kind of detail is not on the map.

Maya turned the map around, trying to look at it from a different angle.

"Having trouble?" a man said, looking over at her. He looked to be in his fifties, with antique round eyeglasses. He was dressed in an impeccable suit and had a kind smile.

"I was just trying to find a spot my friend marked on a map for me to investigate."

"Let me have a look. I know the area well," the man said. Maya had folded the map so that only the section she was reviewing right now was visible.

"Oh, I see, yes. Oh. I understand completely." The man looked up at Maya and smiled again.

"What you're looking for is the building behind this one. It used to be a famous restaurant, but now it's just abandoned."

"Oh, how would I get there?" Maya said.

The man turned around, searching for something.

"Ah, yes, you see that corridor down the back? If you follow that corridor, you'll go past the restrooms and there will be an exit at the end. That will take you into an alley where you will find the restaurant. I'm afraid it's been closed for quite a few years though." The man gave her an apologetic smile.

Maya nodded. "I understand. Thank you so much for your help. I'll go have a look just so I can tell my friend I found it. Then I can let him know that it's been closed for a while."

"No problem at all. Glad I could help you, and sorry about the restaurant." The man waved and wandered off.

Maya put the map away and strode down the corridor while the instructions were still fresh. She walked past the bathrooms and found a plain white exit door at the end of the corridor. She opened it and walked through, stepping into the blinding sunlight. Once her eyes adjusted, she could see an old Italian restaurant called 'Mama's Pizzeria'.

The place was all boarded up and looked like it had been abandoned for a long time. The terracotta tiles on the roof were dirty, faded, and crumbling. Maya walked around the building, trying to find a good way in or at least a good viewpoint she could use.

She completed a complete circuit of the building and didn't spot anything.

There has to be a way. He found his way in here originally without the WallSpy.

Maya did another route, this time noticing there was a small gap in between the boards in one of the windows, and just enough light to give her a view inside the building.

Got it.

Maya peered inside, seeing a dusty floor with tables and chairs covered by blankets. She picked a spot and teleported in. The air was stale and musty, but she was inside the old, abandoned restaurant. She walked around, doing a kind of victory lap.

This is perfect. No one can see inside. I can easily teleport into the restaurant, and no one will even see me. If all the locations are like this, I am onto a winner.

Maya did a quick tour of the building, noting the different rooms, and then teleported out to behind the building. As expected, there was nobody around in any part of the laneway. She walked back into the shopping mall and headed back to Kora's suite.

MAYA FOUND Kora and Anders chatting over coffee.

"Did you make me one?" Maya asked as she closed the door.

"Yeah, I left some in the pot for you." Anders pointed to the coffee pot. Maya poured herself a cup and joined the other two.

"So, what's the verdict?" Maya said, looking at them both.

"Anders is going to fill you in. I think it'll work." Kora walked back to her desk, put down her coffee and got back to work.

"She doesn't like this still, huh?" Maya asked.

Anders nodded. "Yeah, I suggested that she research the inventor a little bit more and that just made things worse. She really admires this woman, and it looks like without this blueprint the research is gonna be set back quite a long time."

"We'll do something once we get the mission done. We'll make it right."

"I have no doubt."

"So, what's the plan?" Maya said taking a sip of her coffee.

"Well, it's simple and brilliant. We need to find the right person to scan, and then we hack into their email server and send that person an email directing them for a security update. Not only can we get the scan, but we can also issue them a new ID card with access."

"Right," Maya said, nodding along.

"And if they can continue to work, then we've effectively tested our access kits."

"This is a great plan," Maya said.

"But if it doesn't work, then we need to make sure we intercept her before she goes to the real security team. They'll realize that she wasn't due for a new access kit and card, and then they're on high alert."

"We can do this, I think. But it won't give us very long to act after that, will it?"

"No. Every day we delay after we get the scan increases the chances that this employee talks to someone about their refreshed access and figures out that there's something wrong."

"I think it's worth a shot at least finding the right person and we'll take it from there."

"Okay, I'll start the prep. We'll get this done." Anders glanced over at Kora, a concerned look on his face. But then he brightened up and left the room.

27

THE STAKEOUT

Maya stopped in front of the building. It was a large factory complex, with a long drive and multiple buildings. She looked over at Anders.

"This is where we split up. Can you go find a nice vantage point and deploy your surveillance gear? And I'll find this teleportation spot."

"Sounds good, see you soon." Anders waved and walked back to the van. Maya watched him drive away, then turned back, walking up the long concrete driveway.

This place looks abandoned. I guess that's why Eduardo picked it.

She walked down the driveway, noticing about twelve empty car spaces along the side. The main building had a small glass door and a few windows up high, but no other points of entry. Maya pulled out the map again and had a look.

Hmm. The precision is not great, but I don't think it's the main building he's referring to here.

Maya kept walking, panning her head from side to side to try and spot something else. As she got closer to the main building, she saw that there was a second building, this one behind. It was a lot smaller and had no doors or windows.

This has potential.

Maya walked alongside the building, looking for any other points of entry. As she rounded the back, she found one tiny window at the top.

How strange. How did he get into this building?

She continued a full loop around and then returned to where the window was. *Maybe there's another way of accessing it. Underground, even. No matter.*

Maya pulled out the WallSpy from her backpack and settled it onto her head. She switched it on and activated the WallSpy function. It took a moment to figure out what she was looking at.

The room was stacked high with boxes. Boxes and boxes. But she spotted an empty space toward the middle of the room. She teleported inside effortlessly, then removed the WallSpy and stashed it in her backpack The air was stale and there was dust everywhere.

The boxes were all sealed, dark plastic tubs. She walked over and lifted the lid off one peering inside.

Looks like paperwork, but why?

Maya closed the lid, a little confused. She spun slowly around the room, taking it all in. It was just shelving with boxes. She retraced her steps and noticed a small section on the side of the room. She walked closer, peering at the walls and the floor, studying them.

The floor had a square outline on it.

Maybe it's a trapdoor or a hatch?

Maya got down on one knee and tugged at the square section. With a little effort she managed to lift it up and push it aside. Underneath was a staircase going into a pitch-black tunnel.

I'm not sure if I want to explore that right now.

Her curiosity somewhat satisfied, Maya pushed the hatch cover back where it was. stood up and teleported to the back of the building. Outside once more, she took in a deep breath of fresh air.

Phew, that's much better. Time to head off and find Anders.

Maya walked a couple of blocks and then checked her phone. Anders had sent her the location of where he was. She followed the directions, ending up at a dark grey warehouse. It was next to the one that Eduardo had tested her on so long ago. The thought of his name brought up more feelings, but Maya did not let herself get swept away.

She walked around to the side of the warehouse, as per Anders's instructions, and found a door propped open. She walked inside and then ascended two flights of stairs before coming out into an open space. It looked like it was originally for an office, but there was no more furniture. Just bland, grey, thin carpet and white walls with the odd glass partition here and there and glass-enclosed meeting rooms.

She found Anders sitting on an old leather chair. Next to him was some sort of telescope.

"This is our spy equipment?" Maya said as she approached.

"Yeah, yeah, I've got some old-school stuff here and there's also a few cameras stashed around." Before him, Anders had propped up his laptop on a plastic tub. On his screen were some camera feeds. After a little bit of looking and thinking, Maya realized they were positioned on nearby buildings looking at the facility they were observing.

"I see what you've done here. Good system."

"Thanks," Anders said. "We can use the telescope to pick up people we want to follow, and then we can track them on these other cameras. Once we record enough footage today, we'll hopefully have some information about their movements and timing."

"How long do we need to hang around for that, to get a good pattern?"

"You'd want to wait a week to get their whole schedule, but

we probably aren't gonna do that. I'd say we pick a target today and then we confirm tomorrow."

"Works for me. Let's go with that." Maya found an old office chair in the corner, rolled it over, and set it next to Anders.

"Alright, let's take turns to avoid crazy boredom. One person watches the cameras, the other person gets to peek around in the telescope," Maya said.

"Let me guess, you're the one using the telescope?" Anders said.

"Of course. You can watch the cameras until I get bored of this." Maya swung the telescope closer to her and peered through the lens.

"Wow, the clarity of this is really good, but there's not much to see," she said, leaning back and taking in the whole view again.

"Yeah, it's probably more helpful if you spot someone that you want to see in more detail. But it's also good to observe the location. Maybe it'll help you with more teleport options," Anders said, hopefully. Maya nodded.

"That's a good way to look at it."

THE MORNING PASSED without anything interesting happening. They saw a lot of people streaming through the main gate, as Maya had that fateful day, with very few accessing the second building without going through the first building.

"Well, I guess it's a good sign that fewer people have access directly to the secondary building. It will be easier to find the right person to replicate," Maya said, thinking it through.

"True, but then it also may be harder to sneak in if there's fewer people using that entrance."

"Also true. I don't know. I have a feeling I'll know the right person when I spot them." Maya looked up suddenly.

That woman looks familiar.

She grabbed the telescope and took a look.

"She is the same one I saw before, and she's carrying lunch bags? Hmm, interesting." Maya watched the woman carefully juggling the bags, fishing out an access card, and then entering the building.

"Well, it is lunchtime," Anders said. "I'm kind of famished myself you know."

"Hang on a minute," Maya said. "You grab some food but show me how to review the footage from earlier today before you go."

"Sure, here's the controls, you can just rewind it," Anders said, demonstrating.

"Okay, thanks. Go. Go get food." Maya waved Anders off and pulled his laptop onto her lap.

She reviewed the recorded footage, winding it back until early in the morning. It wasn't too hard to find things to review because there was not a lot of activity in that area of the grounds.

Not that one, not this one.

She kept flicking backward. Then, something looked promising. She paused and peered closer at the screen.

That's it. How do I make this bigger?

She played around with the buttons until she could magnify the image. Then she leaned back in her chair triumphantly.

Anders is gonna love this. I've figured it out.

Anders returned soon enough with a bag of food. It looked similar to the ones that the woman had just carried into the facility.

"Did you find the same lunch place?" Maya asked.

"I think so. There's nothing else really around here and the bag looked familiar."

"What is it?" Maya said, curious and hungry.

"Oh, it's just like a sandwich place. They do rolls with different things. I got you a falafel something."

"Okay, thanks." She waited for Anders to sit down, and he handed her some kind of sandwich wrapped in a lot of paper. "Have a look at the screen."

"Oh hey, it's that woman. Is she doing a coffee run?" Anders said around a mouthful of sandwich.

"Yes, she is. A coffee run in the morning, and a lunch run at midday. If she has a coffee run this afternoon, that's amazing."

"We could try and replace her in one of the runs," Anders said, thinking out loud.

"No, no, that's a terrible idea because they will know all their orders and you'd have to interact with multiple people. That's just a disaster waiting to happen."

"Now that you put it that way, sure. But this is great. It means this woman is the only one going in and out regularly to the most secure area."

"If I look like her, and I go in any time of the day, nobody will think twice about it."

"Probably not. She does seem like a good initial target," Anders said. He pulled out his sandwich and started chomping on it.

Maya glanced over. It was a long round roll with some kind of meatballs inside. She shrugged.

Anders opened his mouth wide, taking a big bite. "Oh, this is really tasty!" he said, shocked. "I guess that's why they keep going back." Anders carefully swallowed the giant mouthful and washed it down with some water. It didn't take long to finish the rest.

"So, here's the plan," Maya said.

"Let's hear it," Anders said cautiously.

"I'll go down there when she comes out for the coffee run. I'll tail her to the location and back."

"Alright. Sounds fine to me. Are you going to use the disguise?"

"Of course. It's the perfect chance to road test it."

"Okay, well, I'll be here. I'll have my many eyes watching." Anders pointed to the camera feeds with a wink. Next, he leaned into his coat and handed Maya an earpiece. "Put this on so you can talk to me if you run into any trouble."

"Sure." Maya popped in the earpiece, waved, and walked away, heading toward the stairwell. She descended the stairs quickly and after she escaped out the back door she reached down and activated the button on her belt.

After a quick shimmer, the illusion washed over her. Maya pulled out her phone and tried to do a selfie. Kora's grinning face smiled back.

"Perfect," Maya said, putting her phone away.

Before walking onto the street proper, Maya tried teleporting up to the office area that she was using for surveillance with Anders. He turned quickly, shocked to see her appearing next to him.

"Everything okay?" he said.

"I think so. Is the disguise tool working?" Maya said. Anders stood up and peered at her from different directions.

"Yes, looks fine. Did you think it wouldn't work?"

"I just wanted to be sure, and also to check if teleporting impacted it at all. Okay, back to it." Maya waved and then teleported to the back of the building. She walked around the building, emerged at the front, and wandered down to the street.

There wasn't a lot of foot traffic, only the occasional car. The street was quite exposed, so she walked past the facility and paused at the corner, looking for somewhere to wait. She could see a row of shops diagonally opposite. A sandwich place, a coffee shop, and a convenience store.

"That's the ticket." Maya walked over to the coffee shop. It was bustling. Mostly people waiting around and then leaving with takeaway cups. Maya walked in and avoided bumping into people. Soon enough she made it to the front of the line.

As she was about to order, she noticed that there was no one actually taking orders. They were just making coffee. She glanced over and saw there were some instructions about ordering through your phone.

Great you've been queuing for nothing. These people are just waiting for their coffee.

She moved off to the side, figuring out how to do that on her phone while occasionally glancing around to look. Maya successfully submitted the order, and then just stared around the room. It was nicely furnished with a soft green carpet and wooden tables, the occasional plush velvet chair.

There were some booths to sit at, but mostly it was just wooden chairs with green backs. There was a notice board where orders were being published. She found hers and tracked its progress, occasionally turning back to look at the newcomers entering the cafe.

It was taking a long time, but Maya resisted the urge to just put on her phone, continuing to watch the room. She was broken out of her distracted state by hearing a voice call out.

"Daphne, coffee up!"

Ooh that's my fake coffee name.

Maya smiled and walked forward to retrieve her coffee. She was almost bowled over by a woman running through the cafe.

28

IDENTITY ACQUIRED

Maya couldn't dodge in time.

If she hits me it's going to blow the illusion.

At the last instant, she managed to teleport a few inches away, just enough to avoid getting hit. The woman was clearly a Speedster.

"Oh, Roberta, just in time. Here's the six coffees you ordered," the barista said, handing a large tray over to the Speedster. Maya shifted and noticed the woman's face.

It was the one they'd been tracking. The one that was doing all the food and coffee runs.

Roberta, eh? Better remember that.

Maya grabbed her coffee slowly and stepped back. Roberta walked at normal speed out of the shop, and Maya followed soon after. She didn't track Roberta all that closely because she knew where she was going. Maya followed her from the other side of the street and once Roberta had disappeared into her building Maya completed the circuit, getting back to the back of her building and teleporting up to Anders.

"Hey, where's my coffee?" Anders said as Maya appeared with a coffee cup.

"Sorry, this was just a test." Maya slowly sipped from the cup.

"That's pretty good coffee." She glanced over at Anders. "Did that look weird?"

"No. I think Kora said as long as you interact with objects slowly, the illusion can maintain itself."

"That's good to know." Maya pushed the button on her belt and the illusion disappeared. She relaxed back in the chair, taking another sip of her coffee.

"Fine, I'll get my own coffee." Anders skulked away.

"Satisfied?" Anders said as they watched Roberta head out for coffee again the next morning.

"Extremely. Are we ready on the scanning front?" Maya asked, sipping her own coffee.

"We are. You can run the scanning process as Kora in case they've been briefed with your appearance." Anders gulped down the last of his coffee and packed up his laptop. He stood up and stretched out.

"Kora and I moved the equipment last night. She has the communications prepped. I'll advise her to send it out to Roberta within the hour."

"Great. How's Kora feeling about all this? She seemed disturbed yesterday."

"Oh, she's not a fan. I've never seen her this uncomfortable about something." Anders sighed.

"I'll talk to her tonight. We'll run the operation soon and fix everything. I promise."

"I know you will. It's not me you have to convince. I better get moving. I'll call you." Anders started walking off and stopped a few yards away. "Oh and wear your lab coat." Anders waved and continued out of the building.

Maya slowly packed up the telescope and dragged the furniture back to where it had started. Clutching the telescope, she teleported to the safe room nearby.

I'm not sure I'll get used to this.

The transition from place to place was still jarring.

I think it's the smell and air. It's not supposed to change so quickly.

Maya glanced around the room, satisfied that nothing had changed since she was last here. She stuffed the telescope in a spot in the corner and opened one of the plastic tubs. She pulled out a white lab coat and draped it over a nearby box.

Next, she reached down and activated the button on her belt. She took Kora's appearance instantly.

Feels weird doing this as her, given how she feels about it. Oh well, after this one time, I'll be Roberta instead.

Maya carefully draped the lab coat over herself and let it settle. Then she teleported out of the building and pulled out her phone to check her appearance.

I look more like Kora than Kora does. The lab coat look does wonders.

Maya walked confidently down the driveway and off to the street. The location they had picked for this false security update was a flashy office only a block away. Maya picked up the pace, not wanting to be late. She reached the revolving doors in a few minutes, picking her moment to dart through.

The suite they had rented was on the first floor. Maya took the lift up and found the office, Room 106. She unlocked the glass door and then pocketed the key in her lab coat.

The key works, that's a good sign.

The reception area was tiny; a single desk and a few wooden chairs with blue cushions. Maya walked through the area to the screening room. It was all white, with a tiled floor. The scanner was set up on a workbench with the computer connected.

Looks good. Very professional.

After a loop around the room, Maya returned to the reception area and lounged near the desk, playing on her phone.

AN HOUR LATER, Maya looked up and saw Roberta walking over, cautiously. Maya put on a smile, waved, and opened the door for Roberta.

"Hello, am I at the right place?"

"Of course, come in Roberta. We appreciate you helping us out today."

"Oh, hang on. Have we met?" Roberta said as she entered.

"Yes, what a coincidence. I think you rushed in to get a coffee order yesterday?" Maya said with a chuckle.

Roberta returned the smile. "Yeah, I was a bit of a whirlwind. When I get stressed, my power leaks out sometimes. Sorry."

"Don't apologize. Come through, this won't take long at all." Maya guided Roberta over to the screening room.

"This is our new screening room. We can do full biometric scans and issue you a new security pass." Maya paused so Roberta could take it all in.

"What about this one?" Roberta said, holding her pass up.

"It will still work. Let me have that for a few moments, and I'll give you both passes at the end." Maya took the security pass and walked over to the computer. She scanned in the details of the card.

"Fantastic, this all looks to be lining up." Maya copied all the security profiles off the card for future use.

"Could you stand on the mark?" Maya asked, pointing to an 'X' taped onto the floor. Roberta walked over quickly.

"Given all the activity lately, we're trialing some new security procedures. As someone who is frequently in and out of the building, you seemed like the best candidate to test the new process," Maya said.

"You have no idea. I feel like I'm even an assistant to the other assistants!"

"I know how that feels. This won't take long, can you look at the cameras, please," Maya said. Roberta turned slightly, looking at the cameras. Maya started the scan and got a green light.

"Can you turn to your right, please, and stand side-on," Maya asked.

"Sure. So what team are you in? I didn't catch your name." Roberta turned and showed her profile.

"I'm Daphne. I'm in the, uh security response team," Maya said. She started off the next scan.

"Oh, I haven't heard of that team. Is it new?" Roberta said.

"Stay still, please. And yes, it's a new team assembled to proactively address security concerns. We were very... reactive before." Maya completed the scan.

"Oh, this is all exciting. I can't wait to tell people," Roberta said, beaming.

Oh no. No, no, no.

"The thing is, since this is a new program, we'd ask you to not discuss it publicly for a few days," Maya said. "Turn again, please, so we can scan your back."

"Why shouldn't I discuss it?" Roberta turned around as requested.

"Well, it's a bit embarrassing, but we'd like to see if things work properly before it becomes public knowledge." Maya completed the next scan.

"Yeah, tell me about it. Valerie's been on a rampage. I honestly don't understand it."

"Exactly. I am picturing her reaction to me making a

mistake now, and it sent a shiver down my spine," Maya said, completely truthfully.

"She's scary. We're not supposed to ask about her powers, but isn't it weird?" Roberta said.

"What have you heard? Please turn once more, so we can get your profile from the other side," Maya instructed.

"Oh, that she has an extra power. But the rumor is that she never used to have it," Roberta almost whispered. But she turned around as requested.

"No way!" Maya said, completing the scan. While the scan was compiling, she clicked the other button Anders had shown her. A new pass started printing.

"It's unbelievable, isn't it? Imagine if we could all get new powers. That would be crazy."

"Too crazy. Total chaos," Maya said absently, focused on the card printer. A fresh card popped out, with Roberta's picture on it. Maya grabbed the card. It was still warm to the touch.

"I think we're all done here," Maya said. She retrieved the new card, and the old card, and walked over to Roberta.

"Here you go. Your new card, and your old one." Maya handed the cards to Roberta. She held up the new one and studied the photo.

"This photo isn't bad at all. Usually they're the worst."

"Well, it's a test phase, I'm sure they'll fix that," Maya said with a laugh. Roberta laughed along with her.

"Can you use the new card for a day or two, and then go back to the old one?" Maya asked.

"Sure. You'll be in touch?" Roberta said.

"Yes, we will monitor and email you in a few days to let you know how the trial went." Maya gave Roberta a big smile.

"Thanks, I'll keep it under wraps," Roberta said with a wink and walked out. Maya escorted her to the main door, opening it for Roberta and waving as she left. After Roberta had completely gone, Maya pulled out her phone and called Anders.

"How did it go?" Anders said.

"The scan was perfect. But we have a problem."

"What's wrong?"

"She's a gossip. I bet she is going to tell someone immediately."

"We still have time, but that may speed things up for us. Take the card and data to Kora, and I'll swing around later and pack up."

"Thanks. See you later." Maya hung up and looked around the room.

Is this even going to work? How am I going to pull this off?

Maya downloaded the scan to a drive and left the building.

MAYA WALKED into Kora's suite.

"I come bearing gifts. Data and coffee," Maya announced. Kora didn't respond, her eyes were glued to her monitor. Maya dropped the coffee and data drive on Kora's desk.

"Did you talk to Anders?" Maya asked. Kora shook her head.

"Well, the scan went perfectly. I have the data here. Anders will be going back to pack everything up. But I think Roberta will be talking too much about this. If word gets to Valerie, this is over."

"Time will tell," Kora said, not looking up.

"What's going on?" Maya said, looking directly at Kora. For the first time, Kora looked up.

"I think we should abort the plan. Anonymously return the blueprints and prototype devices."

"We discussed this. I can fix it after the mission. No harm done," Maya said, smiling at Kora.

"There's already harm done." Kora swiveled the monitor around, showing Maya. There was a news article.

"Researcher sunk by missing plans," Maya read out.

Maya looked over at Kora and sighed.

"Okay, so there's been an impact already, but I can fix this. We'll set up our own fake foundation and give her a grant that way."

"She's brilliant. This is a breakthrough invention, and we're just meddling in her life. Aren't we smart enough to find a better way than this?"

"Probably, but...we're going to be done really soon. We'll make it right. We should just finish what we've started."

"I don't agree. We should just return everything. If we do it now, she can..." Kora paused, looking for the right words. "I can't reconcile this, I just don't believe in what we're doing. I don't believe in it."

Maya paced around the room before addressing Kora again.

"I'm sorry, I understand where you're coming from. But we're already in it. We've got the image of Roberta." Maya started firing up, gesturing as she spoke. "We've got the access pass. I can get in. I can do something. I can pull out the Wall-Spy. I can infiltrate the facility. We're so close. Let's just do it before this opportunity goes away."

Kora shook her head sadly.

"We don't see eye to eye on this. I'm sorry, I can't support this plan any longer. I'll figure out what I've already promised you, so you can send the email to Roberta. But I'm done. If you need help on something else, I'm always here. But I'm stepping away at this moment. I hope you understand," Kora said quietly, in a flat tone that Maya had never heard her use before.

This is really it.

"It's okay, Kora. I understand. I don't want to force you to do anything that you don't want to do. And... I know we don't agree on how this is playing out, but I promise you I'll make it right. You just have to trust me."

"I do trust you. I just don't believe in the way you're doing it. I want to go for a walk." Kora stood up and left the room without another word. Maya watched her go.

Is she right? Should we just change what we're doing? I'm so confused.

29

ROBOT COMBAT

The next morning Maya found Anders doing surveillance on the facility. He was monitoring the cameras and some other data on his laptop.

"How's it looking?" she asked, handing him coffee. He took a sip before responding.

"So far, so good. I think it looks like Roberta is using the new security pass and it's working."

"That's good news. It works, and she won't have a reason to ask for help," Maya said.

"I wish I had eyes inside the facility to see what she was doing. But I don't." Anders sighed and continued alternating through the different camera feeds.

"We've got a bit of time. Let's finalize the last details. Did you recover the vaults we were testing out?"

"No, it was too risky. Even if we got in and out cleanly, those vaults could attract Valerie back to us. I had to abandon them."

"Well, at least we learned how the hacking tool works. Although we didn't recover that either, did we?" Maya drank her coffee again, not making eye contact.

"No, and frankly we're better off without it." Anders leaned back and took a large drink of his coffee. "You teleported out of the vault with the WallSpy, so we shouldn't need to crack the vault." Anders winked.

"But what if they've got an even thicker one?" Maya said, concerned. She started playing with the lid on her coffee cup, twisting it around.

"Well, that's a risk we're going to have to take. There's no way we can get another one of these vault hackers, or even retrieve the one that we lost, without painting a giant sign on our backs saying, 'About to steal from the Haste facility'." Anders trailed off as his joke ran out of steam.

"You're right. This would have worked so much better with Eduardo. But I guess I can do it myself."

"I'll be providing remote support, and you've got teleport locations nearby you can access," Anders said in a hopeful tone. Maya brightened a little.

"That's true. I'll have to do a test tonight to make sure I can teleport from near the facility grounds to those locations easily."

"Exactly. Don't leave it your chance. In fact, since we're not going to move today, I think you need to shore up your teleportation as much as possible. It's gonna be the thing that saves you. And once you get inside this place, it's gonna be the thing that gets you back inside anytime you want."

"That's right. Once I can come and go as I please, they can't keep me out. They can't secure the place at all."

"Yeah, then they'll just move everything," Anders said, finishing the thought.

"I guess they could. Another reason why we need to move on this sooner rather than later." Maya stood up and started pacing around.

"If they think the risk is too high, they'll absolutely do this. They've got the resources of the Master Sage behind them."

"I keep thinking back to what Roberta said. Everyone's

figured out about Valerie. Word is going to spread soon, they won't be able to keep this contained. The Master Sage will have to change things, might take the heat off me a little bit." Maya took another big sip of her coffee.

Anders stood up, stretching his legs.

"I'll leave you to prep all the gear. I want to go back to my teleport practice. Today's challenge is to get across to the training center in three hops."

"Good luck and call me if you need anything. And don't make yourself unconscious," Anders added.

"I'll do my best, but no promises." Maya waved and teleported away.

Her first location was the nearby building, where she had been stashing some of their surveillance gear. It was an easy jump and perfectly secure.

Alright, you can do this. You've done all these teleports by yourself, singly. There's no reason you can't just chain them together.

Maya pictured the next location and teleported. She arrived easily enough, a little bit fatigued, so took a moment to catch her breath.

Okay, next location.

She stumbled a little, but she was in the abandoned Italian restaurant, Mama's Pizzeria.

Okay, so far so good. One more hop back to the command center. You can do it.

Maya focused herself, concentrated, and pushed. She appeared in the command center, tripped over Eduardo's chair, and landed flat on her face.

Look, not the most graceful landing, but you're here. What can I do to get my training to the next level? I'm sure Eduardo had more space down here. Let me have a look through the data he left me.

Maya fired up Eduardo's computer and paged through all the files. She was specifically looking for any schematics or information about the training center he'd slowly built up.

She'd already tried all the rooms in the main space, and she'd seen some of the nearby spaces which were not designed for training but were just accessible.

Paging through the plans, she noticed something.

There's another level downstairs. For combat training. That's the ticket.

Once Maya read through the instructions, she realized there was an application on the computer that could unlock the room. Maya located the application, simply called Combat, and activated it.

She heard a quaking sound in the room outside and teleported over to investigate immediately. A section of the floor opened to reveal a hatch leading down. Maya peered into the hole. There was another corridor underneath, with minimal lighting.

Here we go.

Maya teleported down and then started walking down the corridor, seeing where it led. She could see one door at the end of the corridor. It was locked with a keypad.

No problem. I'll just fetch some tools.

Maya teleported back to the command center, grabbed the spare WallSpy and teleported back to the keypad door. She put on the WallSpy, activated it and the WallSpy function, and peered through the doorway. On the other side was a small foyer and then a larger room that she couldn't quite make out.

Teleport time.

She arrived in the foyer and then put the WallSpy away. Maya wandered into the large training room. It was white on every surface, with gleaming tiles. In the center of the room there was a control panel on a white pedestal.

Maya teleported over and examined the panel. There was a dial, which went from zero to twenty, and a start button.

Okay. Let's give this a go.

Maya turned the dial to one and pressed start. At the back

of the room, a piece of floor opened and a black humanoid figure came up through the floor. It looked like a kind of robot mixed with a crash dummy. Once the robot was in the room proper, it came to life, walking smoothly over toward Maya.

I guess this is level one. Let's see what it's like.

Maya readied herself and let the robot approach. It didn't seem to have any kind of stance. It was just walking normally. It wasn't even heading directly for Maya, just meandering nearby.

Suddenly, it turned and threw a punch with its right hand. Maya couldn't react fast enough to completely dodge. She threw up her arms to block the strike. It worked, but the impact hurt. The robot then launched into a series of attacks, each one slightly faster than the one before.

Maya had to block each one, her training guiding her movements. But every blocked attack made the robot attack even faster.

I'm gonna get pummeled soon if I'm not careful. This is only level one!

Desperate for some breathing room, Maya teleported back to the start. The robot slowed and became still. Maya took a few breaths and watched the robot. It was motionless.

She stepped back into the training area, watching the robot as she cautiously approached. It was still lifeless. Maya walked closer, not taking her eyes off the robot for even a fraction of a second. Suddenly, it threw out a punch again, but Maya had an idea.

She teleported behind the robot and struck it in the back of the head, as Eduardo had done in a few of their fights. The robot slumped to the floor and a bell sounded in the room. The floor opened up, the robot disappeared under the floor and the room was reset.

Oh, this doesn't seem too bad.

Maya teleported back to the control panel, turned the dial to two, and hit start again. This time, two robots rose from the back of the room. After a few moments, they activated, each heading in opposite directions toward Maya in a pincer movement.

Now I know the trick, this is going to be easier.

The robots moved in a smooth, uniform manner, each coming from a different direction. She waited for them to get closer so she could do the same move she'd just done.

However, instead of walking past her, they suddenly dashed forward at incredible speed. Maya could do nothing but block the two attacks. Of course, that meant they started doing faster and faster dashing strikes. Maya was about to be overwhelmed.

Come on, don't get pinned down.

Maya teleported away, buying herself a few seconds before they continued their assault. This time she was ready. She watched them closely, and they dashed in again. Too fast for her to react the way she'd like, but she picked a spot behind them and teleported.

Their attacks missed completely, but Maya was too far to hit them after she landed. They turned and dashed again, both coming from the same direction. Maya picked another spot and teleported there as they dashed. This time she was closer still, but that also meant that she had less reaction time for their next attack.

They spun and moved in even faster than before. Maya couldn't really think, she just teleported and found herself exactly behind both robots. With a very fast sweeping strike, she knocked them both down from behind. They dropped to the floor and were cleaned up as the room reset.

Maya bent over for a few seconds, drawing in deep breaths, and recovering.

That was level two. You've got a long way to go.

She gave herself a few moments to recover, then teleported back to try again.

I wish I'd found out this days ago. The shorter teleports are less straining overall. This is very useful training.

She activated level three and three more robots rose.

Here we go again.

HOURS LATER, Maya was facing off against a single robot. It was the last of its group, dashing around the room randomly. She couldn't predict where it would land next or when it would actually attack her. All she could do was pay attention, slowly shift her stance and footing to be ready, and watch.

After a minute or two of this, she grew fed up with that process.

Time to take the fight to this stupid robot.

Maya teleported closer, baiting the robot into an attack. It did it instantly. She reacted without thinking, arriving behind the robot and knocked it down.

That was it. Level six.

All six robots were cleaned up and the room reset once again. Maya teleported back to the control panel and looked at the dial, considering level seven.

Nope, not going to happen today.

She teleported back to the command center and eased herself into Eduardo's chair, resting. She suddenly felt an intense thirst. Maya teleported to the kitchenette, got herself a cup of water and drank it greedily then refilled the cup and drank it again. She pulled out her phone and called Anders.

"Hey, where are we up to?" Maya said.

"The gear is ready. Our kits are ready. The plan's still a little bit free-form, but it could be done."

"Wow. Don't go all super confident on me," Maya said, laughing.

"I'm just trying to be upfront. It's not the best plan because we have to throw it together. But the foundations are solid. We've got tried and tested access. You can look like the person whose ID you're using. And we can time your movements for when she's not in the building. But after that, there's a lot of unknowns. We still don't have an accurate picture of the interior of either building."

"I know. Let me head over and we can talk about final details."

"Okay. I've ordered pizza, so get yourself here."

"Will do," Maya said, hanging up.

How much can you push yourself? At least one more step.

Maya picked the location a quarter of the way to her hotel and teleported. She arrived without any trouble but felt fatigue settling in.

Alright, just one more hop, then you'll walk the rest of the way. Or get a taxi. Or Anders can pick you up. Just do one more and don't pass out. I know you can do it.

She had scouted out the next evenly distanced jump back to the hotel, which would get her about halfway there. But she hadn't tried it yet.

This is it. You can do this.

Maya pictured the location in her mind and teleported. She arrived and then staggered, leaning against the wall. She was in a tight and dark space. And she felt frightened for a moment before she remembered where she was.

After calming her breathing down, she forced the door open and looked around. There was nobody there. She had teleported into an old broken photo booth that nobody used anymore.

Maya was wandering around a dilapidated cinema foyer. For some reason, it was still open but barely showed any movies and had barely any customers.

Perfect for my purposes, but not for the people trying to run this business.

After a few steps, Maya felt a little bit steadier on her feet.

Maybe you can walk the rest of the way to the hotel? Come on. You don't need to call for help. Just take your time. Put one foot in front of the other.

With a groan, Maya slowly walked the rest of the way back to her hotel.

30

GEARING DOWN

Maya leaned back in the chair, looking up at the stars. She was sitting next to Anders on the rooftop of their hotel building.

"I'm impressed you got us up here." Anders whistled with admiration.

"Well, you did walk up here yourself. I just opened the way. Their security is designed to keep people from accessing the roof from within the building, not from another building.

"Lucky for us." Anders leaned back and took another sip of his beer. Maya sipped a glass of red wine.

"So, it's all happening tomorrow? We're ready?" Maya said.

"All the gear is set up in our surveillance spot. We'll watch the building for any signs of abnormalities. We've got a pattern now from the last couple of days."

"When am I going in?"

"We're going to wait for Roberta to leave for the day, and then shortly after you're gonna pop back in as her. No one will suspect a problem because she's in and out of the building all day."

"They'll assume she forgot something. What will you be doing?"

"I'll be running surveillance from the same location. We'll be in radio contact, I'll also be watching your feed from multiple cameras, and you'll have a tracker. I just want you to know I've got all bases covered."

"Good." Maya took a gulp of her wine.

"If you run into trouble, just teleport out. We've measured the distance between the facility and the nearest safe room that you've been testing. It's within your safe teleportation distance."

"That's reassuring," Maya said, focusing on the sky and getting lost in the stars.

"You know, we can stop if you're not confident. There's always another way. Someone else can infiltrate."

"But no one else can get as far as me. Kora's backed out of this. You could walk in with the disguise, but your walk will not be as convincing as mine."

"True, but I could hack my way through a couple of rooms. Maybe even get to the vault," Anders said.

"But it's a real gamble whether you can even get into the vault. And there's no easy exit for you. You've got to pull yourself through the whole building, potentially with enemies on your tail. It's way too risky."

"Well, it's not ideal." Anders took a long sip of his beer. "I'm just trying to say, there are other options. Don't feel like you have to do this."

"But I have to do this. It's not really an option. Eduardo is dead. I couldn't save him." Maya gulped down most of her wine. Anders sighed.

"I'm just saying if you're not comfortable we don't have to go tomorrow. There's always another option."

"Well, let's agree to disagree because I think there's no other option. Here's to a crazy heist." Maya held up her wine glass and Anders clinked his beer bottle against it.

"Cheers to a crazy heist, and good luck."

THE NEXT MORNING Anders drove Maya silently through the streets toward the building to commence their setup. He parked a block away, locking the nondescript white van.

After he stepped out, Anders gave her a reassuring smile and they walked casually down the street, ducking down an alley, entering through the back of the building, and ascending to the top floor, as they'd done many times before.

"No teleporting today?" Anders said.

"No, not today. I'm saving that for later."

"Understood. Let's kick off surveillance and then coffee."

"Good. I already need another one." Maya followed Anders through the relatively empty space, arriving at the corner where they had stashed their gear.

"I thought you put it in this corner," Maya said.

"I did." Anders looked around, confused.

"Okay, so your laptop's in your backpack but where's the telescope? Where's the WallSpy? Where's the hologram belt?" Maya said, listing off thing after thing he had stashed.

"Right, I remember packing them into that cabinet." Anders pointed to a cabinet in the opposite corner of the room. He ran over, but Maya teleported and made it there first.

"If this is the cabinet, we're in trouble," she said. Anders arrived seconds later, staring and the cabinet in disbelief.

"This was definitely it. I loaded it all last night myself. Someone's cleaned us out."

"Alright, it's not safe here. Let's get out of here," Maya said.

Anders nodded. "Yeah, let's go." Anders made a start and

Maya teleported to the base of the stairs, waiting for him to catch up.

She looked left and right but didn't spot anyone in the area. Within two minutes, Anders met her at the bottom of the stairs.

"Just walk casually back to the van. Don't draw any attention."

"Yeah, we should figure this out in the command center."

"Good plan. Hurry up." Maya glanced at both sides of the street, then wandered back to the van, not seeing any suspicious people on the street. They hopped in and drove away. After a few blocks Maya started to relax.

That's better. Now I can breathe again.

"This is not a coincidence that someone found all our gear just before the heist."

"I agree. The timing is too perfect. What's happened?"

"I don't know. You've still got your laptop, right?"

"Yeah, it's in my bag."

"Let's get down to the command center and see if you can still review the camera footage."

"Absolutely. That will tell us a bit more about what's happened." Anders parked the van in the middle of the city, and they ran down the abandoned subway stairs, hustled through the station, and into the training area and command center.

Once there Maya brought up the one camera feed Eduardo had managed to get inside the facility.

"Valerie's training again. Surprise, surprise."

"Is that live footage?" Anders asked.

"Yeah, it is. See what you've got." Maya watched Anders open his laptop and load up the camera feeds.

"Nothing right now."

"Go back a couple of hours," Maya said.

Anders went through the footage carefully. "There's Valerie all around the perimeter of the building. She's been patrolling."

"They are on high alert. But not high enough alert to spot the cameras you've hidden around the area."

"That's true. This is odd. I don't think they've been tipped off, necessarily. But maybe whatever alerted the person to our presence to steal our gear was also picked up by Valerie and her team. They're on edge."

"Well, we can't do the heist like this."

"No, we can't. You can't disguise as Roberta since there's no hologram device. You can't walk around without being spotted from a mile away. We've got the pass, which may still work. But it's too risky, especially with Valerie patrolling around."

"They know something's happening, or they think something's happening." Maya rubbed her hands over her face. "This is just messed up. What do we do now?"

"As much as I hate saying it, we've got to talk to Kora about this. She'll be able to give us a better idea of how on alert they are. What's happening in their systems. She has a limited view at least, more than we have," Anders said.

Maya sighed. "Alright, let's just let's head back. I'll find my own way there. I might do some training on the way home."

"Alright. I'll race you," Anders said, forcing a smile.

Maya waved and then teleported to her first stop on the way home. It felt the same as she'd done last time. But she didn't really dive into that. She was preoccupied with what just happened.

I don't know how Kora's going to take this. All that pain she's felt about us stealing this device and building it. We can't even return a working device. Oh this is just a nightmare.

Maya did the next teleport, making it to the halfway point. She felt tired but not completely exhausted.

Hmm, well I've scoped out the next spot. I'm not going to do any other teleporting today, since there's no mission. I can push myself. Worth a try.

She put the location in her mind, concentrated, and teleported. Maya staggered and then fell onto her bottom. But looking around, she had made it.

I did it!

She was in an abandoned courtyard of an old office block. The rest of the building was closed for refurbishment, but it had been a year or two since that had happened, and no one came here anymore.

Maya picked herself up and looked around.

Well, this worked.

She was a bit wobbly on her legs.

Better not push it with another teleport. I guess I have to get a taxi or walk. No way to beat Anders now, though.

It took Maya a few minutes to get back to the street. And then there were only a few more blocks of walking to get back to the hotel. She didn't notice the walk at all. Her mind completely focused on scenarios and what had happened.

She walked through the hotel lobby in a daze, called the lift, rode it up, knocked on Kora's door, and walked in. She could see Anders waiting in the middle of the room, and Kora standing, looking nervous.

"Okay, Maya's here. That was pretty quick," Anders said.

"Thanks."

"So, as you might expect, there's been a problem," Anders said to Kora. She looked from Anders to Maya and back to Anders again.

"Go on," she said.

"The mission was supposed to go ahead today. We had everything prepped in a building not far from the location. We completed surveillance for days, without any incident. I stashed all the gear there in a cabinet. You wouldn't think to look there unless you knew something. I wasn't just leaving stuff out for people to find."

"I understand. And then what happened?" Kora said.

"We got there this morning, and the gear was all gone.

Valerie has been around, but not anywhere near our building, just patrolling the facility and visibly training," Anders said.

"And the cameras Anders had put up around the building were not disturbed. It's like they're on alert but they don't know what for. They don't know about our operation at all," Maya added.

"Interesting. So, all your gear is gone. What was there?" Kora asked.

Anders started to list off the items. "Telescope. One of the WallSpy units. The hologram belt."

"What about the scanning equipment?" Kora asked.

"I left that in our suite."

"Yeah," Maya said.

"Is it still there?" Kora asked.

"Let me go check." Anders quickly left the room.

"Good thinking. What led you to suggest that?" Maya asked.

"Just a hunch," Kora said, not adding any further. Moments later, Anders returned.

"It's all gone. The scanning setup is gone."

"Well, we should have surveillance footage, right?"

"We've got nothing set up in our rooms, but the hotel should have something in the lifts or in the lobby," Anders said.

"Let's have a look," Kora said. She started tapping around her computer and brought up an image feed. "Okay, this is the three lifts. When do you think it was stolen?"

"I doubt they would have stolen it while we were here, or yesterday when we were out. Maybe this morning? They took it as soon as we left."

"How long between when you left this morning and when you returned just now?"

"Probably an hour?" Maya said.

"Well, that's it. Let's check the footage of everyone who's ridden the lift in the last hour," Kora said, her eyes glued to the screen.

31

A CHALLENGER APPEARS

Maya and Anders watched over Kora's shoulder as she paged through the security footage. Not that many people came and went, but for each one they tried to guess where the person had traveled on the floor and gauge if they had been heading toward Kora's or Maya's suite.

"We'll know when we see it," Maya said.

Anders nodded. He was too focused on the footage to say anything else. Kora stopped suddenly. There was a woman's features in the frame.

"She looks familiar," Kora said. "I just can't quite put my finger on it."

"Do a search. Use the tech you used on Eduardo to find a match," Maya said.

Kora grabbed the screenshot, enhanced the image, and put it through a search algorithm. It didn't take long to hit a match.

"Uh oh," Kora said.

"I've never heard you say that," Maya said.

"Me either," Anders added in.

"Who is it?" Maya said looking over at Kora.

"It's Irina Thomas."

"Irina Thomas?" Anders said. "Why does that name ring a bell?"

"Who are we talking about?" Maya asked.

"He's starting to get it. Irina is the inventor of the hologram device," Kora said.

"Oh no." Maya facepalmed. "She came to take it back, didn't she?"

"Looks like it. We still have the plans, don't we?" Maya said, looking at Kora.

"Yeah. Of course we do, I secured them." Kora searched through her computer.

"What? Impossible."

"I think we're in for some trouble," Anders said to Maya.

"What's happened?" Maya said, leaning in.

"The plans are gone."

"Did you get hacked?" Maya said, incredulous.

"I think so. Nobody hacks me. Who is this?"

"Well, you were right, Kora, we certainly crossed the wrong person," Maya said dejectedly. She started pacing around the room. "Let's think this through. We lost the ID pass, the scanner, the hologram belt, and one WallSpy. And the plans to make another holographic device."

"Sounds about right," Anders said with a glum expression. "Anything else you want to add, Kora?"

Kora stood up and glared at them both.

"Fine. Okay. I may have some part in this."

"What?" Maya blurted out. "That's not what I was expecting to hear."

"Well, I researched Irina and felt bad about stealing her life's work, as we discussed on a few occasions."

"Go on," Maya said slowly.

"So, I anonymously apologized, and told her we would return her equipment soon."

"Did you tell her you built it?" Anders said.

"I did," Kora added.

"And you didn't suspect she was a better hacker than you?" Anders said.

"No," Kora said with some difficulty.

"Well, this is a right mess." Maya continued pacing around. "We've got nothing now. We can't pull Roberta back out. She'll get too suspicious. Kora could approach her, since I was disguised as Kora, but the voice will be wrong."

"That's right, I can't do your voice. I'd have to grab some voice tech," Kora said.

"I can't figure this out right now. I need to go train, to get my mind on something else. Sorry, I'll leave this to you to figure out for now."

"All right, I'll call if we have updates," Anders said.

"This mission keeps going from bad to worse." Maya pictured the teleport spot she had prepared halfway to the command center and went straight there.

She arrived and felt a little bit woozy, but she was just too angry to care about that. She teleported the rest of the way to the command center. Somehow, she appeared in Eduardo's chair.

Hmm. That worked okay. Maybe I should train more when I'm angry.

Maya used the computer to open up the staircase in the middle of the training room. Then she wandered down to the combat training area. She turned the dial up to ten and hit start.

As expected, ten combat robots rose from the ground. They quickly turned to face Maya, and then began to form a ring around her.

Good. I really feel like punching something.

Maya let them approach, tracking their movements to determine who would be attacking first. She got it wrong. Turning to check on a robot behind her, Maya almost didn't notice a different one attacking.

She reacted just in time, teleporting out of the way. She prepared a counterattack, but the robot was too fast, and Maya was out of range.

Before Maya had a chance to adjust further another robot attacked. This one kicked off a continuous assault. All Maya could do was teleport and teleport. She could stay half a step ahead of their attacks, but not fight back.

On and on the fight went. The robots not tiring, but the constant teleportation was wearing on Maya. They were in a mode of stalemate. But the robots could keep this up far longer than Maya could.

You need to change something. How can you break the pattern?

Maya dodged an attack and stood still. She used all her senses to judge the next attack. Turning her head slightly, she could see the robot fist closing in. This time she waited as long as possible. Just before the hit connected, she teleported.

Since the robot was so close and committed to the attack, it was easier for Maya to calibrate her teleport. She barely moved, just enough for the attack to slide past harmlessly. It left her in the perfect place to strike back. One precise attack and the robot was down.

Need to push hard and use your edge. They'll topple one by one.

Maya teleported once for space and then tried the same tactic again. Staying still, allowing the strike to practically hit her, and just move slightly over. It worked, and she was able to easily counter.

Now we're talking.

The next robot landed the hit, disorienting Maya. But she

shook it off and tried again, doing better, and taking it down. From there it was just a process of elimination. The robots rarely tried to attack simultaneously, even though Maya was still easily outnumbered.

Eventually, she was the final one standing, the floor opening up to drag away the robots and reset the room. Maya sucked in a few sharp breaths and then slowed her breathing.

That was full on. What will twenty be like?

Maya teleported up to the kitchenette, gulped down two glasses of water and then took a third one back to the couch to sip slowly.

Pretty tired now, time to check in with the team.

Maya pulled herself up and started to prepare to teleport back.

Maya appeared on Kora's couch and immediately slumped down.

"Ouch, that was a bit much," Maya said.

"Oh, welcome back," Anders said. He was in the kitchenette making coffee.

"Smells like coffee. I'll have one," Maya said breathlessly.

"We've been doing some investigating," Kora said from her desk.

"What have we learned," Maya said from the couch, not sitting up.

"Irina is also a cybersecurity expert. Something I should have taken into account earlier," Kora said.

Maya laughed.

"What's so funny?" Anders said, bringing coffee over. He set down a cup for Maya on the tiny coffee table and leaned against a nearby wall, sipping at his cup.

Maya gazed over at the coffee.

Too hard to sit up right now. Coffee can cool down.

"Kora met her match. It's funny when you think about it. Worst possible person to have those skills, I'd say."

"Worse than Valerie?" Anders asked.

"Way worse. If Valerie was better at this stuff, sure she could detect more of our remote spying. But she'd be easier to punch."

"True. What else have you found?" Anders looked to Kora.

"I think the gear is active, but she's set up somewhere else. I don't have a location yet."

"Do we need it back? Is there a plan 'B'? Or even 'C'?" Maya slowly dragged herself into a seated position, and carefully reached for the coffee. She took a slow and minimal sip.

"If you had your full power set, we could be a bit more aggressive with the infiltration. But right now, we need to be more cautious. I don't see a good way in without the hologram kit."

"Because I need to avoid detection for a long time?" Maya said.

"Exactly. When it was you and Eduardo, you could infiltrate from two directions and reinforce each other. You could jump over to the other track, so to speak. But this way, it's much riskier."

"Are there any other teleport users that we know of?"

"No. And even if there were, I'd say there's probably not enough time to build trust," Anders said. He looked at Kora, and she nodded in agreement.

"Then, our options are either to get the equipment back or find new equipment to support my solo infiltration?" Maya said, looking from Anders to Kora.

"Yes, that's the best scenario. Taking either of us with you complicates the mission too much. We can support from outside. And arrive in style if required." Anders sounded confident.

"Well then, our focus should be on getting the equipment back?"

"I'm all for that. But there is one condition," Kora said.

"Let's hear it." Maya sipped her coffee again.

"We ask for it back. We negotiate with her. We don't try and steal it again." Kora looked extremely focused.

"Fine by me," Anders said, checking with Maya.

"Agreed. Even if we wanted to be sneaky, it's too risky. She would steal it back most likely and do worse this time."

"That's my assessment also." Kora turned back to her computer, bringing up some new applications.

"Good. I'm going to lie here for now, and one of you is going to find us some dinner." Maya fell over on the couch and closed her eyes.

I won't fail in this. It's just another challenge.

MAYA AWOKE to a wave of different aromas. Kora and Anders were hunched over the tiny coffee table. Maya sat up and laughed.

"This is the best arrangement?" she said.

"All the other tables are occupied." Anders gestured to the room and Maya saw it to be true. All of Anders's gear was set up as well.

"What have we got?"

"Paella for us. Gazpacho for you," Anders said.

"Amazing! I've wanted to try it." Maya shuffled over and took a spoonful of the tomato soup. It was colder than expected but refreshing. "Just what I needed." She expelled a satisfied sigh.

"Likewise." Anders was digging into a large bowl. It was full of rice and topped with seafood.

"Thanks for sticking with me through this. It's been a weird time."

"Not weird," Anders said.

"Just another week in the life of Maya," Kora said with a grin. She shoveled in another spoonful of Paella.

"One day this will all be over. I'll have a boring life," Maya said.

Anders burst out laughing. "Unlikely."

"It can't always be like this, can it?" Maya said, doubtful.

"Take care of the Master Sage, and I'll believe you can live a boring life," Kora said with a chuckle.

"I reserve the right to live a boring life. The Master Sage needs to get an attitude adjustment," Maya said.

Anders laughed again. "Let's make it happen."

"With a few more powers, things are going to be very different around here. I won't be swept around by his whims."

"Sounds good to me," Anders said over a mouthful of food.

"We'll be with you all the way. Not to mention the other friends you've made," Kora said.

"Thanks. Each step gets me a little closer. And then I become more of a force to be reckoned with." Maya eagerly dove back into her soup.

MAYA LAY ON HER BED, almost asleep. Her whole body was tense and desperate to sleep. But her mind was racing, and her thoughts were running over each other.

What do you do now? Can you keep going down this path?

Maya heard a knock on her door, and then it opened.

"It's just me," Anders said.

"I'm awake," Maya said. Anders stepped into the room. Maya could only really see his silhouette in the dark.

"Kora thinks she found Irina. We wanted to check with you. Are you still keen on us meeting her?"

"Yes," Maya said without hesitation. "Thank you. Plan it as best as you can, let's go in the morning."

"Perfect. Have a good rest."

"You too. We can figure out the rest tomorrow," Maya said.

Anders nodded and pulled the door closed.

Time to see if we can turn this enemy into a new friend.

32

THE GLASS EGG

aya, Kora, and Anders stood outside the concrete bunker. It was out of town and surrounded by nothing. Just empty streets, and concrete.

"I wonder what this used to be," Maya said.

"Who knows. But I suspect this place isn't hers. There are a few mysteries here," Kora said.

"It's nice to have you along in person," Anders said.

"I couldn't miss this one." Kora strode off toward the front door. Maya and Anders rushed to catch up with her.

The front door was made entirely of a dark steel with no obvious way of opening it or even knocking or ringing. Maya glanced up and noticed the cameras positioned above the door.

"She knows we're here. Hello!" Maya waved at the cameras. She looked back down at the door, and nothing happened.

"Maybe this is a test," Kora said. She looked around.

"No access points," Anders said.

"We don't need to hack in. Hand me the WallSpy," Maya said to Anders. He reached into his coat and handed it over.

"Give me a minute." Maya slipped on the goggles and activated them, looking through the door. She could see a blank hallway beyond.

"Seems safe enough." Maya teleported beyond the door, removing the goggles instantly. She was in a plain concrete hallway. Turning around, she noticed a simple latch on the door. Maya unlocked the door and swung it open.

"Interesting," Kora said, stepping inside, and walking ahead.

"I think she means thanks." Anders stepped inside and closed the door behind him. They walked together down the corridor, following Kora.

"Did she send you some sort of invitation? Or do you think you finding this location was a message?" Maya said.

"Both. It was too easy to find this location. It's a meeting point for sure, and also a way to see us in action." Kora stopped before another door. It was similar to the front door, cast in what looked like very thick steel.

Kora turned to Maya.

"Did you want to take care of this one as well?"

"Sure." Maya pulled out the WallSpy, placed it over her head, and activated it again. She checked the other side of the door and saw nothing much on the ground. Well, nothing much in the rest of the room either. But she did notice a little latch on the heavy door, which meant she should have no problem opening it from the inside.

Maya teleported in and looked around the room. She noticed that it was just an anteroom connected to something larger beyond. Maya stashed away the WallSpy, unlatched the heavy steel door, and yanked it open.

"I wonder how many of these we have to go through," Kora said, stepping into the room. She marched ahead immediately. Maya waited for Anders to come through. The two of them followed closely behind Kora.

The room they were in consisted of stark white walls and

concrete flooring. It opened out onto a bigger room. By the time they caught up with Kora she was standing in the room and before them, standing, or rather lounging, was Irina.

"So, you found me," Irina said.

"Don't get your hopes up. She's not real," Kora said. Kora walked over and waved her hand through Irina. The holographic image distorted with Kora's contact.

"Oh, she's good. She already adapted the tech," Anders said

"Joke's on you," Irina said. "I've lured you here. Now all of your stuff is unguarded. I wonder if you know what it feels like to be robbed?" Irina said.

"Yeah, we were already robbed. By you," Maya replied.

"Don't bother, Maya. It's just a recording," Kora said. Irina didn't react, and then started talking again.

"If you want to meet in person, I have a test for you. Rather, a challenge. I need a communications relay. It'll make this sort of tech possible in real-time. What you're watching now is just a recording." The recording paused before continuing on.

"If you can bring a relay back to this location within twenty-four hours, I'll meet with you, and we'll discuss how we can work together. I really do hope you succeed, because I love that equipment and you seem like interesting folks. Good luck, and I will see you soon, hopefully." Irina smiled and then the hologram disappeared.

"Where was it projecting from?" Anders asked. Kora strode ahead, examining the wall at the back of the room. Anders joined her. Maya sat back and waited for them to complete their search.

"Found it. It's not the part from the belt unit, she's rigged something else up. Interesting method, but nothing that's useful to us." Kora turned around, an annoyed look on her face.

"I really wanted to talk to her. This is just frustrating."

"Well, I can get my hands on that relay. That'll get her talking," Anders said. "And think of the possibilities of being able to operate a remote hologram. That's pretty cool, right?"

"In theory, yes, but there's a lot of drawbacks, and you need to see who you're interacting with. Not to mention the voice. It's interesting but has very limited applications until we can solve the bigger problem," Kora said.

"Fair enough. Maya, what do you think of all this?" Anders looked at her with a thoughtful expression.

"I think that we're low on options and she seems quite resourceful. Kora felt bad about stealing from her, so let's get her something instead and see how things go from there."

"Do you think she'll double-cross us?" Anders asked, looking from Kora to Maya.

"She'd better not," Kora said, determined.

"I've got a good feeling about this. I mean, not a good feeling about us losing our kit and being lured into this location, but for a potential new ally, I think it's worth going after this relay. Sounds like pretty interesting tech. What do you think, Kora?"

"It's going to be in the same league as the other stuff we've been taking. Things are hard to get a hold of, and everyone notices that they're missing."

But it's not obviously for a heist, is it? The relay by itself?" Anders said.

Kora paused, considering his question. She turned to face Anders. "You're right, this should go under the radar in terms of us. Sounds like we're going on another mission."

"Where will we find such a thing?" Maya asked.

"Has to be a big tech company. Probably R&D. But Kora will narrow it down for us." Anders winked at Kora.

She shrugged. "That's what I do. Let's get out of here before Irina changes her mind and finds a way to lock us in."

"Speak for yourself," Maya said with a laugh. She waved

and teleported outside the building. She walked around to the front and waited patiently for Anders and Kora to emerge.

"Show off," Anders said as he walked out the main door.

"You're lucky we didn't get stuck," Kora said. At first an annoyed look on her face, then she grinned.

"All right, Kora, Anders, let's get this search underway."

MAYA WAS JOLTED around as Anders took a corner a little bit too hard. She looked over at Kora, sitting next to her.

"Sorry, he drives everything like it's a sports car," Maya said.

Kora gave her a wry smile before becoming businesslike again. "I expect what we are going for will be a similar size to the vault hacker."

"That's quite good actually. I was able to teleport that with me. Should help us getting out."

"Agreed, you should definitely escape with the device once we secure it, and then help us as required."

"I appreciate you coming out on this one. I know you're usually doing stuff remotely."

"I just want to make sure this one succeeds. I think we really need a win here." Kora smiled and Maya returned it.

The van suddenly stopped, forcing the two women to lurch forward in their chairs.

"At least we've stopped," Maya said, shaking her head. The van turned off and Maya heard Anders coming around the side and opening the side door of the van.

"Welcome to Epic Tech," Anders said with a flourish.

Maya stepped out into the dark alley. It was actually hard to see anything. "You've picked a good spot." She stepped aside and let Kora get out.

Anders closed the van door carefully. "Yeah, the lack of

moonlight certainly helped us as well. We're only a block away from the building, so I think you're in easy teleport distance."

"Kora and I agreed when we find the device, if it's not too big, I'll bring it straight back to the van."

"That's a great idea. Lugging it back would really slow us down. Hopefully, it means this is a bit of a smoother operation."

"Anders, you shouldn't have said that. Now something bad's gonna happen." Maya shook her head, unimpressed, and Kora laughed.

"It'll be fine. Let's go." Anders lit the way with a small head-lamp, and they followed along in single file, traversing the nondescript, empty alley. Maya almost tripped over some garbage bins but spotted them just in time.

As they reached the main street, it was still pretty dark. There were barely any streetlights, only a scattering of build-ings around. Anders shut off his headlamp.

"Isn't this a bit secluded for big tech?" Maya said, looking around.

"Oh, these ones are special. They built out in the middle of nowhere. Quite an impressive facility. You'll see in a minute." Anders led them down the street slowly. There was enough light around to navigate without tripping over each other, but they still had to take care.

As they rounded the corner of the next block, Maya stopped. She could see what Anders meant. The building was a giant glass egg with multiple floors of open-plan office space. All perfectly visible from the outside.

"There's still people working," Maya said. "Isn't this a bit risky?"

"They won't see us. Besides, all the valuable stuff is under-ground," Kora said, looking at Anders and he nodded.

"That's right. We're heading around to a service entry. The geeks won't even see us."

"Okay, lead on," Maya said. They followed the perimeter

of the building, keeping their distance so they blended into the shadows. There was a more traditional structure at the back of the egg which was a secure door with a concrete housing.

"Only secured by a simple card reader." Anders pulled out a gadget and in moments doors unlocked. He held it open.

"Ladies first." Anders waved them in. Kora went first and Maya followed. Anders closed the door quietly behind them.

They were in a service tunnel. It was concrete with grey blocks on the walls.

"They didn't bother making this pretty, did they?" Maya commented as they walked down the corridor.

"Not at all." Kora led the way. At the end of the tunnel, they descended two flights of stairs and arrived at another security door. Anders went to pull out his hacking tool, but Kora raised her hand.

"Let me get this one." Kora pulled out her own device, which looked like a little egg, and attached it to the card reader. The door opened instantly, and she strode through, holding it open for them.

Maya stepped into a locker room.

"This is not what I expected." Maya walked around, noticing a few open lockers. She peered closer at one of them. "These are uniforms? Equipment?" Maya said, trying to figure it out.

"Yeah, the security teams gear up here. They don't want to spook the office geeks." Kora turned a corner and led them out another door into another tunnel. At the end of this tunnel was a very large glass security door with a card reader. Maya could see what looked like labs behind it.

"Here we go," she said.

"Yeah, this is the good stuff. Can you do the honors?" Anders asked. Kora pulled out her egg again, unlocking the door with ease.

"Is that one of your concoctions or did you steal one of their devices?" Maya said.

"Oh, this? I built it. But for fun. I put it in the egg housing, you know, to fit the theme." Kora winked and Maya chuckled.

"Why not?" They walked into what looked like a very different area. There were glass labs spread out all over the floor. There were still a few people working away.

"Follow my lead." Kora walked confidently through the middle of the room.

33

A NEW ALLY

Maya cautiously followed, looking over the staff that were working. None of them seemed to look up and pay them any attention.

"Anyone else find this weird?" Maya said quietly.

"No. Why do you think Kora is walking ahead of us." Anders glanced over at Kora and Maya followed his gaze.

Of course she's using her power. She's manipulating them somehow. Relax. Just follow along.

They soon reached the end of the room and Kora unlocked the next set of glass doors with her egg. They passed through another similar lab area.

"If all the secure R&D is down here, what's going on upstairs?" Maya asked quietly.

"Maybe this is the sacred stuff and that's the generic stuff," Anders said.

"Keep it down," Kora hissed at them.

Maya stopped talking and just focused on what was ahead of them. They passed through this room and through another set of glass doors and then down another flight of stairs.

At the bottom of the stairs was a thick steel door with a card reader. Kora unlocked it like the rest and immediately a guard pointed a gun at them.

"Easy, relax," Kora said. She walked up to him confidently and patted him on the shoulder. The security guard lowered his weapon and stepped to the side.

"Come on," Kora said, leading them through the tunnel. This section was different. Back to concrete flooring and walls. But they started to come across heavyset doors in the corridor. Each with a number on it.

"These are storage rooms where they keep the good stuff," Kora said. They wandered down a long corridor and then came across a very large metal door with no way of opening it.

"You're up Maya," Kora said.

"Awesome!" She slipped on the WallSpy, activated it, and peered through the door.

"There are two guards on the other side. I guess they're the ones that usually open it," Maya said quietly.

"Take these." Anders handed Maya two stun wands.

"Perfect. I'll see you soon." Maya teleported behind the two guards, quickly flicking the mode on the WallSpy to give her regular vision and jammed them both in the back with a stun wand. They collapsed to the floor, effortlessly.

Maya looked around to see if there was anyone else watching. She didn't see anyone. What she did see was a giant cavernous space filled with shelving and boxes.

This might be a bit of a needle-in-a-haystack exercise.

Maya unlocked the giant doors and swung them open. Anders and Kora carefully picked their way past the downed guards.

"Do you know where to look?" Anders asked.

"I do. Follow me." Kora led them through the maze of shelving and aisles of boxes. Somewhere in the back corner she stopped, bent down, and pulled a box off a shelf. She opened the lid and peered inside.

"This is it. Maya, could you take that back for us?"

"My pleasure." Maya shuffled the box closer, got down on one knee, and held the box securely in her hands. She pictured the spot in the van she wanted to arrive and teleported.

Maya found herself seated in the van with the box at her feet. She let go a deep sigh.

Phew. Wasn't sure how well that was going to work. There are very tight tolerances in here.

She opened the lid and saw that the device was still inside.

Fantastic.

Maya activated her radio.

"I'm back in the van. Do you need any help?"

"I don't think we do, actually. Why don't you hang tight and monitor from the van?" Anders said over the radio.

"Roger that." Maya shuffled over and reached across to the front seat to grab Anders's laptop. She opened it and saw the feed coming through on his camera. It was on his shoulder, so she got a pretty decent viewpoint. Only, it wasn't much of a show.

He followed Kora back through the facility. They stepped over the two guards that were stunned. They walked through the labs, where the researchers paid them no attention. And they finally came to the back door, opened it, and stepped outside.

Maya closed the laptop with a sigh.

It's not so fun in the van.

Soon enough she heard their footsteps coming around the corner, Maya jumped out to greet them.

"I see it was a rather boring exit," Maya said.

"Boring exits are the best kind," Kora said.

"Agreed. How was it in the van?" Anders asked.

"Uh... Kind of boring. I'm sorry you've had to sit in the van so much."

"Don't worry. Usually, your missions are a little more exciting to monitor."

"Yeah, a bit more boring would be nice. I agree. What's the plan?" Maya said, looking at the two of them.

"Let's head straight back there. I'm curious to see if she'll show up," Kora said.

Anders shrugged. "Works for me. Let's go."

Kora jumped in and sat next to Maya. Anders went around to the driver's seat. He started up the van and drove away. Rather sedately at first, and then was soon back to his normal style.

"Anders it's getting pretty late, if you keep zooming around corners, people are going to start getting suspicious. It's a van."

"Okay, okay, I get it," Anders grumbled.

Maya leaned back in the chair. "I know he tries, but he always goes back to the same driving. I think he's in the wrong profession. Maybe he should be testing race cars or something else," Maya said quietly.

"Probably."

"But it's good that he's here. And without him, I wouldn't have met you. And I'm so very grateful for all the help so far."

"Don't mention it. Besides, I would have found you anyway. You're making waves, Maya."

"Yeah, I am. Often more than I'm looking for."

"That's the way of the game changers. Just go with the flow and understand the impact you're having."

"I think it's gonna take time or a lot of alcohol. Maybe both."

"Yeah, I think both are required." Kora gave off a little laugh. "And just hurry it up Anders, why don't you? I want to see if Irina's waiting for us," Kora heckled, winking at Maya.

"Speed up now. Slow down. Speed up. Fine." Anders sped up the van.

"Gotta keep him on his toes," Kora said quietly.

Soon enough, they parked outside the warehouse building in the middle of nowhere. Maya picked up the box with the comms relay.

"It's pretty heavy. Why don't you guys go ahead and I'll meet you there?"

"If it's anything like last time, we're gonna need you to unlock the doors," Anders said.

"If she's here, the doors will be unlocked," Kora corrected him.

"Alright, Maya. You've still got the radio. We'll call you. Good luck." Anders and Kora walked off, and Maya stayed seated in the van. She almost opened Anders's laptop to watch their progress but decided not to.

It won't take them long. Let's see how they go.

"How's that door coming along?" Maya said over the radio.

"It's unlocked. Kora was right, I think," Anders said.

"I'm always right," Kora chimed in.

"Let me know when I should make my grand entrance," Maya said.

"Copy that."

There was radio silence for another minute or so. Finally, Anders spoke up over the radio. "Okay, bring it in."

Maya kneeled down and cradled the box as she'd done before, and then teleported into the middle of the big room at the back of the warehouse. She was flanked on either side by Anders and Kora, and Irina was standing only a few feet away.

"Impressive. I bet that made the heist a little bit easier," Irina said, watching Maya.

Maya stood up, walked over, and offered her hand. "Maya Mills, nice to meet you in person."

"Irina Thomas, likewise." Irina shook Maya's hand very firmly and smiled. Her otherwise serious face lit up for a brief moment before going back to business.

"You've done well without the comms relay. It's the missing piece that I need."

"Well, we held up our end of the deal. What have you got for us?" Anders said.

"What I said. A proposal," Irina said with a wink.

"But we've just met. Don't you have to buy me a drink or something?" Maya said, grinning.

Irina threw her head back and laughed. It was such a genuine, melodic laugh that cut through the rest of the tension.

Maya swung the door open.

"Now this is our training center. Well, my training center, really." She held the door open and waited for the rest to enter the space.

"It's quite big. How'd you procure this site?" Irina said, looking around.

"My mentor built this space up, so I'm not a hundred percent sure. But somehow, this whole site is stuck in development limbo, and he secured part of it for himself. Here and below are training spaces for my skill set, teleportation. What you'll be most interested in is over here, the command center."

Maya teleported over the command center and waited for her friends to catch up.

"Seems like a fun power," Irina said.

"It can be now that I'm getting used to it. Please come inside." Maya held the door open once more, and Irina, Anders, and Kora all filed in.

"This is where Eduardo and I used to plan our ops. Anders would help too. Kora's got her own setup somewhere else."

"I know," Irina said, glancing over at Kora and winking.

"This is probably our best base of operations because it's secure. No one knows about it, and there's a lot of equipment already here. Plus, Eduardo's crowning achievement, well, in terms of this heist anyway." Maya fired up Eduardo's computer and opened the camera feed.

"Somehow, he managed to get a feed into one of the training spaces in the facility we're trying to target. Oh look, Valerie's back again," Maya said, trying to sound playful, but pushing away the sudden anger at seeing Valerie again.

"She's the thorn in your side, huh?" Irina said.

"Yeah. To date, we've managed to outwit her and defeat her more often than not. But she got us when we were preparing for the last heist. And she killed Eduardo."

"Your mentor? I'm so sorry." Irina paused and started looking faraway for a moment. "I understand now, how important this is to you." Irina started to drum her fingers on the table, deep in thought. "You know, since you've got this video feed, I could use it to backdoor more comprehensively into their system. At least the security system."

"How would you do that?" Kora said, walking over, challenging Irina with a glance.

"Well, I've done it before, so maybe I can do it here as well. It sounds like this mission requires a bit more visibility inside the facility."

"It does. That's really a weak spot right now," Anders said.

Irina nodded. "Now, things are coming together for me. I can help you with the hologram tech. I think I can get you access to their security camera feeds, or at least more than the one that you've got. And with the relay, we may even be able to project a hologram. A low-quality one as a distraction."

"Sounds pretty good to me," Maya said, looking around the room. "What does everyone else think?"

"I'm game," Anders said. "Kora?"

"Seems fair for us. What do you get out of this?"

"Well, it's the next evolution of my tech, and you're gonna supply the funding and the hardware that I need. And an investment in my future projects." Irina turned to face Maya, holding out her hand. "Do we shake on it?"

Maya shook her hand firmly. "It's a deal. Look forward to working with you more collaboratively." Maya chuckled.

"With me on the team, you can't lose. Now, tell me more about this Valerie character." Irina pointed at the feed. Valerie was practicing curses.

"It's a long story. What's the short version?" Maya said. She ran through the details in her mind. "Valerie hates me, and she was originally a Speedster, but she's been given the LifeDeath power by the Master Sage as part of an experiment."

"Ooh, that does sound like quite a story. Why don't you fill me in while I investigate this camera feed," Irina said, sitting down at the computer, and getting to work.

34

ANOTHER TRIAL

Maya pulled Kora aside into one of the training rooms.

"Is there a problem?" Kora said once they were alone.

"No problem. Yet. We've given Irina a lot of information about the bloodlines," Maya said, pausing to gauge Kora's reaction.

"Yes. She's trustworthy."

"Are you sure? I want to double-check before we jump in completely." Maya let the concern show on her face.

"I've looked exhaustively into her. Before, when I was feeling guilty and looking for excuses to justify what we did. And, also after, when she stole things back from us."

"And what did you find?"

"She's totally clean. Skirts the law, as we all seem to these days. But no ties to the Master Sage. No clan affiliations. Just known for her research. Specializes in hologram tech mostly. But as you have noticed, has a keen aptitude for security as well," Kora said.

Maya studied her expression.

Kora admires her so much. Go with your gut on this. Trust Irina.

"Okay, Kora, I trust you, and by extension I trust her as well. There's been so many surprises and setbacks that I just wanted to double-check." Maya sighed.

Kora put her hand on Maya's shoulder. "I understand. She's a good one. A rare, good one. You don't have to share everything, but you can trust her. We'll do this together."

"Thanks, Kora. Let's go get this kicked off." Maya opened the door, and Kora walked out first. They quickly made their way back to the command center.

"All good?" Anders asked as they entered.

"Pre-operation nerves is all," Maya said.

Anders nodded.

"No worries. But I think this is our best plan yet." Anders pointed to the main screen and Maya looked up.

"Irina has found a way to project a hologram through the surveillance system. It won't stand up to close scrutiny, the camera technology they're using isn't quite there."

"What can it do?" Maya asked.

"Take a look at this." Irina put an image up on the screen. It looked like Kora was standing out in the main training area.

"Wow, that's pretty good. I can't see anything wrong with it," Maya said.

"It's great for fooling people watching security monitors. It won't be great in person. Go take a look," Irina said. Maya teleported out to see for herself. She saw Kora standing in the room, motionless. As Maya approached, she started to see through the illusion. She studied it from all angles, and looked up to find the camera that was projecting it. Satisfied she teleported back into the command center.

"I see. It will work from a distance, as you said. But when you get closer, the quality is not there. It's a very flat image, and there's no movement either."

"Exactly. There's no person giving the movement and life to the hologram. But it has its place."

"Thanks, this will be handy."

"Great. I'll be monitoring the security feeds from here and will deploy the hologram as required based on the mission." Irina hit a few keys and the hologram changed over to show Roberta.

"Phew, you kept the scan," Maya said.

"There's another one too." Irina looked at Maya and winked before hitting a few more keys. The image on the screen changed over to Valerie.

"What!" Maya blurted out.

"Okay, I'm seriously impressed. How did you get the scan data?" Anders said.

Irina was beaming with satisfaction. "Lucky for us, Valerie trains a lot. I had all the angles. And my innate understanding of this tech."

"Would that work for me? Using the belt?" Maya asked.

"Yes, it should be as good as the Roberta scan. I've added a button to switch between profiles. Best not to use that in view of a camera." Irina laughed and Maya chuckled as well. Irina threw over the belt. Maya caught it and examined the changes.

"Absolutely. Thanks for doing this all so fast."

"My pleasure. My work has been theoretical for so long. It's refreshing to be able to quickly iterate it with working tech."

"I'll have to buy you a drink after this and pick your brain," Kora said.

Irina smiled and her eyes lit up. "I'd love that. A post-mission debrief and information sharing."

"Do we have enough for a test?" Anders said.

"Yes. Can we do it down here?" Kora said.

"Sure. It will take a bit of time to prepare, but we can," Irina said.

"Thanks. The last time we did a dry run it ended badly."

"Understood. Give me a few hours to finalize the setup." Irina started immediately, bringing up multiple applications and working away.

"I think we all have other preparations to make," Anders said.

"Of course. I'll go train, let's meet back after lunch," Maya said.

"Done. See you then," Kora said. She and Anders left immediately, and Irina waved without looking.

"Would you mind opening the downstairs training area?" Maya asked.

"Done. Good luck," Irina said.

MAYA TURNED the dial to fifteen, took a breath, and pressed the button. Fifteen robots rose out of the floor and converged on her location. They took up a lot of the space in the room. And once they closed in, there was nowhere safe.

One dashed in with an attack, and Maya teleported into the space behind it, only to have to move again to avoid getting struck by a different robot. Teleporting again and again, she was always one move behind. The robots were perfectly in sync and attacking any spots that she could move to. It was exhausting.

As fast as she could teleport, the faster they changed their swings and rhythm to anticipate her movement. She got clipped a few times, throwing her off balance, always managing to just teleport away before the next hit. But just getting more and more stuck in the endless loop.

I can't do this, it's too much. How did Eduardo beat this? Did he even beat this? I just don't know.

The thoughts rattled around, but she had no time to dwell on them. She was just teleporting by instinct alone. Shifting from place to place, trying to find a way to use this pattern against them, but having no time to actually think.

Suddenly, she had a crazy idea.

Might as well try it. What's the worst that could happen?

The next move, instead of teleporting into a blank space on the ground, she teleported into the air above them all. The robots swung in unison to attack all the gaps on the ground. Maya was not there.

As she came down, she elbowed a robot in the back of its head, and it fell down. The robots quickly adjusted to continue their assault. Maya grinned.

I need three dimensions to solve this problem. I've been limiting myself to two only.

She looked around the room for the first time with fresh eyes, seeing the width, length, and height, and understanding that she could move to all those spaces. She picked another spot, above the edge of the ring of robots, and did the same thing.

She teleported into the air and struck on her way down, the robots completely missing her. They struggled to adapt to her new technique. And one by one, she took them all out. She stood at last, alone in the room as the floor devoured the robots until the next time.

As Maya stood triumphantly, her stomach gurgled so loud she thought it was echoing around the space.

I guess it's time for lunch.

Maya teleported back up to the command center. Anders, Kora, and Irina were there, munching sandwiches.

"Here's yours." Anders handed Maya a parcel. It was a sandwich wrapped in brown paper. She bit into it hungrily, not even examining the sandwich to see what was in it.

"Mmm, tasty," she said, noticing that it was cheese and salad with mayonnaise and something else she couldn't quite pick.

"Good session?" Anders said before taking a big bite of his chicken sandwich.

"Yeah. It got me thinking about how I can do this better."

"Good, good. That's the kind of thing we want before trying out the mission."

"I'm strangely excited." Maya grinned before launching into another bite.

"Wonderful. Are we about ready here?" Anders looked around the room and Kora nodded.

"The operation is set up," Irina said. "Whenever you want to start, Maya, we can start."

"Great, I'll just finish off this sandwich. What do I need to know before I go out there?"

"Anders will talk you through the mission while you're out there. We'll be running support remotely. Anders is also on standby to join the mission, if you find an alternate exit that he can use safely," Kora said.

"What gear am I taking in?" Maya polished off her last bite and stood up.

"Well, you're going to have a tracking camera with a GPS so we know where you are, and we can see what you're seeing all the time. You'll have the hologram belt, a security pass to move through the building, and one WallSpy. Kora and I had a little collaboration and we shrunk it down a little bit," Irina said, looking at Kora.

Kora threw a pair of glasses over to Maya.

"Is this it?" Maya turned the glasses around in amazement.

"Oh, don't forget this." Anders threw a chunky brick-like object encased in plastic over to Maya as well.

"This connects to the glasses. It's not all that simple," Anders said with a chuckle.

"But she believed it. Did you see that?" Irina said to Kora.

"Oh, I saw it. Maya, you expect too much."

"No, I'm..." Maya said a bit sheepishly. "I'm just so amazed by what you two can do that I believed you shrank it down that much."

"Loving the faith in our abilities, we'll get there but not overnight."

"Next version then." Maya winked and then geared up. "Okay, I'm ready to give this a go."

"Fantastic. Go ahead," Anders said.

Maya walked through the door, curious to see what lay before her. The training area looked mostly the same.

"Maya, we set up a door in the corner of the room that links through to the test area."

"Okay, walking over now." Maya cautiously walked through the space, unsure of what they might have changed. It was an easy trip. She didn't notice anything special on the way.

She arrived at a door that wasn't there before. It had a keypad reader on it.

I guess I know what to do here.

Maya pulled out the security pass from Roberta and swiped it over the reader. It beeped and the door unlocked. She stepped through quickly.

So far so good.

Next, she entered a horrible concrete corridor.

"Looks authentic," Maya said over the radio.

"Sorry, we didn't really have time to redecorate. But we've redone cameras and everything else you need," Anders said.

"Thank you. You might want to activate the Roberta hologram," Anders said.

Maya facepalmed.

"Yes, that would be a good idea." She reached down and activated the belt, switching it into the number one position. She noticed a shimmer around her.

"Okay, looking good. Continue," Anders said.

Maya walked down the hallway, noticing the security

cameras. She pressed on to the end of the hallway and found another door with a card reader on it.

She tried Roberta's access card.

It beeped twice and a red light flashed.

"I've hit a snag, Roberta can't get any further," Maya said.

"Try the WallSpy," Anders suggested.

Maya pressed the button on her glasses, activating the WallSpy. She looked through the door at the room beyond. She noticed several security cameras and a dummy cardboard figure of a guard. After a few seconds, the guard swiveled to face the door.

"What's the camera coverage of that room like?" Maya asked.

"There's a blind spot in the left corner, just past the door in front of you."

All right. I can work with that.

"You should also look around. In the far corner near the next door, you'll hit a blind spot as well."

"Alright let's try this out." Maya switched the hologram belt to position two. She noticed another shimmer.

I should be Valerie now. Now let's try teleporting into the other blind spot.

She looked at the position again with the WallSpy and then teleported, while the fake guard was facing the wrong way.

"The guard is going to see you in a second. What are you going to do?" Anders said.

"I'm going to do this." Maya teleported into the space above the guard and then quickly teleported to the other end of the room, stopping at the other door. Activating the WallSpy, she looked through and spotted a clear spot, teleporting straight there.

"Okay, how'd I do?" Maya said, catching her breath.

"You scored well, based on what the ladies are saying and

seeing through the cameras. Why did you choose to do that as Valerie?" Anders asked.

"If they see her being a bit weird or being places that they shouldn't expect her to get to, they'll just write it off as Valerie being mysterious and powerful. If they see Roberta doing weird stuff, they're going to raise the alarm."

"Good thinking. All right, well, I think that's enough of a test. We've got to prepare for the real thing now."

"Thanks, team." Maya teleported back to the command center. She deactivated the WallSpy and the hologram belt, taking them both off and leaving them on the desk in front of her.

"That worked well. Thanks for setting this up. It was a good test, don't we agree?"

"You got this," Irina said. "I have enough data to confirm that we've got a shot."

"That works for me. I'm just going to go collapse for a few minutes." Maya teleported to the couch in the training area and sunk into it.

NOT A COFFEE RUN

Maya stared out the window, her eyes fixated on the Haste facility. She turned to Anders.

"So, you're sure this location is secure?"

"Yes," Anders said, his voice weary from repeating it. "The only reason we were compromised here was because Irina had tracked her device. We've triple-checked everything."

"Okay, good," Maya said, turning back to look at the security camera footage. She played with her watch again. It was still only early afternoon.

"This will go better than the test run, Valerie is just her usual craziness today. Nothing special. Roberta is all normal. Just remember the plan."

"We wait for Roberta to leave for the day, then I swoop in. Kora and Irina are monitoring the internal cameras. They'll let us know when the timing is right."

"That's it. You know it all. That's the plan."

"I just hate waiting. And I can't do anything except wait, and sit, and stare. I can't train. It'll waste my energy. Can't do anything productive. Because I'm preoccupied with the mission."

"I know. It's frustrating. But the success of this mission is highly increased if you go at the right time. So, we just have to hold on."

"I know. I understand the logic. I'm fully on board. The waiting is killing me." Maya sat down and pulled out her phone, trying to scroll through and find something to distract her mind.

"Look, we've got the plan. Just hang on. Oh, that's interesting," Anders said.

"What happened?" Maya said, instantly curious.

"Roberta left," Anders said.

Maya made a dismissive sound. "She's just gonna get coffee."

"Possibly. But she seems like she's rushing more than normal. Look at this." Anders spun the laptop around. Maya could see Roberta power walking out the front.

"Why is she walking like that? She's a speedster, can't she just zip away?" Maya said.

"Yeah, I don't know, it's weird. Maybe there's some restrictions on this district because of the high concentration of Speedsters."

"Hmm, that's odd. I'm gonna take a look."

"Are you sure that..." Maya didn't hear Anders's next word because she'd already teleported to the opposite corner of where Roberta was last seen on the footage.

She had remembered a sheltered nook in the facade of this building and luckily no one stepped inside normally. On this occasion, she was also lucky that there was no one there.

Better cool it before you blow the mission. But since you're here, you might as well have a peek.

Maya went down to the street and saw Roberta hurrying away. Maya looked both ways and darted across the road, keeping her distance but making sure that she could keep

Roberta in sight. Roberta turned another corner and went down a side alley.

Hmm, this is weird.

Maya followed, pausing when she got to the corner. She waited three seconds and then walked along, pretending she was on an errand, glancing to the side to see if she could see anything. The alley ended in a dead end. And Roberta was nowhere to be seen.

Maya finished her walk, looped around to a different alley that was empty, and teleported back to the building with Anders.

"What happened?" he said.

"She's gone. She went down an alley and vanished."

"Okay, that's definitely not a coffee run," Anders said, his eyes lighting up.

"Yeah. Maybe she just got called away early today. I don't know."

"I'll call the others." Anders picked up his phone. "Hey, Kora. What's it like inside? Is it still busy?" There was a pause where Anders was listening. "Oh, okay. You see, Roberta's left. Maya managed to tail her, and she didn't go on a coffee run, she just vanished." Anders paused again.

"Mm-hmm right, okay, I'll pass that on." Anders closed the phone and turned back to Maya. "So, it's interesting. There's barely any movement in the building. It looks like a skeleton crew. Maybe it's a holiday or people are on leave or something's happening elsewhere. But they said from what they can tell it's a good time to go in. Not many people around to even see you, let alone challenge you."

"But what if it's a trap? Roberta leaving early, the facility being understaffed. Isn't that like too good an opportunity? I don't know."

"Unfortunately, the ideal circumstance for us could be engineered as a trap. This is unusual behavior for Roberta. We've been watching her for days. So, are we taking the bait? Or are we capitalizing on an opportunity? It's fifty-fifty. It's your call."

Maya sighed, tapped her foot a few times, and stared out of the window. She went within, trying to figure out her gut reaction. She was conflicted.

What do I do? Do I leave the opportunity, or do I wait? What if I miss this window? Maya's eyes snapped into focus. She turned back to Anders.

"I'm gonna do it. This could be a mistake, but we've waited so long, we've been cautious, we've adjusted the plans so many times. It's time. We just have to do it."

"Okay. I'll make the call." Anders looked her over and checked her equipment. His hands lingered on her shoulders, then he pulled her in for a hug. "Take care. Get out if you run into trouble. It's okay."

"Thanks," Maya said.

"I'll be watching."

"I know."

"Good luck," Anders said with a smile.

Maya teleported to the nearby safe building. She activated the Roberta hologram, pulled out her phone, and checked how she looked.

All good. Let's make this happen.

She teleported to the outside of the building, hurried back to the street, and then rushed over to the Haste facility, heading straight for the secure door that Roberta always used on the rear building.

Maya fought the urge to look left and right and behind her as she walked.

Just act natural, rush like Roberta, but don't appear panicked.

She walked quicker than she would have liked but reminded herself that Roberta walked like this. She'd studied the walk, she'd seen her in person. She had to trust that it was going to be possible.

Maya arrived at the access door, smoothly pulled out her access card, and swiped it. The door unlocked. Maya shoved the door open, stepping inside. The hallway was a mix of black and white.

The walls were black at the top and white at the bottom and the floor was a chessboard style, checker pattern, of black and white tiles. She found herself in a long corridor, and she hurried down it, looking around to note any particular landmarks.

There were none. She turned a corner, and it ended up in a T-junction.

Left or right, which way?

She chose right, following the corridor through to another locked door. She swiped her card on the access reader and it opened.

So far so good. Keep going.

She emerged into what seemed like a lunchroom. It was pretty big. Enough to cater for twenty or three people with multiple rectangular tables and plain black chairs. There was one man seated at a table.

"I'm sorry," Maya muttered quietly, rushing out of the room. The man didn't seem to do anything strange.

I think I got away with it.

She arrived at another door, swiped her access card, and walked through easily. She found a sign at the next junction printed on the wall. Left said Labs and the right said Vault.

I guess Vault is the one. Let's try that.

It looked like there was no one around. So, Maya activated her radio.

"Do we have eyes in the lunchroom? That man spotted me, but I don't think he noticed anything."

"We don't have eyes in that room. But I think we've got nearby corridors. What did he look like?" Kora said.

"Black shirt, blue jeans, brown hair. He's in his forties," Maya said, trying to remember the man's description.

"We'll keep an eye out. How's your progress?" Kora said.

"I'm heading on a path that says vault."

"Okay, good. Hopefully, we'll see you on our cameras soon. We don't have access to everything, but we've got a lot. Fingers crossed," Kora said.

Maya hurried ahead through the twisting corridor. She came to another T-junction. One option said 'Training rooms'. The next one said 'Vault'.

Vault it is.

She turned, swiped her access card again, and continued. At the end of the hallway, she saw a security guard standing in front of another access door. She hurried toward him, not trying to hide.

"Okay. He probably recognizes you, but he'll pick your voice is wrong."

"Um, okay."

"We might have to take him out. Just be cool." Maya put her phone on her ear, rushing ahead. She waited for the security guard.

"Roberta, what are you doing?"

"Uh-huh, okay, yeah, no, it's urgent, I get it," Maya said softly into the phone. She looked apologetically at the guard and pointed to the door behind him. He stepped. across to block her way.

"Roberta, who are you talking to? You're not supposed to go in here," he said, his voice being more concerned.

"Maya, close the phone. Put it away..." Anders started to speak.

Maya suddenly teleported behind the man and struck the back of his head. He tumbled to the floor and stayed still. Maya looked around.

She could see a camera further down the hall but couldn't tell if it was viewing her current actions.

"Little issue with the security guard. He's out. I'm not sure if this spot is on camera."

"We're not seeing any alarms. Press on," Kora said.

"Copy that." Maya swiped her access card and the door opened. She grabbed the guard by his feet and dragged him through the open door into the next room. She pulled him around the corner, waiting for the door to close. Maya took a deep breath, turned, and looked at the room.

It was a much bigger space, and it was dominated by one thing in particular. A giant vault. Maya let go a sigh of relief.

Okay, you made it to the vault. This is amazing. Let's get in there.

"I'm in the vault room," Maya said with excitement.

"That's great news. None of our cameras go any further down, so we won't be able to track what you're doing. But we can keep an eye on the response elsewhere in the building," Kora said.

"Thanks, I'll see what I can find."

"Hold up," Anders said. "We have a problem."

"What is it?" Maya said quickly.

"It's Roberta. She's heading back into the facility. How many people saw you?"

"Well, just two. The man eating his lunch and the guard I took out who's currently unconscious in the vault room."

"We don't have a lot of time. What do you want to do, Maya? You can back out now and hopefully teleport back. Or you can push on."

"I'm here now. I'll push on. Just let me know what's happening. I don't want any more surprises."

"We got your back. Good luck and keep it up," Anders said.

Am I making a mistake?

Maya hurried closer to the vault door.

36

IN THE VAULT

Maya approached the vault doors. Her hand trembled.

Am I excited? Or scared? Or both?

She reached into her pocket and pulled out the WallSpy glasses. She activated the glasses and looked through the vault door. It was fuzzy, but she could make out the interior. There seemed to be kind of a hatch in the room as well.

Maya wasted no time teleporting inside. She felt a bit of pushback and resistance but found herself inside the vault as she saw it. She put the glasses away and looked around with her own eyes.

The vault was incredibly simply built. It was just polished steel on all the surfaces. In the center of the room was a hatch, as she had seen from outside. Maya walked over and tugged at the hatch. It was a bit stuck, but it wasn't locked. She yanked a bit harder, and it jumped up.

She pushed it over on its hinge and looked below. It was a ladder heading further down.

"I'm in the vault. It's a hatch. I'm going down."

"Whaaat?" Anders said. "It was distorted and cut out. Are they blocking the signals?"

"I can't troubleshoot this. I gotta push on." Maya grabbed the ladder and started climbing down into the dark passage. It was a long way down.

She climbed for a complete minute before her feet touched the ground again. She was in a pitch-black tunnel. No lighting whatsoever. She pulled out a penlight and clipped it onto her shoulder.

With the light, she looked around.

Is this a cave, or a cavern, or some kind of excavation? How old is this?

Maya walked forward, slowly turning left to right to let the beam of light swing over the ground. She couldn't see anything at all. Just the rough, dirty ground and the roughly hewn stone walls around her.

This is giving me flashbacks of the BloodStorm Cave. And the ritual.

A cold shiver ran through her. She pushed those memories aside and kept on. She came to a door. It was made from an impossibly black metal. There was no card reader, but there was a wheel she could turn.

Maya grabbed the wheel, the cold metal chilling her. She turned it, but it didn't budge. She yanked harder and harder, and it started to turn. She felt the lock release. Pulling the door open, she emerged into yet another pitch-black space.

Maya stepped into the room beyond, searching around. It was dark, the only light coming from her. She could see some kind of wall up ahead or a window. She walked closer, unclipping the light from her shoulder and holding it in her hand so she could better direct the beam.

She kept it on the ground to avoid giving away too much of the light. She pressed herself up against what felt like a window and shone a minimal amount of light to look through. The glass was totally black.

Did Eduardo know what was down here? I wonder how much he wanted to tell me and didn't get a chance to.

Maya focused herself on the job ahead. She found it hard to see through the glass.

It's tinted. Try something else.

She felt along it, trying to find some kind of lateral opening or button or anything. There was nothing. Once she'd passed that strange metal wall with the window, she found herself in a stony area again. Using the light, she peered around the room. It was just rough stone, nothing special. She ventured to the other end of this long rectangular room to see what was there at that end.

Nothing, just stonework.

The way forward had to be related to the window. There had to be a way of opening it or unlocking a passage or door. Maya examined every angle and every surface of that steel wall. There was nothing she could press.

She looked at the window from every angle, trying to peer through to see what was beyond.

Nothing.

Maya put the WallSpy glasses back on and activated them. She looked through the window and could just see murkiness. She tried looking up and down, left and right to find something to which she could anchor. There was just space.

Leaving them on, she did a loop of the room, seeing if there was anything beyond the walls. She could see nothing.

Maybe the walls are so thick I can't see through them. And this glass, this window, maybe it looks at nothing. Am I in a dead end?

Maya resisted the urge to bang her head against the wall. She turned and looked around, putting the glasses away.

Think. This is the only way through. Unless it's a dummy vault.

There's a trick here. It's meant to fail intruders. It's probably something that only the Haste Clan can overcome.

Maya looked around again with renewed interest. This wasn't a blockage. This wasn't the end. It was just a different problem to solve. She checked all the walls and the floor. Nothing was there.

The special glass was quite tough. She thought about hitting it but that didn't really line up with her theory.

Hang on a minute. What if I look up?

Maya looked at the ceiling instead. It wasn't the earthy stone on which she was walking. It was sheets of smooth metal. She activated her light and pointed it at the ceiling, reviewing it closely.

There has to be a hatch or a door or a panel or something. Speeders can run up the walls. Jumpers can leap to the roof. Flyers can fly to the roof. It's the only place that makes sense. People who teleport can't get through the roof because they can't see the destination. Okay, this I can work with. Just find the answer.

Maya laboriously checked all the ceiling surface, but didn't notice any obvious buttons, switches, panels, or imperfections.

It has to be something you have to touch to activate. How am I going to get up the wall?

Maya looked at ways to climb or jump. She couldn't do it. The walls were hard to hold. She tried teleporting up to the roof and pressing on the ceiling. She successfully did it, but nothing happened.

How am I going to tackle this? I can't teleport to every space in the room.

She tried activating her earpiece again. There was just silence, then static.

How am I gonna get through this? What am I gonna do?

Maya heard footsteps and quickly turned to face what was coming. The footsteps came closer and closer until a figure emerged in the room. Maya didn't bother hiding. She shined her torch at the figure, seeing that it was Valerie.

"I was wondering when you were going to show up. You made it pretty far," Valerie said with a satisfied smirk on her face. She strutted into the room, exuding total confidence.

"You led us on a merry chase. 'Roberta' was seen all over the facility. But I wasn't fooled. I knew you'd come straight here."

"I'm glad we provided you some entertainment," Maya said.

"Odds are kind of stacked against you, aren't they? There's no way out of this room. Your mentor is dead. Radios don't work down here. You're trapped. I have complete power over you." Valerie slowly advanced.

"I have just about mastered the LifeDeath power, and I'm guessing you're a fair way away from mastering teleport, one of the more interesting and difficult powers." Valerie smiled and walked closer again.

Maya kept her eyes on the woman, trying to remain calm.

Don't let her get in your head. Yes, you're outnumbered and outpowered. There's always a way.

"Well, I was wondering how I was going to get past this room. Thanks for showing up to give me a hand," Maya said, forcing a smile.

"Why would I give you the secret to this room? It's a security measure. One of the oldest types. One you cannot penetrate with technology."

"So you say, but I won't be stuck in here," Maya said.

"You'll get stuck in here if I want you to get stuck in here." Valerie kept advancing, preparing a curse on her right hand.

It's a Binding curse. She's trying to lock me down.

"I know you know what this is, and the thing is, if I hit you with this, it's all over. Are you as fast as Eduardo? I doubt it. So, I'm pretty sure you're gonna suffer the same fate. Or maybe a worse one. I have no idea what the Master Sage has in store for you." Valerie laughed and advanced on Maya again.

Maya slowly retreated, not taking her eyes off Valerie for a moment.

"You don't have access to your speed yet. I'm still faster," Maya said, trying to sound confident.

"Perhaps, but there's nowhere to run. This room is pretty small. And I've got reinforcements lining the passages behind me. Wherever you pop up, you're gone. You can't possibly escape now."

Maya took another step back.

Buy yourself time. Okay, you need a plan. She might be bluffing about the reinforcements, but she's probably not. It's easy for her to get a security team assembled. Someone's probably coming to help, but I don't know how they'd get through to me. It's on you. You have to find a way to disarm her or disable her and get out of here.

Maya stared at Valerie defiantly.

"If you can't touch me, you can't curse me," Maya said and teleported to the other end of the room. Valerie swiftly turned and advanced on Maya once more.

"I think you've forgotten something. There is one attack that I can do where I don't have to touch you."

Oh no, she's gonna do a Lifedrain. I'll have to keep moving so she can't connect properly.

As soon as Maya saw Valerie start to concentrate, she teleported behind the woman. Valerie, grunted, with disapproval, swung, and started to focus again.

This will work for now, but how are you going to stop her?

Maya teleported again, disrupting Valerie's concentration.

"I can do this all day. You're never going to latch onto me like that," Maya said, probing and pushing Valerie.

She's starting to get frustrated.

"Fine, I never liked that move anyway. I've got other things with me." Valerie put on some dark glasses with her left hand and let the Binding curse drop off her right. She reached into her pocket and threw a little ball on the ground.

Maya recognized it instantly.

Well, that's not good.

Maya teleported out of the room, hiding behind the great door that she had come through. The white light flashed brightly, but Maya was protected. She teleported back into the room into a far corner. She couldn't quite see Valerie though.

Of course, use the darkness.

Maya switched off her light. In the absence of the light, the room was very dark. Feeling unsafe, Maya quickly teleported.

"Urghhh!" Valerie said. "I almost had you there." She wheeled around, looking excited.

I'm not sure how much longer I can keep this up without a way to fight back.

Maya thought through what she had on her. It was mostly infiltrating gadgets.

But you have a stun wand. But it probably wouldn't work. At least you can try.

Maya reached in and pulled out her stun wand from her utility belt.

"Oh, you're gonna fight back now, are you?" Valerie said in a mocking voice.

Maya held the stun wand in one hand, cautiously watching Valerie's movements. She teleported next to Valerie and then back again, trying to gauge Valerie's reaction speed.

She's very fast, but not as fast as if she'd had her full Haste blood-line power.

"Trying to tease me, are you? Thinking you can get in a jab with the stun wand? Good luck. I don't think it's going to be worth it." Valerie stood still in a ready position, beckoning for Maya to come closer.

"Come on, try your luck," Valerie said in a singsong voice.

You can't attack her from behind. She's expecting that. How about this?

Maya teleported herself above Valerie, swinging down with

the stun wand. It connected with Valerie's head and then Maya quickly teleported away. Valerie dropped to one knee, clutching her head.

"Cheap shot. I didn't expect that, but now I will. It's not enough to put me out of action either. You wasted your best chance." Valerie groaned. Shook off the stun wand and stood up, stretching.

"I hope you got something better, otherwise you're all mine."

"No, she's mine," said a voice from the doorway. Maya turned and saw another Valerie standing there.

37

THE POWER OF THREE

The New Valerie grinned at Maya.

"Help has arrived. I also told the security teams on the way to stand down. They really fear you, Valerie," New Valerie said. Regular Valerie looked livid, her face contorting in anger.

"Who are you? How dare you impersonate me!"

"Maya, come over here for a minute. And activate setting two on your belt." New Valerie beckoned for Maya to join her.

She knows about the belt. It must be Kora. Did they make another one?

Maya teleported over to New Valerie and activated her belt. She noticed a shimmer and then they were almost identical.

"Three Valeries. It's definitely three too many," New Valerie said. She swapped places with Maya, and they kept switching positions.

How did she get the voice right? I have much to learn it seems.

"If you think this makes any difference, you're sorely mistaken. I don't care who is who, you're both going down." Valerie started advancing on them, preparing a Binding curse.

"What's the rest of the plan? Do you have something to use against her?" Maya said quietly.

"I just wanted to make sure that you were alright and had a path out. If you need to, just leave. I have something to slow her down." New Valerie put up her fists in a ready position. Maya copied the pose.

Can I do it? Should we just get away while we can?

Maya struggled with the decision as Valerie edged closer. Watching the woman's expression, Maya suddenly decided.

I can't run from her anymore.

Maya advanced to meet Valerie. She watched for any attacks and then led with a sweeping kick. Valerie went to block with her active curse hand.

Oh no. Quick.

Maya teleported back, Valerie's hand blocking nothing. Valerie grunted in frustration. New Valerie threw something into the room. It exploded and smoke started billowing out.

"Make your choice, Maya," New Valerie shouted.

"We fight," Maya said. She approached Valerie from behind. Valerie was choking on the smoke, trying to wave it away with her hands. Her curse was still active.

Pretend to attach from behind, and go from the front. She won't expect it.

Maya advanced and started running toward Valerie.

This had better work.

Maya made no effort in masking her sound. She wanted Valerie to expect it and turn around with an attack. As she closed in, Maya teleported. She feinted and teleported again. Crack.

Valerie's fist made contact with Maya's arm. It stiffened instantly and Maya teleported away.

"One arm down. Did you think that would work?" Valerie taunted. She had recovered from the smoke and was standing tall. New Valerie rolled something else along the ground. Arcs of electricity jumped up from the ground. Valerie took a defensive pose and an aura shimmered around her.

She's using her Lifeforce to buffer the attack and prevent her muscles locking up from the electricity.

The electricity faded and Valerie looked unharmed.

"Those tricks won't work. It will take true power to take me down. Which neither of you seems to possess," Valerie said. She eyed Maya's arm.

"Time to lock you down even more." Valerie stalked toward Maya.

Time for a new plan. What can you do?

Maya edged backward, cradling her useless arm.

Oh, leave it. Focus on what else you can do.

Maya let her arm dangle at her side.

I hate this. But just move past it. Your arm will recover.

Valerie reached into her pocket and threw something of her own. Maya didn't wait around to see what it was, she teleported back to the entrance of the room, next to New Valerie. An explosion rocked the space, knocking Maya down. She pulled herself up in time to see Valerie's attack. Maya tried to teleport but Valerie grabbed her arm.

The sensation of trying to teleport with another person was strange, and it failed. The delay was all Valerie needed. She hit both of Maya's legs with a Binding curse. Maya fell down, pain arcing through her.

"And now it's done. I could kill you right now, I think. If I wanted." Valerie circled around Maya, delighting in her victory. She was completely ignoring New Valerie.

"Get out while you can. She only wants me," Maya called out.

New Valerie shook her head, withdrawing two stun rods. Wordlessly she advanced on Valerie.

"I'm going to get such a great bonus for this. Maybe even a

new power?" Valerie threw her head back and laughed. "I can't believe it ended up this easy."

This can't be over. Is this it?

New Valerie was there in a flash, attacking with both stun rods. They connected. Valerie fell to the floor.

Yes! Nice one!

Maya was about to congratulate New Valerie when she noticed something odd. New Valerie clutched at her chest and then collapsed.

"I'll recover. Faster than her," Valerie grunted with satisfaction.

Maya continued to watch New Valerie with growing dread.

"What did you do to her?"

"Binding curse on her chest. She will live. But it will be painful," Valerie said. She was motionless on the ground. New Valerie was breathing in ragged gasps.

No. Not like this.

New Valerie began to shimmer and change. Now Irina was lying on the ground.

What? Irina?

Maya looked at Irina in shock.

Why did she come to help? She shouldn't have. It's not her fight.

Maya's eyes noticed something off with Irina's body. It took a few moments to puzzle it out.

She's not wearing a hologram belt.

Suddenly Maya had an epiphany.

She's a shapeshifter. It's why she is so obsessed with hologram tech. And was able to mimic Valerie perfectly. I can't believe it.

Irina was bent over in pain, oblivious to anything else. Valerie was struggling too.

You have time now. Before Valerie recovers. Do something. Anything.

Maya tried to move. She couldn't. Her legs and right arm

were disabled. Her left arm could do nothing by itself. It surely wasn't strong enough to put her whole weight on.

Maybe you can access part of your LifeDeath or Chakra power to reduce the curse?

Maya sent her focus inwards, trying to feel her other powers. There was always an awareness of them. But they were beyond reach. Helping, but not available. Maya strained, reaching for them. Trying to access their power.

But it was useless.

You have to use the power you have now. Master it.

Maya shook her head at the thought.

I can't master Haste now. I can't even move. In moments, Valerie will be back up. She will drag us out of here and into a prison.

Maya looked over at Irina again. She was in pain. Maya's heart went out to their new friend.

Why would she sacrifice so much for us? To reveal her secret?

Maya made a resolution in that moment. She would not let Valerie beat her.

You don't need to move your body. You can teleport.

Maya focused her will and tried teleporting next to Irina. Her power built, but it fell off. It met resistance. Maya felt the source of that resistance and gasped.

It's me. I am stopping myself.

She closed her eyes and focused, relaxed her mind, and dove inside. She thought about teleportation, how it was the perfect expression of freedom. She thought of the one thing she wanted more than anything else.

Unconsciously, all those years she had longed for it while asleep. And again, during the other times she had been captured by the Master Sage. She'd even wanted freedom from the burden of responsibility she had felt when others were hurt because of her. Anders almost died. Now Irina was in a critical state and defenseless.

Stop holding yourself back. Let go. Have the freedom you deserve. I give you permission.

Maya shed a tear and teleported. She arrived next to Irina and felt a surge of happiness. Of relief.

You did it. If you teleported with three limbs cursed, you can do anything. You're free.

A surge of something else went through Maya. A powerful rush of forces breaking free. She stood slowly, drinking in the power that flowed through. It had been held back long enough.

Her three powers mixed. Her LifeDeath infusing her body once more, her Chakra building and flowing. Her Haste power coming into the mix as well. Maya looked at her wrist, seeing the new Mastery Mark.

You did it. You really did it.

Valerie was stirring but Maya paid her no mind. She reached down and removed the curse from Irina, her LifeDeath power flowing through without thought. Irina's relief was immediate. She looked up, bewildered.

"It's okay now. Let's get you back." Maya held Irina's hand and teleported. There was a brief tug at her, but the resistance melted away. Maya and Irina arrived in the command center. Kora yelled out in surprise.

"We're okay. Irina got quite a shock. Keep an eye on her for me, will you?" Maya said with a smile. Kora regained her composure and smiled back.

"Go finish the mission. We're fine here," Kora said.

Maya gave her a little wave and teleported back.

Valerie had dragged herself up.

"What did you do?" Valerie said, shaking off the last remnants of the shock.

"I mastered the Haste bloodline. You can't defeat me now," Maya said slowly, enjoying the expression on Valerie's face.

"Here's an example." Maya teleported right next to Valerie, quickly tapping her once with each hand, and teleporting back to her original location. Valerie staggered, her left arm disabled with a Binding curse.

"How?" Valerie said, a mixture of surprise and frustration.

"I have my powers back. Three mastered powers working in combination. It's not something to be trifled with."

"You can't get away with this." Valerie used her other hand to remove the curse, restoring her body.

"How does it feel to be the one that's powerless?" Maya said, staring Valerie down.

"I'm not powerless. You just have an edge right now, that's all." Valerie struggled to her feet. Maya turned to look at the doorway and then looked back at Valerie.

"What are you going to do? Where could you possibly go? There's no running, I can just catch you."

"Well, you're not the only one with a contingency plan." Valerie pulled out a device and pushed the button. Maya heard an explosion and the room started crumbling around her. She teleported away, making sure she didn't get stuck in the rubble.

After the sounds subsided, Maya teleported back into the room. There was no sign of Valerie. The rubble filled most of the room, and the ceiling had now collapsed.

Time to take advantage of this moment to explore the facility.

Maya teleported into the ceiling cavity now that she could see into it. There was a crawlspace ahead of her that she wormed her way through, and then a ladder to climb down, which she did slowly, rung by rung. Down and down, she went. It was such a long climb that she wondered if there was some kind of other trick that she missed. But she eventually saw earth beneath her. She put her feet down and looked around.

After a few steps, the rock turned to cobblestone. She was in a massive underground warehouse that looked old.

This has to be hundreds of years old.

It was lined with shelves, boxes, and crates. All kinds of storage with unknown treasures within.

I'm here. How do I find the needle in the haystack?

Maya visualized what the teleportation amulet looked like. It was a lightning bolt and a star fused together within a circle. But Eduardo had not known where it was stored.

Time to go hunting.

38

THE MYSTERIOUS VIAL

Maya felt a familiarity when moving through the space.

When have I seen this before?

It came back to her in a flash.

My Chakra vision. I saw the Master Sage down here hiding something.

Maya tried to recall the vision. It was floating there, beyond her sight. Maya reached back and pushed hard. Suddenly the vision burst into incredible detail. She could see him walking through the space, holding the amulet in his hand. He passed by several spots, pausing at them, but moving on. He finally entered the second last aisle.

Walking with purpose he strode down the aisle, bending down and selecting a box on the ground. It was a simple black box with a keypad. He entered the code and unlocked the box. After dropping the amulet inside, he closed the box carefully and it locked.

Standing up, the Master Sage, paused, looking around. His eyes lingered on another box on a different row. But he refocused himself and sped out of the aisle at an alarming speed.

Maya's vision returned. She rushed off to the aisle, running to the box. She spotted it, nestled behind a larger wooden box. Maya input the code quickly.

The date of the BloodStorm. Not very creative.

The box unlocked and Maya looked inside. There were a few items, which she ignored. The one that held her attention was the amulet stashed at the back. She reached in and grabbed it, feeling a flow of energy pass over her.

What is this? It feels... ancient.

Maya put the amulet over her head, letting it rest on her chest and tucking it into her clothes. She felt a lightness on her chest and took a deep breath.

Time to go.

Maya teleported herself back to the command center. Irina and Kora looked up, startled.

"Everything okay? What happened?" Kora asked.

"Valerie is either buried or she escaped. Can you bring up my tracker?"

"Your tracker?" Kora asked, then gave her a knowing nod. She brought up a map view on her computer.

"It's on the move. I'm guessing that's Valerie?"

"Yes. Is the video feed working?" Maya asked, staring at the map.

"Let's have a look." Kora brought up another window. There was a view of a car window on the screen.

"Looks good. Signal is decent. They're heading up into the mountains, judging from the map."

"I only need a glimpse of the destination to follow her in," Maya said with determination.

"She's already a fair distance..." Kora said looking at Maya.

"I have this." Maya reached in and pulled out the amulet to show them.

"Now we're talking. And it works?" Kora said.

Maya nodded.

"I can feel it. Wherever Valerie is going, I can follow."

"Is that why you left her an opening?" Irina said, curious.

"Partially the reason. The other one... I'm not sure. I feel sorry for her. I'm not as ruthless as them."

"Sorry for her?" Kora blurted out.

"She's being manipulated. It's the classic Master Sage move. That could easily be me. I want to stop her, but I don't want to kill her. It doesn't feel right."

"I understand. But you can't save everyone. No matter how powerful you get," Kora said softly.

"A problem for another day. It looks like she's stopped?" Maya said pointing at the screen.

"Yes. Let's see if we can get a decent look at the location." Kora tried adjusting the camera settings.

"It's a fixed angle, we gotta hope you put it in a decent position."

"It's on her shoulder, it should be fine." Maya watched the monitor. She could see a rocky mountainous area, with a little grass. Similar to the facility that she had infiltrated with Eduardo.

"I think it's a sister building to the one I already infiltrated."

"Looks that way. Let's see her get inside," Kora said.

The video feed passed through a large gate toward an entrance. Maya noticed some guards quickly get out of Valerie's way.

"Unlock the vault," Valerie demanded. One guard rushed off. Then the video feed went black.

"Must be scrambling tech. But we got enough. Are you ready to follow?" Kora asked.

"The sooner the better." Maya turned to Irina.

"Thank you for your help. You really saved the day." Maya bowed.

"You're welcome. I'm glad I could make the difference. I

only ask that you keep my secret." Irina gave Maya a nervous smile.

"Of course. It's your secret, I won't say a word to anyone. Wish me luck." Maya waved and teleported to the entry of the facility.

A stunned guard moved to yell, but Maya was on him instantly, knocking him out. The other guard reactively swung out a stun wand, but Maya easily dodged it, appearing behind the man and taking him out efficiently.

You got this.

Maya strode through the main door, finding herself in an open foyer.

Black-clad security staff looked up in alarm, raising weapons. They fired blue energy beams at Maya. She teleported behind each one, efficiently knocking them out with a custom Binding curse strike at the back of the neck. She looked around, satisfied, and continued through double doors into a hallway.

Maya teleported to the end of the hallway, not wasting any time. She threw open the double doors and entered the next space. It was a series of research rooms, with glass walls. One was filled with computer equipment, others had different machinery she didn't recognize. There were researchers in white lab coats working away. Maya didn't see Valerie anywhere.

Teleporting to the end of the room, Maya glanced back again.

Valerie isn't here. She's come for something specific.

Maya noticed the next door was locked before her. She concentrated for a moment, throwing out her combination Chakra wave and curse move. The door disintegrated before her.

I'm going to call that the Decay Wave.

Maya stepped through the door, teleporting along the next

hallway. She paused before each door, opening it to look inside before continuing.

No sign of Valerie. She must be close.

At the end of the corridor, Maya found a door leading to a stairwell. She glanced down, teleporting to the bottom of the stairs. A thick vault door barred her way.

Let's see what we can do here.

Maya focused her Chakra, condensing it into a small ball in her hand. It glowed blue as she poured more into it, making it denser and denser. It began to shimmer and have flecks of gold through it. With concentration, she pushed it into the door.

The Chakra ball connected with the door, burning a hole through it. Maya kept her connection to the Chakra, forcing it to stay compacted. Once it had passed through the door, she let it loose. It ballooned out into an explosion of force.

The vault door was ripped off its hinges and flung at Maya. She teleported past it, watching it slam into the stairwell behind her. The explosion had also wreaked havoc in the vault itself. Shattered glass vials were all over the floor. A green liquid also coated the floor, draining out of the destroyed vials. There was some trashed equipment.

At the back of the room stood Valerie, momentarily stunned. She stood at a doorway, which linked to another room. Spotting Maya, Valerie ran. Maya teleported to where Valerie was standing, assessing the room beyond.

It was dominated by a massive control panel with an array of buttons and dials on it. An extensive pipe network lined the walls. Valerie was not visible. Maya teleported over to the control panel to get a better look.

"Code validated. Destruction sequence initiated," a female voice announced. Maya looked around. She noticed flashing red lights in the room now.

"You lose," Valerie said from the back of the room. Maya

walked around to have a look. Valerie was standing in a doorway. Maya couldn't make out what was behind her.

Is it another room? It's all shiny.

"I got what I needed. And now I'm here."

"Cute touch, by the way." Valerie held out the tracker that Maya had used and crushed it with her hand. "This facility will not give up its secrets. But I will benefit." Valerie held up an undamaged vial.

"Valerie, he's using you. You're just a tool to him. Eventually, you'll break or get thrown away."

"Like you? Seems like you turned out alright. I'll take my chances."

"We have no idea what this does to your body. You're experimenting on yourself."

"Like I said, I'll take my chances. I need to get stronger. Next time I'll beat you. And you'll know your place," Valerie hissed at Maya, smashing a button next to her. A silver door slammed down locking her away.

You could teleport into her room if you wanted to. Grab that vial.

Maya considered it. But something cautioned her against it.

You got what you needed. You've destroyed another research facility. Take the win.

Maya teleported to the entrance of the building. There was a squad of people standing outside, waiting.

"Take her down!" a woman shouted. A wave of water hurtled toward Maya, with a column of fire coming from a different direction.

They're not mucking around.

Maya teleported back to the underground facility where she had found the teleportation amulet.

Better hunt around for more useful intel before they do something here too.

Maya took a few steps then stopped dead still. There was

someone else down in the stacks, hunting around. The figure paused and walked over to Maya.

"Fancy seeing you here," the man said with an amused chuckle. He was wearing a flowing robe with sandals.

The Master Sage. He's here.

"You've been quite busy, haven't you? Teleportation is such a nuisance. Of course, you'd have to get that one, wouldn't you." The Master Sage gave her a pained smile.

"I am just making the best of what I have. Your viral video expose was quite childish," Maya countered.

"Oh, I enjoyed that. A lot. Even more so because it wasn't me that did it." The Master Sage kept eye contact the whole time. Maya watched her emotions like a hawk. She didn't feel a blip of anything.

I think he's telling the truth. That tracks with what Kora said.

"Why are you here?" Maya said. The Master Sage stepped closer.

"I came to inspect the damage myself. We'll have to relocate all this stuff now." He gestured to the room around him. "Why did you come back?"

"I know there's more here. I know what you've been doing with bloodlines. Once I get the evidence..."

"You'll expose me? Good luck with that. I own this world. Don't you get it?" The Master Sage gave her a look, like he was chastising an over-energetic puppy.

"What you've done isn't sustainable. I know you weren't the original Master Sage. I know about the war," Maya said, stepping backward.

Don't let him get too close. You need reaction time.

"Ancient history. There were differing opinions, but only I had the staying power to follow through. To the victor, the spoils." The Master Sage made a grand gesture around him, stepping closer again.

You're not going to learn anything useful. He's just stalling you for something. Get out while you can.

"Just, stay away from me. Leave me alone," Maya said.

The Master Sage chuckled.

"You've broken into three of my facilities, destroyed two of them. I think you should leave me alone," he said with amusement. He stepped forward again.

"You kept me in a coma for twenty years, threw me into a locked academy, subjected me to a level eighteen Degeneration Field, and stuffed me into a glass chamber. What do you want with me?"

"Isn't it obvious? I want you by my side. We can rule together forever. And bring forth a line of perfect bloodline users. Everything will be ours, and nothing will challenge us." The Master Sage clenched both his fists in delight.

He looks deranged.

"So, Valerie is your plan B, then? For your glorious dynasty?" Maya said, outraged.

The Master Sage stepped closer again.

"She's not as good as you, but she's got the right motivation. I am, what did you say, just making the best of what I have." He gave her a broad grin and dashed forward.

Maya noticed the movement and teleported away.

She arrived at the command center, her heart thumping.

You're safe. You made it out.

39

HOPE

Maya and Anders strolled into Kora's hotel suite.

"We come bearing gifts," Maya announced.

"Coffee," Anders explained. He had a tray with four takeaway cups on it. Kora was lying on the couch, relaxing. And Irina sat at the desk, hacking away at the computer.

Anders distributed the coffees, and Maya pulled up some chairs. They sat around the coffee table.

"So, how's everyone?" Anders asked.

"We're good. Irina's been staying over to help out," Kora said.

"Awesome. Any changes over at the Haste facility?" Maya asked.

"No, the place is locked down, and has become a construction zone. I don't think you're going back in there. Not anytime soon." Kora gave an apologetic smile and Maya sighed.

"So close, but maybe I can try again later." She took a sip of her coffee.

"Any sign of Valerie?" Anders asked.

"Not even a blip. She's quite underground. Maybe she's trying out her new bloodline," Kora suggested.

"I'm not sure she's ready for that yet. She still hadn't mastered LifeDeath," Maya pondered.

"The minute she pops up anywhere, we'll know about it," Irina said, looking over at them. She grabbed her coffee and sat next to Kora.

"Something new you've discovered or is that just how things work?" Anders asked, looking over at Irina with interest.

"I think now's the time we tell them." Irina looked over at Kora, and Kora nodded.

"Tell us what?" Maya said, concerned.

"It's all yours." Kora deferred to Irina, whose eyes lit up.

"Kora showed me the database you were given by the Life-Death clan."

"Oh yeah, what a waste of time that was. Everything but nothing." Maya shook her head.

"That's because they had to fulfill their deal, but still wanted to screw you over. It worked too... until I figured it out." Irina beamed a triumphant smile at Maya who stared, speechless.

"I know a few of the tricks of the trade, so when I started poking around this database, I started to realize there was more under the surface that was obscured. I had the skills to bring it out and it proved my theories correct. All the data is available now."

"What does that mean?" Maya said.

"You can get meaningful results now. And it's updated over time with new information."

"They gave that to me?" Maya said, astonished.

Irina shrugged.

"They probably didn't expect you to figure it out," Anders said, chuckling.

"Did you find anyone?" Maya blurted out.

"We haven't run everything. We've been able to verify Valerie's last few locations, which was helpful and also was a way of confirming our other data."

"Come on, tell them the fun thing," Kora said.

"Well, Kora mentioned that a friend of yours came up through the data. Nadia Hunt."

"Yes. She's an old friend of mine, I haven't seen her since the BloodStorm happened."

"Well, we know that she was underground as a test subject. But we also know that she was released back into the population and was last spotted in Sweden," Irina said.

"Sweden? Why there? So, she's still alive?" Maya said, incredibly quickly, the words blurring together.

"It looks that way, and she has the Elemental bloodline."

"Which power?" Maya asked.

"Ice," Irina said.

"That is unbelievable. I can't believe she's alive. And she's out there somewhere and she's got powers. Wow." Maya sat back in her chair, thinking it over.

I can't believe it. There's someone out there. One of my people. And it's Nadia.

"What else have you got? Is there a photo?" Maya ran over to the computer. Irina quickly hopped onto the chair and brought up Nadia's profile. There was a photo.

"Wow." Maya sank back down into the nearby couch. "How old is she?"

"Forty-two," Irina said.

Maya nodded. "Sounds about right." Maya stared into the distance, looking at nothing.

"Are you alright?" Anders squeezed in between Maya and Kora.

"I feel like I last saw her recently. Months ago. But it's been twenty years. She's lived a whole other life," Maya said quietly. She sighed.

"It's really hitting home now, now that you have an anchor," Kora said.

Maya nodded slowly.

"Irina, we need to find Nadia." Kora stood up and leaned over Irina, looking at the monitor.

"Can't you do the thing you did with Eduardo? Search all the video footage for her?" Maya asked.

"Not so simple. We have a low-quality photo, no precise location data, and no access to the right security feeds. It'll take time," Kora explained.

"Exactly. But we're experts at this. Nobody else can do what we can do, especially with facial recognition," Irina added.

"The second you find her, I'm there," Maya said emphatically.

"Why don't we pause for a minute," Anders said.

Maya whirled around and glared at him.

"Easy, easy. I know she's your friend, but it's been twenty years. And wasn't she also a captive test subject of the Master Sage? I'm just saying we should do a proper investigation before you catapult yourself in there!" Anders held his hands up, shielding himself.

Maya relaxed back into the couch. "Fine. But she's the closest thing I have to family right now."

"Of course. We all support you. Let's just do it right," Anders said. He looked over to Kora for support.

"Don't forget you're wanted, and your face was plastered all over the news," Kora said.

"You two can help me with that," Maya said.

"True, but you can't operate in the shadows anymore. Not completely," Kora said with an apologetic smile.

"Fine," Maya grumbled.

Anders shuffled along the couch, making himself comfortable.

"So, you know you never really explained your encounter with the Master Sage. At the Haste facility," Anders said.

"He was just trying to stall me, so he can nab me again. He knew he couldn't stop my teleportation," Maya said.

Anders looked to Kora, and then back to Maya again.

"You know, it might help us if you shared more from that conversation."

"Alright." Maya let go a deep sigh.

"He said he wants me to join him. Help him create a dynasty of super-powered people that rule forever." Maya shuddered.

"What!" Anders blurted out, looking sheepish after.

"Talk about textbook tyrant right there. He's not even trying," Kora muttered.

"Why would he even think that's what you would want?" Anders said.

"I think he's trying to make my life hell. So that the alternative looks better. And he has a plan 'B'."

"Valerie," Kora said.

"Right. Her Haste bloodline makes the bloodline integration process work better. And she's obsessed enough to keep plowing ahead," Maya said, her voice weary.

"He's so twisted. What a joke. What happened to him?" Irina said.

"Imagine you lost a war but were the sole survivor. With no opposition, you could further cement your ideas and double down on your flawed philosophy. A few thousand years later, here's the result."

"What are you going to do? There's no changing his mind, is there?" Anders said quietly.

"I'm not sure. All I can do right now is get stronger. And build my team up to be stronger too." Maya smiled at them all.

"We're in this together, you can count on us," Anders said.

"We're in this too. You've already got three bloodlines, I'm a

Charmer and your friend Nadia is an Elemental. You've basically got the whole set already," Kora said with a wink.

"And Anders is a good errand boy, and amateur racecar driver," Maya added.

"Hey!" Anders shouted. The rest of them burst into laughter.

Maybe you can do this?

VALERIE PUNCHED the wall hundreds of times with pinpoint accuracy, her strikes so fast she was a blur. She leapt back to admire her handiwork. The cement wall looked like it had been the target of incredibly coordinated machinegun fire. Valerie looked over her hands, and they were completely undamaged.

"Satisfied?" Valerie said, looking over at Elias. He nodded.

"You have clearly mastered the LifeDeath bloodline, and regained access to your Haste abilities. Everything is working as expected."

"I like the raw power and recovery you get with this bloodline. It will be easy to incorporate that into my abilities."

"You would do well to consider the full power set and the synergies between the different abilities," Elias said.

Valerie turned to fully face him. "I don't really buy the curses. They are a waste of time."

"Maya developed a devastatingly effective style, using her increased speed and positioning to land debilitating curses, disabling her enemies effortlessly," Elias said, looking up from his notebook to observe Valerie's reaction.

She glared at him, before dashing at the wall, hitting it with an explosive strike combining her extreme speed and additional power and resilience. The pattern of strikes was replaced by a giant hole in the wall.

"I'm not her. I don't need to keep my enemies alive when I can destroy them."

"Very well." Elias made a few extra notes in his notebook and put it away. "I'll give you the all-clear. They'll administer your new bloodline in the morning."

"Excellent." Valerie heard Elias walking away and put him from her mind.

I'm coming for you, Maya. And this time I won't hold back.

THE STORY CONTINUES

THUNDERED

BOOK FOUR OF THE BLOODSTORM

Power courses, lightning strikes: will Maya illuminate the truth?

LET'S CONTINUE THE JOURNEY TOGETHER

Hey there, fellow adventure-seeker!

Want to stay in the loop and hear about my bookish escapades before anyone else? Just pop your email into my newsletter. You'll get all the fun updates, behind-the-scenes peeks, and even some exclusive goodies.

Plus, my website is always there for a quick fix of story magic. Let's have some fun on this wild ride of words together!

www.vaughanwsmith.com

ABOUT THE AUTHOR

My name is Vaughan, and I believe that writing should transport you to a fantastic place, and bring you back feeling better than when you left.

I live in Sydney, Australia and I'm constantly devouring new books, TV shows, and movies. My favourite genres are Fantasy, Mystery and Thrillers, and Science Fiction.